THE UNLUCKY
ONES

ALSO BY HANNAH MORRISSEY

Hello, Transcriber

The Widowmaker

When I'm Dead

THE UNLUCKY ONES

A BLACK HARBOR NOVEL

Hannah Morrissey

MINOTAUR BOOKS
NEW YORK

This is a work of fiction. All of the characters, organizations, and events portrayed in this novel are either products of the author's imagination or are used fictitiously.

First published in the United States by Minotaur Books, an imprint of St. Martin's Publishing Group

THE UNLUCKY ONES. Copyright © 2025 by Hannah Morrissey. All rights reserved. Printed in the United States of America. For information, address St. Martin's Publishing Group, 120 Broadway, New York, NY 10271.

www.minotaurbooks.com

Designed by Omar Chapa

The Library of Congress Cataloging-in-Publication Data is available upon request.

ISBN 978-1-250-36974-1 (hardcover)
ISBN 978-1-250-36975-8 (ebook)

Our books may be purchased in bulk for promotional, educational, or business use. Please contact your local bookseller or the Macmillan Corporate and Premium Sales Department at 1-800-221-7945, extension 5442, or by email at MacmillanSpecialMarkets@macmillan.com.

First Edition: 2025

10 9 8 7 6 5 4 3 2 1

For you.
For being here with me.

Mercy did not exist in the primordial life. It was misunderstood for fear, and such misunderstandings made for death. Kill or be killed, eat or be eaten, was the law . . .

—JACK LONDON, *The Call of the Wild*

THE UNLUCKY
ONES

PROLOGUE

He said I would never leave you.

It's been almost eight years since my ex-husband spat those words at me, and I hear them as clearly as if he's speaking them to me now. I feel the way they sink into my skin like a row of teeth, breaking and burrowing underneath, taking harbor in my hollow spaces. I even smell the reek of urine as he unzipped his jeans and pissed on my belongings, material things that mattered enough for me to return to the duplex we shared so I could shove them all into a laundry basket and escape from him and the miserable city he'd brought me to—a place that swallows people whole.

Black Harbor.

Your sidewalks glitter with rocks of crystal meth; frost-colored and sharp, they catch the light of the streetlamps and shine like shards from a fallen star. Wind rolls off the whitecaps of Lake Michigan and pushes heroin needles into your curbs, where they nestle among malt liquor cans and food wrappers and the occasional fingernail that's been torn off in a fight.

You're not unique in that regard, you know.

A lot of places have crime. A lot of places have cold winters and coldhearted people. And yet . . . you have me. All those pieces of myself that I surrendered.

A little glass shamrock.

A bracelet with my name spelled out in beads.

My wedding ring.

Years ago, I stood on your coal-blackened railroad bridge and dropped them into the river. Not all at once. Sometimes weeks, even months would pass between my ceremonial offerings. But I always came back. I always had one thing left to give.

Until I almost gave my life.

As if summoned, the scar on my right leg pulses. Raised and pinker than the rest of me, it resembles a wire. Sometimes, I suspect it's what keeps me tethered to you, although there are nearly a thousand miles between us.

My feet pound the pedestrian walkway. The streetlamps illuminate the path as it snakes toward the Brooklyn Bridge, a famous, floating masterpiece. It's just after 4 A.M. There are a handful of runners and walkers, early-morning commuters, but for the most part, the bridge is mine.

Cables shoot toward me, reeling me into the gothic double arches. I feel myself being pulled to the bridge's center. My hands slice the air. My stride lengthens and I drink in the mist that lingers from last night's rain as I race against ghosts that, until recently, I hadn't realized had followed me here.

I thought I'd escaped you.

I thought I'd escaped him.

I'm sprinting now. Away or toward, I don't know. The memory takes hold of me and suddenly, I am tiptoeing back into that duplex, as unsuspecting as a rabbit about to walk into a trap. The house was silent, empty (I thought), filled with a swirling quiet like when you press a seashell to your ear. The handgun was on the dining room table, next to the vestiges of Tommy's breakfast. Beyond it, in the kitchen, beer cans were spread across the countertops. There were more on the floor, another on the mantel by a stuffed possum. He'd been on a bender since I left to stay with my sister.

Stale cigar smoke stung my eyes. It was threaded into the fabric of the curtains, the soiled throw pillows, the paint. I was only here to collect my things—my laptop, clean work clothes, books—anything he hadn't shredded or burned as revenge for me having cheated on him. For me trying to leave him.

I was so blinded by my mission that I didn't see him sitting on the couch. He scared me when he spoke, startled me into dropping my basket full of belongings, and as he closed the distance between us, I saw the anger that eclipsed his eyes.

He yelled. He berated me. He pissed on my things. I deserved it; I had committed a cardinal sin. I had slept with another man. Worse, I had fallen desperately, irrevocably in love with another man or at least I had fallen in love with the idea of there being more to life than existing in the squalid duplex filled with dead animals and a husband that marched me upstairs every three days to fulfill my wifely duties.

He didn't care that it hurt me. Afterward, my spine would curl as I folded myself as small as possible, as if minimizing the space I took up would minimize the pain that tore through me.

Finally, after all this time, I've come to understand that what hurt him the most wasn't that he had lost me to someone else—because in the end, I had chosen to go alone. It was that he had simply lost me, the one thing he could bend and push to its breaking point.

Then, he uttered those five words that froze my blood: *You'll never leave Black Harbor.*

Recalling memories from that time in my life feels like watching a TV series with each episode reaching a dramatic climax as the screen fades to black. It's as if my brain has rearranged them that way, edited them, and only lately have I been discovering my deleted scenes. Thorny details have started to surface, tearing the thin fabric of protection I have draped between past and present, details sharp enough to wrest me out of a dead sleep.

Now I know that it didn't end there, with Tommy defiling my things. For the past several nights, I have woken drenched in sweat and tangled in my sheets, drowning in the shame of what I did and what I let him do to me. And suddenly I'm back there, in that duplex with him.

My knees digging into the hardwood floor.

His hands cradling the back of my skull.

The handgun on the dining room table, always loaded. Always threatening.

All eyes are on me, glass marbles fitted into sockets of all the animals he's killed before, and I am just another one of his trophies.

Don't struggle, it will only make it worse. I wonder if that's what they told themselves, all his taxidermied creatures, before he stood over them and watched them bleed out.

I run over the East River now. From here, Manhattan skyscrapers look like shoeboxes standing on end. Little pinpricks of light blink on as the city awakens. I stare down at the path, my feet clipping in and out of my frame of vision. Orbs from the streetlamps reflect in the puddles, stretching into ghoulish things. But I'm not afraid.

There isn't much that scares me anymore.

I slow down at the bridge's center. Hands on hips, I turn slowly, taking it all in, this metropolis wherein I have carved a life for myself. A life far away from you.

But if I'm being completely honest, a part of me—perhaps a part of me that I left up there on your railroad bridge—has been dying to return. To fight, for once, instead of fleeing. To show you how I have been remade. To charge into your maw and let you swallow me whole again, and this time, you'll note that I have grown quills.

A warm breeze feathers the hair around my face. I lean over the railing and close my eyes. Then, as if by muscle memory, I extract a talisman from my pocket. The key is nondescript. It looks like any old house key, except I know it is the one that unlocked the duplex. How many years has this key been with me, hiding in plain sight among all the others on my key ring?

I hold my arm straight out over the water. A tremor runs through it. The key is an anvil, heavy with the weight of your ghosts, the memories that have been haunting me. I can't hold on to it any longer. I don't want to.

I watch the bones in my hand contract, shifting like gears in a machine.

"Fuck you, Tommy."

The key falls and disappears quickly from sight. I don't even hear it plink into the water, but worse than that is the realization that terror isn't the most terrifying feeling in the world.

It's feeling nothing at all.

You'll never leave Black Harbor. For years, I've wondered whether his words were a prediction or a promise. Either way, he was wrong. Because I'm the one who left. And he never will.

That's a promise.

SUNDAY, JUNE 30

1
KOLE

The sucker punch happens as soon as he walks in. A metaphorical sucker punch, but still, it has the same effect as a row of knuckles slamming into his skull: his eyes water, his nose crinkles, his head snaps back. The stench of rot is so visceral it could bring a grown man to his knees. And it has. His eyes shift to the edges of the room where ribbons of steam rise from puddles of fresh vomit. At least the baby cops got their retching out of the way before his arrival. They stand outside now, brushing their tongues over their teeth and guarding the perimeter.

That being said, he's smelled worse.

The Mineshaft is derelict even by Black Harbor standards. An afterset on Heeley Avenue, it's a hangout for biker gangs and dope dealers, a "gool" of sorts where opposing baddies call a truce and shoot the bull—or the bum, which was apparently the case last night.

The body's in the back, although the palpable reek makes it seem as if it's right under his nose.

Sergeant Nikolai Kole takes another step inside, his steely gaze already searching for bullet casings and blood. The floor appears to be covered in it—blood, that is—as if someone dunked a paintbrush in a bucket of it and went to town like a knockoff Jackson Pollock. It's just paint, though; helter-skelter splatters of red and white make his job extraordinarily more difficult than it needs to be.

"Well, this is fucking annoying," he grumbles to no one in particular.

Two paces away, near a cow skull hanging cockeyed behind the bar, Investigator Fletcher pauses. "What's that?"

Kole gestures to the floor. Fletcher nods, understanding. They just got here and the guy's already sweated through his black tactical T-shirt. It suctions to him like cling wrap, making Kole suddenly aware of his own shirt sticking to his chest, back, and biceps. Thank God he isn't wearing body armor on top of it; he'd croak from heatstroke.

The Mineshaft is a genuine hellhole, and if there's one thing you can count on with those it's that, no matter the time of year, hellholes are always hot. Now, being the weekend before the Fourth of July, with temperatures skyrocketing into the high nineties and not a drop of rain since May, it's a fucking inferno.

Admittedly, this is the first time Kole's ever set foot in this particular hellhole. The fact that the Mineshaft operates like a bar but identifies as an afterset is a loophole that has chapped the Black Harbor Police Department's ass for years.

Investigator Riley enters the frame, fanning herself with the complaint form. Beads of sweat dot her lip. "Afterset, huh? There's a lot of empty liquor bottles for a place without a liquor license."

Kole matches her gaze to the three hundred or so plastic cups and shot glasses that litter the tabletops and the floor. Liquor bottles lie on their sides as if waiting for someone to give them a spin. "You know the defense is gonna want all these tested for DNA," he says.

Riley snorts. "Ain't nobody got time for that."

"This place should've been shut down a long time ago," says Fletcher, and Kole would love nothing more than to throw a dart at his thick skull. Shutting down the Mineshaft was a fool's errand, reasons being that (1) they've got bigger, scarier fish to fry, and (2) it's members only. Any cop stupid enough to go undercover would *get his a$$ beat*.

According to the "House Rules" anyway. The letter board is on the back wall, behind the bar.

> **THE MINESHAFT—H0U53 RU⌃3$**
> NO
> HANDS ON MY MF DOORS
> FIGHTING IN MY MF HOU$E
> GLASS BOTTLES
> WEAPONS
> PICTURES
> COPS
>
> WHEN THE HOU$E IS TALKING SHUT THE F%CK UP!
> OBEY OR GET YOUR A$$BEAT!

"House Rules," he knows, is a play on words. The Mineshaft's owner is a guy named Joseph Orien, but everyone calls him Big House, because he's built like a brick shithouse and he basically grew up in the big house, aka Sulfur County Prison, getting locked up for things like assault and grand theft auto. They'll have to get in contact with him. But first, Kole wants to identify the poor bastard who's stinking up the joint. Maybe Big House will know him and how he got himself murdered and they can all go home.

Yeah, right.

"You get the name of the caller?" he asks Riley. The call filtered through Dispatch at 0446 hours. Patrol responded to a noise complaint, only to hear a rumor from several people outside the establishment that someone was dead. Officers arrived and forced entry, and Kole's phone rang at 0542 hours.

There's only one reason his phone rings that early, and it's never anyone inviting him to breakfast.

Riley squints to read the form. She states the complainant's name and adds: "Lives over on Meacham."

Kole's head tilts back as though the address tells him most, if not all, he needs to know about her. Just two streets over, Meacham's a tough area, its inhabitants fairly transient. Not a lot of good comes out of there, but a lot of bad passes through.

"Why don't you two head over there. See if she's willing to share whatever she knows." Then, "Where's Winthorp?"

"Him or her?" asks Riley.

"Him, the one I'm responsible for."

"Axel's with Patrol on the perimeter," offers Fletcher.

"Good, tell him to start canvassing the neighborhood. Look for other dead bodies, and any live bodies who might've seen or heard something. Check doorbell cameras, surveillance cameras . . . he knows the drill."

They depart with their marching orders, and Kole plunges farther into the place, weaving through a maze of tipped-over stools and bright-yellow evidence placards. A new scent infiltrates the air. It smells like cleaning products.

A propped-open door in the back leads to a closet-sized bathroom, inside of which is a body cocooned in trash bags and duct tape. It's lying supine, head pushed against the base of the toilet and feet angled toward the door. A pool of blood leaks out from underneath, matching the stuff splattered on the stucco walls.

Kole catches a flash of blond hair in his peripheral vision. Medical Examiner Rowan Winthorp is squeezed between the door and the pedestal sink. "You beat me here," he says.

"I rode in with Axel." Rowan snaps on her black latex gloves. "Figured we were going to the same place."

"What do you make of this?" Kole asks, pointing to shallow pools of liquid glistening on the trash bags.

"Bleach," says Rowan, and Kole notes the discarded container. "I'd say whoever doused this guy was in a hurry, probably trying to erase their fingerprints." Then, she plants one foot on either side of the body, and hovering over the torso, she drags a knife from the top of the head to the chest. She peels the two halves of plastic apart to reveal a Caucasian male with dark hair, the whiskey nose of an alcoholic.

Kole steps aside, giving her room to work. He leans over to get a good look at the victim. Beneath the blood and the bruises, he recognizes the poor bastard. The edges of his vision darken, forcing him to home in on the dead man's face. It's been years since he last laid eyes on him. He's a little older, a little heavier in the jowls—clearly he's spent a lot of his time at the bottom of a bottle—but otherwise, he looks the same.

"Friend of yours?" poses Rowan.

"Not exactly."

"But you know him?"

Kole sighs. Yes, he knows him. Or, he knows of him, rather. They've never so much as exchanged a word, but the hate that Tommy Greenlee harbored for Kole these past eight years hovers over his corpse like a toxic aura. For a fleeting second, Kole feels mildly guilty for how things turned out. It passes, though.

Guilt is a wasted emotion.

"I slept with his wife."

Rowan's eyes widen. "The transcriber?"

Kole flinches. "Everyone knows about that, huh?"

Her silence is telling. He crouches down to examine the body up close. Tommy's lip is split. A dried river of red glares on the bridge of his nose. His eyes are the most disturbing part, though. The iris and pupil are gone, having dissolved into two blackish-brown stripes. It's called tache noire and means "black stain" in French, a phenomenon that occurs when the eyes are not fully closed and postmortem drying occurs. The eyes are literally melting, losing their structure.

Kole's gaze travels to the shredded chest. He must have been shot five or six times. Maybe more. The work is sloppy. Whoever killed Tommy Greenlee was angry.

In their mind, he deserved to die like this.

"Gang-related?" Rowan's question pulls him out of his trance.

"Could be." The truth is, while gangs have always been prevalent in Black Harbor, tensions now are worse than ever. Teenage boys are being recruited at an alarming rate; they're naïve about how expendable they are until they're getting whacked in an alley. Houses are being shot up on the daily and cars are being stolen right out of people's driveways. Maybe it's the heat lately, but it feels like the city is ready to erupt. Perhaps this—his gaze flicks back to Tommy—is the start of it.

Rowan considers her watch and pronounces time of death. "June 30, 0718 hours." She will go more in-depth at the medical examiner's office in Milwaukee, he knows, where there's room to breathe. "At least he's pliable," she says, lifting his arm and checking for marbling and contusions.

"Silver lining," Kole mutters.

With this heat, the stages of rigor will be expedited. He isn't a medical expert, but he's been around cadavers enough to know that the cessation of the body's natural thermoregulation means that gasses are being produced at a faster rate, creating holes for flies and other insects to lay their eggs. Cell structures are breaking apart. In a matter of hours, this will all be a liquified mess. They need to get Tommy into a freezer before any clues to what happened are completely erased.

As if they're reading each other's thoughts, Rowan says: "Help me roll him over."

Kole slides his arms beneath the shoulders while Rowan grabs the trunk. Together, they heave the body onto its side. She slices the garbage bags some more with her knife and tears away the plastic, then peels up the victim's shirt. The flesh on the back is bluish-purple, a result of blood pooling at the lowest point. She presses her fingers to it. Kole has seen where sometimes her prints remain, blanching the skin. But not this time.

"Lividity is decent," she notes. "Not blanchable yet, even though this heat's speeding everything up. My guess is he was killed around 1 or 2 A.M."

Kole nods. It checks out. If there's a witching hour in Black Harbor, that's it. He looks up as something gold catches his eye. The water in the toilet bowl is pink, but nestled in the neck of it are two brass bullet casings. It's at this moment—with his arm sunk up to his elbow in a toilet and he's silently cursing every life decision that landed him in this predicament—when his mind wanders to Hazel, the one person connecting him to the rapidly decomposing corpse on the floor. It's been nearly eight years since he watched her leave Black Harbor behind for good. He never thought she'd come back, and yet, as he stares at the spent casings now glistening in his palm, an impossible thought screws itself into his mind: perhaps she already has.

2
KOLE

"Knew you couldn't stay away." Milo Crue is pouring a fresh cup of coffee when Kole walks into the SIU hideout. He lets himself into the lieutenant's office and sits down.

"Have a seat," says Crue sarcastically. His previous comment is warranted; Kole was just out with them last night, hours before getting called in for the homicide, assisting SIU with investigating a gang shooting on Geneva Street. Although the Special Investigations Unit and Violent Crime Task Force operate separately—with SIU fighting the war on gangs and drugs, and Kole's VCTF tackling homicides—more often than not, their worlds collide. Yesterday's incident was the typical Saturday-night bullshit with the usual suspects: East Side Anarchists versus Nightmare Kings. As tempting as it is to stand on the sidelines and let these gang members kill each other, inevitably an innocent citizen would get caught in the cross fire. Not to mention the property damage is out of control. These gangs are locusts destroying everything in their path.

"I'd offer you some," says Crue, "but . . ."

Kole makes a face as Crue slides the carafe back onto the warming plate. Saving his soliloquy on how coffee is only good for composting, he dumps the contents of a paper bag on Crue's desk. The two shells he fished out of the toilet roll onto the surface.

"Your guys pick up any of these at the Geneva Street shooting?" Kole asks.

Crue picks up one of the casings with a tissue and reads the headstamp. The marking on the bottom is already branded in Kole's brain: S&W .38 SPL. "Smith & Wesson .38 Special." Crue frowns. "I'll have to check. Shit's pretty old, though. Smith & Wesson hasn't made ammo since the seventies. Where'd you find these?"

"The toilet."

Crue screws up his face and sets the casing down. "Are you serious?" Aside from being disgusted, Kole knows what else the lieutenant is thinking: unlike an automatic, a revolver doesn't eject casings. Whoever shot Tommy emptied the entire cartridge, then must have cast them aside to reload.

"We recovered a dead body at the Mineshaft early this morning."

"I heard." Crue squirts hand sanitizer in his palm. "One of my guys' informants, or what?"

"Tommy Greenlee."

"Why do I know that name?"

"A former transcriber . . . Hazel Greenlee. He's her ex-husband."

A distant look enters Crue's eyes as he searches his memory. "I remember her," he says, finally. "Dark hair? Pretty? Got wrapped up in the Candy Man investigation?"

"That's her."

"She moved away, didn't she? After the whole almost-getting-murdered thing."

"As far as I know."

Crue falls quiet for a moment, and Kole knows what's coming next. "Isn't that the one you . . ."

Kole rolls his eyes. "Yes."

"Is she a suspect?"

"No way." While the thought had indeed entered Kole's mind, its presence was fleeting. Not only would Hazel never return to Black Harbor, this was clearly an inside job. Whoever murdered Tommy Greenlee had to have been a member of the club—which Tommy wasn't. He was either lured to the Mineshaft under false pretenses, or he was there against his will.

He tells Crue as much, who offers: "That, or he knew a member who got him in."

"Or that, yeah." He fills him in on where they're at with the investigation: Riley and Fletcher are interviewing the complainant and Axel is canvassing with patrol officers. The autopsy's scheduled for ten o'clock tomorrow morning.

"What about Big House?" Crue names the owner of the afterset. All BHPD officers, from patrol to top brass, are familiar with him. "You know the DA's office is gonna assume this is his handiwork."

"Maybe it is, maybe it isn't."

Crue nods, apparently satisfied. As much as the lawyers in the district attorney's office would love to draw a line down the middle of the city's criminal activity and classify all violent crime as stemming from Big House and assign all drug-related mischief to Hades, it isn't that simple. Just as the worlds of Kole's Violent Crime Task Force and Crue's drug unit often collide, the same is true for Black Harbor's criminal enterprisers.

Besides, Hades has been off the streets for four years, ever since Kole arrested him for possession of cocaine and running a drug house, and the drug activity hasn't exactly dried up. It just goes to show that Black Harbor will always be a dark and dangerous place. The best any of them can do is try to keep it in check.

Kole stands. "Anyway, I'm hoping I can borrow a couple of your guys to help search Tommy's residence. The warrant's being reviewed now. Should be ready to go in an hour or two."

Crue loosely gestures to the detectives milling around their desks as though to say, *Have at 'em.*

"In the meantime, I want to talk with them, see what their snitches are saying."

He has to keep this investigation moving. They have a matter of hours—maybe less—until the media catches wind of this murder. Soon, everybody and their brother will know about the body that was discovered in the back of the Mineshaft. It isn't always a bad thing. People usually come forward when a story breaks, and sometimes, they actually have valuable information: they know someone who was there, or they heard something. Most of the time, though, it's just someone looking for someone else to give a fifteen-minute fuck about what they've got to say.

"Probably a good idea," Crue endorses. Then, his voice falls to a low register. "It's just . . ."

"What?"

"A .38 Special is kind of a girly gun, isn't it? Little snub-nose revolver like that."

Kole bites the inside of his cheek. He feels his shoulder blades pull toward each other. "There are other guns that shoot that caliber."

"Okay."

"It wasn't her, Milo."

Crue shows his palms. "I'm just saying it could have been a woman, is all. You sure the ex-wife is the only chick Tommy could have pissed off?"

Twenty minutes later, he looks over the names he's got scratched on a legal pad. They belong to people known to either frequent the Mineshaft or live near it. Kole's familiar with most of them. He taps the tip of his pen on the last one. "Robert Pitts. He's gotten into selling the harder stuff lately, hasn't he?"

Malcolm Jimenez nods. "Fentanyl. I managed to get two buys on him, just need a third, but he's ghosted me. My CI says she can't make contact with him anymore. Unless she's playing games."

Kole considers that for a second. The "buys" Malcolm mentioned are controlled purchases—setups in which a drug cop gives a confidential informant cash to purchase illegal substances from a known dealer. The transaction is recorded via hidden camera worn by the CI, who, afterward, surrenders the illegal substances to the drug detective. To play by the rules, you need three controlled purchases to achieve a search warrant for the offender's residence. But criminals have evolved. Their ability to sniff out snitches has developed into something superhuman, which forces the cops to get creative. They swap out CIs so as not to use the same one all three times, they conduct four or five controlled purchases instead of three, and sometimes, they surprise the suspect in the middle of a transaction and hit his house once he's in custody.

"Fuckin' fentanyl," Kole mutters.

"Now there's Xombie to contend with, too—with an *X*," he adds, and Kole makes the correction in his notes. "It's a premade cocktail of fentanyl, carfentanil, and xylazine. Users are dropping like flies."

"You guys stop using Narcan or what? Thought that shit grew on trees around here." As a former drug cop, he has a complicated relationship with the medicine. On one hand, its ability to instantly reverse the effects of an opioid saves lives, which is great. But, is it really? Because after administering it to the same party seven, eight, nine times, he also sees how it not only enables people to stay addicted, it's a Band-Aid that enables the city to avoid setting up serious resources.

"Don't work, brother," says Malcolm. "Not with xylazine."

"Because it isn't an opioid?"

"Correct."

"So, you overdose, you die? End of story?"

"Seems to be the case. It's nasty stuff, too. People get all these sores that won't heal. They literally rot. That's why some of the kids call it *the purple people eater*." He scrolls through his camera roll to show Kole a photo of confiscated Xombie. Kole pinches the screen to zoom in. Three purple pills lie on a paper towel. The monogram CXF is printed on the seam.

"Seized that from a fourteen-year-old," Malcolm adds. "Said he bought it off Robert Pitts."

Kole's chest tightens. This conversation is quickly reminding him why, as much as he enjoyed kicking in doors and raiding drug dens, he was glad to walk away from the never-ending opioid epidemic. Not that stopping violent crime is any less futile. He circles Robert Pitts's name. "Who's your CI that's working him?"

"Dirty Harriet."

Kole's mouth twitches with an almost smile. He knows Dirty Harriet. Orange-haired and feral, she's a human alley cat, adept at slinking around and getting information. Plus, she's got nine lives and no matter how doped up she is, she always lands on her feet. "One of my old CIs," he acknowledges. "I passed her off to Crue."

"Who passed her off to me," says Malcolm.

"Lucky you." He stands and shakes Malcolm's hand. "Thanks for the info. I'll see you in an hour for the pre-warrant briefing."

Malcolm nods, but he's more tense than he was a moment ago. When Kole asks what's wrong, the detective works his jaw and takes a deep breath. "I hate to say it, but things were better when Hades was still on the streets."

The statement is a kick to the groin. Still, Kole manages to maintain his composure and draw himself up to his full height. "You think I shouldn't have locked him up?" His heart rate quickens as he anticipates the answer. His hands squeeze into fists. "I don't know if you noticed, but we were losing the battle on drugs even then."

This time, Malcolm looks almost rueful when he meets Kole's gaze. "And now we're losing the whole fucking war."

3
KOLE

"All right, dish." Kole sits on the edge of his metal desk, feet planted on the seat of his chair. Thumbs hooked beneath his jaw, he stares thoughtfully out the third-story window of the lighthouse that serves as the VCTF's off-site command center. Below is a vast expanse of blue. Lake Michigan has claimed two lives in the past two days. It will claim more by week's end, unfortunately. The Fourth of July is always disproportionately high for drownings. People refuse to accept that Lake Michigan has a riptide, that she's more like the ocean.

A current of warm air blows in his direction. It's almost enough to wick the sweat from his brow, but then the fan rotates. This is week five of insufferable working conditions; unlike the rest of the world, working remotely is one more luxury that the BHPD cannot be afforded. Fletcher tried to pull that shit once, suggesting he type his report from home and come in later. Kole threatened to drive to his house and drag him out here by his ponytail.

He's here now, his T-shirt soaked through with sweat, sitting back-to-back with Riley.

Axel should arrive any minute with the signed warrant, granting them permission to search Tommy Greenlee's residence.

Throughout his years in Investigations, Kole has learned two things about detectives: they are all of them hunters, and there's more than one type. There are the thinkers, like Axel; they like to lay out all their pieces, to look at the whole picture before moving in for the kill. Then there are ones like Fletcher, the hungry dogs; give them the scent of blood and they'll take off like a bullet, hunting tirelessly until they bring in their prize. And, finally, there's Riley. He's never met anyone like her. All stealth and secrets, she's a mystery, one he's accepted he'll never solve. Together, each of their unique talents gives them a fighting chance at tackling the onslaught of violent crime in this city. It's why he hand-selected them for his task force.

"Has anyone gotten in touch with Big House? Was he there last night?"

"Word on the street is he's out of state," offers Riley. "On a fishing trip."

"Convenient. What does the word on the street have to say about when he'll be back?"

"Wednesday."

July 3. Kole makes a mental note. "See if that alibi checks out, please. So what'd the complainant have to say?"

Riley does most of the talking and Fletcher adds color commentary as they tell him about visiting the complainant's residence, where she operates an in-home daycare. "So far it all tracks," says Riley. "She told us she called 911 around quarter to five this morning to report loud music and what she thought may have been gunshots."

"Funny she didn't just assume it was firecrackers." These days, the city is a cacophony of whistles and pops. For two weeks straight, people light off fireworks like it's their God-given right.

"She did at first," says Riley, "which was why she didn't call right away. Not until she started hearing rumors that someone was dead inside the Mineshaft."

"And she heard that from who?" presses Kole, already dreading that this is one of those goddamn heard-it-from-a-friend-who-heard-it-from-a-friend webs they will have to untangle.

"Her cousin, Darren Hogan. He's since gone back to Chicago—"

"So she claims," interjects Fletcher.

"—so she claims," cosigns Riley. "Anyway, apparently it was pretty rowdy at the Mineshaft last night. A fight broke out in the back and the bartender just kept turning up the stereo to drown out the noise."

Kole tilts his head back. That checks with what the neighbors have been saying all morning—those who would talk, anyway—that the street was literally bumping. *I swear to God that fuckin' place was pulsin', the music was so damn loud . . .* he recalls from one interview in particular. "So much for no fighting in the motherfuckin' house," he says, recalling the House Rules.

Riley wears her braids piled and pinned on top of her head. One has come free, drawing a line down the middle of her face. She tucks it behind her ear. "The complainant stated she heard there were close to a hundred people in that bar."

"Clubhouse," corrects Kole. A sardonic smile tugs at his mouth as Riley rolls her eyes.

"So, which one of those hundred or so derelicts was Hogan with last night?" When Riley and Fletcher exchange a glance, he adds: "It's members only. If Hogan's from Chicago, I'm willing to bet he isn't a member. He had to have been someone's plus-one."

"Robert Pitts," says Riley. "That's what Hogan told the complainant, anyway."

The name sends a chill zipping up Kole's spine. "Jimenez is working Pitts right now. He says he ghosted him after two buys." He catches them up on his conversation with Malcolm Jimenez over at SIU. Leave it to Black Harbor to be the last place in the continental US to get Wi-Fi and traffic-light cameras, but the first to hop on the latest drug trends.

"Xombie," says Fletcher. "I've heard about that shit. It eats people alive."

"Sounds like the last thing we need here," Kole acknowledges. He goes on to mention that Narcan is useless against it, but leaves out the part about Jimenez blaming his arrest of Hades for the worsening drug landscape. The mere thought boils his blood, and he's hot enough as it is.

At the tail end of his story, Axel clips up the stairs. His face is red. He fans himself with the signed warrant.

Kole hops off his desk and snatches it from him. "You can blast the AC in the car. Let's get this briefing done so we can see what Tommy's house has to tell us. Fletch, go ahead and see who you can grab from Patrol to set up a perimeter. We'll meet you there in less than an hour. Riley, ride with Axel and me. I'm not trying to start a goddamn parade."

4
KOLE

They approach the duplex two by two. The house is mauve and molting. The entire structure slumps forward. On the ground, shards of glass sparkle in the harsh light. An old beer bottle is pulverized into the lawn, its label faded and torn. The grass is so stiff it feels like needles snapping beneath his feet. In his peripheral vision, Kole watches as other detectives take their places on the perimeter. Fletcher managed to scare up three patrol officers and an evidence technician, and Kole snagged four detectives from SIU. It's enough for them to get the job done, granted there are no dangerous persons holed up inside, waiting for police to arrive so they can open fire.

They've already had two of those this summer.

"The adjoining unit is unoccupied?" Axel falls into step beside him.

"The old guy who lived next door died last year," says Kole. "He owned the place, too, so with no living children to inherit it, he left it to Tommy." He glances surreptitiously at Riley, then, who walks behind them. She looks unfazed, despite the fact that she is the reason the old man had no living children, for it was her finger that pulled the trigger and sent a bullet careening through his son's chest. He toppled off of Forge Bridge, splashing into the river like countless bodies before and after.

Shooting him was less than ideal, but then . . . it was him or Hazel. One of them wasn't walking off that bridge.

He slows his breathing so he can listen. For the sounds of dogs barking or someone moving around inside. The air feels electric; the hair on his arms stands on end and he wonders if it isn't the intensity of the memories attached to this place. Of him sitting in his vehicle, watching Hazel in his rearview mirror as she gets out of her truck and slams the door. Of her bright blue eyes burning into his as she stands next to his window, begging him to leave. It was the first and only time he ever saw her without her makeup. She looked younger than her twenty-six years then, with a constellation of freckles across her cheeks. This is the moment he replays over and over, the one that runs on a loop when he lies awake at night and rehearses what he would do differently if he had the chance to do it all over again. He likes to believe that he wouldn't let her go into that house where she would be hunted down by the psycho inside, that this time, he would ask her to stay with him.

Mercifully, the memory relinquishes its hold. Kole's throat itches. He spits on the ground and swears he hears it sizzle.

"Ready?" Axel tilts his head toward the duplex.

The warrant is a knock and announce. If someone's inside, they've got about ten seconds not to be. Kole stands back, gun drawn, as Axel takes the stairs. The front step cracks under his weight. "Police! Search warrant!"

They wait.

Kole watches the door. If memory serves him right, there were dead bolts on the other side. No reason to believe they wouldn't still be there.

Axel shouts and knocks again.

No answer.

They move in.

"Police! Search warrant!" Axel pounds a total of three times and then tries the knob. The door keens and falls away, inviting them into a dark interior. Kole tightens his grip on his gun. The fact that the house is unlocked is more unnerving than if all the hatches had been battened down. Someone was here after Tommy.

They could still be inside.

Kole enters after Axel. The darkness swallows them. "Police!" he shouts. "If anyone's inside, come out with your hands—" His breath catches. His eyes ricochet around the room. The place is a disaster. Brass casings litter the floor. Steel gun safes have been ripped away from the walls; they lie faceup, their doors open wide. Picked clean.

Someone has clearly looted the place.

Someone who knows the combinations to the gun safes, he realizes, as he notes the locks are intact.

The only real furniture is a sagging love seat, its cushions so chock-full of dust it promises a plume of debris to anyone who dares sit down. A lawn chair is planted in the middle of the room, a half-empty can of Natty Ice in the mesh cup holder. It's collected as evidence, in case the perp decided to sit down and have a beer after all their hard work.

The residence is cleared in a matter of minutes. No parties are located inside. They regroup in the living room—a term that borders on satire for a place so full of dead things. The place reminds Kole of Deschane's taxidermy shop. Animal carcasses stare at them with blind, glass eyes from every corner. Deer heads protrude from the walls, cobwebs strung between their antlers. A pheasant is frozen in mid-flight; a raccoon creeps along the mantel.

Kole chooses his next steps carefully, not wanting to contaminate the crime scene more than they already have.

"How many guns you reckon he must've had?" asks Axel.

"Enough for a small militia," Kole estimates.

"Check this out." Fletcher is paging through a faded green journal. A swatch of duct tape adhered to the front cover with primitive, almost childish handwriting: CLEANING IS NOT AN OPTION! Apparently that rule didn't apply to the rest of the place.

"What's that, a cleaning log?" Kole asks, coming around to read over Fletcher's shoulder. There are columns to denote dates and serial numbers, everything scratched in the same handwriting as on the cover.

"Goddamn, there must be fifty or sixty guns in here," mutters Fletcher.

"And now they're out on the streets."

Kole lifts his eyes to meet Axel's. The statement hangs in the air like an ill omen, but it's a fact. Even as they stand here, the serial numbers are being stripped, each firearm falling into the wrong hands.

Unless Tommy moved them himself. But why—

"Oh shit." Fletcher stops fanning the pages.

"What?" Kole takes the book from him as Fletcher asks: "What kind of rounds were those casings you fished out of the toilet again?"

".38 Special." He's said it over and over to himself so many times now that he recites the calibers on autopilot, as if giving his usual order in a drive-thru. He pages through the journal. Ranging from assault rifles to handguns, it's an inventory of every gun that Tommy Greenlee owns—or *owned*. Possession is nine-tenths of the law. His eyes scan each line, speeding past makes, models, serial numbers, dates of when cleaned and last shot, until suddenly, at the bottom of a page, he stops. The final entry notes:

.38 Special S&W	Revolver	.38SPL	639712	11/18/15	Hazel's gun (MIA)

"Shit," he breathes, echoing Fletcher.

Riley's come around to read over Kole's shoulder. He hears the accusation in her voice, then, when she says what they're all thinking: "Well, are you gonna call her or are you gonna make one of us do it?"

MONDAY, JULY 1

5
HAZEL

I shouldn't be here.

It's early morning, not yet 7 A.M., and the dew has already burned off the grass. Brooklyn is hot but it's temperate compared to Black Harbor. At least there's shade where I've just come from, whether from the trees or skyscrapers, or the ocean haze that hangs in the air like a protective covering. There's no protection here. The leaves on the trees are rough and ragged, gnawed on by insects and the sun's rays. Yards have dried into postage stamp–sized hay fields. I kick a malt liquor can by accident. It skates across the asphalt and careens into an empty airplane bottle of vodka and a Roman candle wrapper. A crinkled Cheetos bag curls into a fist, only half hiding a used heroin needle or whatever the poison of choice is these days.

Monday is apparently garbage day on this side of town—an unfortunate oversight on my part. Sun-faded black bins are stuffed to the gills with sour-smelling trash, all bellied up to the curb, as though waiting for the truck to come along and transport them someplace better than here. Like the landfill.

My stomach clenches as I jog past a particularly pungent area. I can feel the asphalt expanding and cracking beneath the soles of my running shoes, the way it moves and breathes, a giant snake slowly wrapping me up, waiting to strike. The tree line becomes my own personal stalker, its jagged shape ever present in a corner of my vision even as I wind my way through town. Everything is so arid in this tiny, tragic corner of the world. *As dry as a weathered bone,* my grandmother would say.

I spoke to her on the phone yesterday. She brought up Tommy's murder of course; she knew I'd already seen the news. Because my sister, Elle, told her—I'd been FaceTiming her when the story broke—or simply because grandmothers are clairvoyant like that. She sounded just like Elle when she said: "Hazel, don't you dare."

"I won't," I lied. I couldn't break her heart and confess that I was already at my gate, a boarding pass in hand for a one-way flight from JFK to MKE.

That was last night.

But what my family doesn't see, or wouldn't understand, is that I need to find out who killed Tommy. The cops are all over this, but I know things. I know *him*. Ten years he's lived here and never ended up dead. Well, no, that's not quite right. "Living in Black Harbor" is an oxymoron. No one lives here; you survive it. And Tommy was surviving, up until now.

I run past the street where I used to reside. I don't turn onto it. I will go there, just . . . not right this second. There's something about knowing that everyone who once inhabited that duplex is dead that repels me, as though perhaps the place is cursed and if I go there, I'll be next. Besides, it's probably still teeming with police now. They'll be poking around, prying open gun safes and searching for answers to the same question as me: Who killed Tommy Greenlee and why?

The Airbnb I rented is a vacant unit in an apartment building. It's actually quite nice, furnished and boasting original hardwood floors. An antique elevator crawls slowly between the five stories.

Last night, when I arrived after dark, I paid $500 cash to the building manager, a middle-aged man named Robbie wearing a baseball cap and a grimy white T-shirt—the kind that comes in a pack of six. He thanked me and asked, "You're not . . . hiding from someone, are you?"

"No," I assured him, perhaps a bit too emphatically. I quickly turned it around. "That's a weird thing to ask."

He shrugged. "Sorry, but . . . you didn't bring hardly nothing with you."

I looked down at the stuff I had set down. A backpack with my laptop tucked safely inside along with some clothes and my makeup bag. The laces of my running shoes were tied around the straps.

"I'm just . . . here for a hot minute." I smiled and wondered immediately if it wasn't the wrong thing to say, if I didn't perhaps look like all the broken women who probably turned up on his doorstep either seeking refuge from an abusive relationship or wanting to rent this place out by the hour.

He smiled tightly but it didn't reach his eyes. He looked sad and told me to call him if I needed anything, then gave me his card and left me be.

Now, I slow my jog to a stop at the crosswalk. Standing at the roundabout across from the police department, I see my old transcribing window, behind which I used to sit, peering through slits in the blinds, watching the streetlamps wink on and off as I transcribed all the gritty goings-on of the city. The potholes are still in the parking lot—old wounds that refuse to heal. I stay on the sidewalk, not close enough to catch my reflection in the glass. I wonder if someone is there now, sitting in my old chair, listening and typing as detectives divulge the city's darkest secrets.

How is it that eight years ago feels like a lifetime and yesterday all at once?

Doing a slow 360, I stare at the patch of earth where the apartments once stood. Where a nine-year-old boy died in his sleeping bag after overdosing on pills given to him by his neighbor, who bought them off of Sarah Dylan, who called herself the Candy Man. Without the apartments blocking the view, I see where the road drops off into a steep descent, eventually leveling off into a vacant lot that leads to Forge Bridge.

I wonder if I am the only one it didn't take. If I am the only person to have walked across its railroad ties, gripped the iron rungs, breathed in the metallic scent of rust and fish and whatever trash lay below, and left intact. A vague term, I know. "Intact" meaning my internal organs are all where they're supposed to be and my bones aren't shattered. I am shattered in other ways, of course. After all, what are humans but mosaics of memories and scars and the things that broke us but couldn't kill us?

A black plastic bag floats across the street. One of those cheap ones you get at the liquor store, it pitches with a sudden breath of wind, tumbling end over end. Drinking in a deep inhale, I start to run again, chasing the bag to the bottom of the hill. It's gone when I reach the abandoned parking lot. Dried spikes of grass shoot through the cracks. Black starbursts stain the asphalt that's littered with the colorful debris of spent fireworks and fast-food wrappers. I forgot that the Fourth of July is always a two-week-long celebration. Any excuse to set shit on fire. There is something terrifically unsettling about the world being made of kindling, and the way it's still—so still—as if waiting for someone to come along and strike a match.

My gaze finds the bag again. It's snagged on a branch in front of the coal-blackened jaws of Forge Bridge and I can't help but think maybe it's a warning for what's going to happen to me this time.

Hardly anyone leaves Black Harbor.

And they sure as hell don't come back.

6

KOLE

He stands shotgun for the autopsy. The body has been scrubbed clean and laid out on a mortuary stretcher. All five bullet wounds have been documented and Liz, the forensic pathologist, has already completed her examination of the clothes by the time he arrives. Now, there's a soft squelching sound as she presses her scalpel hard into the flesh for the Y incision that extends from shoulder to shoulder, meeting at the breastbone and extending down to the pubic bone.

Kole isn't squeamish, but this part always gets him. Grabbing the flap she just made, Liz pulls it back up toward the neck. It looks almost as if Tommy was wearing a skin-colored shirt, which she has just reefed upward to expose his organs. She takes photographs before reaching for the garden shears. They're the same brand as the ones he has in his garage. The medical ones cost five times as much, Liz explained to him once, and "these crack a rib cage all the same."

Peering through his face shield, he spares a glance at the steepled structure of bone before she splits it apart. It reminds him of Forge Bridge, the way the ribs converge to create a carapace.

"Aha! Gotcha, you little bastard. That's the kill shot, right there," says Liz, pointing to a blood-covered bullet in what appears to be a urine sample cup. Kole watches as she sets the cup next to the other four that each contain one bullet. "Right in the liver, which . . ." She tilts her head. "Looks like he was doing a fine job of destroying all on his own."

"Cirrhosis?" Kole offers.

"Steatosis for sure," she mutters, and then adding for his benefit: "Fatty liver. I'll test him, but I'd bet my left nut this guy's blood-ethanol ratio is through the roof."

Kole frowns. He feels his eyebrows scrunch toward the middle of his forehead.

Liz laughs, her breath fogging her face shield. "Relax a little, Nik. You look like you're bracing yourself for this dude to jump off the table and throttle you."

Absent-mindedly, Kole touches his neck. "I don't like autopsies."

"Why not?"

"Because I don't need to see someone's face pulled off their face."

Liz smiles. "We haven't gotten to that part yet. Besides, I'm not exactly peeling his whole face off. I'm just folding his scalp down to his eyebrows."

Sufficiently skeeved out, Kole takes a step away from the table as a wave of nausea rocks him back on his heels. All of his current demons—the stress of the investigation, his abysmally sleepless night, the chemical stench of the morgue, and dread over the fact that there are now hundreds of unregistered firearms in the wrong hands—are on the same freight train and it's just careened into him.

He's been managing the stolen guns situation since 7 A.M. They entered all the serial numbers from the cleaning log into NCIC last night. Now Fletcher's working with an ATF agent to scour pawnshops, online marketplaces, and the black market—anywhere a used firearm might pop up.

To add insult to injury, none of the bullets that blanketed the floor were a match for the casings Kole fished out of the toilet yesterday morning.

"You could have sent someone else, you know." Liz's voice sounds distant.

"I know, but . . . I need to see this for myself."

"You know that's what 'autopsy' means, right? 'To see for oneself'?"

"I didn't."

Liz shrugs. "The more you know."

Cautiously, Kole creeps toward the table again. "So, if he hadn't been shot to death, he would have died from alcohol poisoning?"

"Eventually. If he kept drinking the way he was. By my estimation, this guy was consuming twenty-five to thirty units of alcohol a week. Some people come home from work, drink four or five beers a night, go hard on the weekends . . . that'll do it." She pokes at the swollen liver that resembles an overinflated whoopee cushion. Then, she cups a gloved hand beneath the stomach and shifts it back and forth. "Hear all that sloshing? He was off his ass when they shot him. Probably didn't even feel a fucking thing. Which is . . . a small mercy, I suppose."

"I suppose," mutters Kole, because he doesn't know what else to say at this moment, except to wish that Tommy Greenlee had succeeded in drowning himself at the bottom of a bottle—or a can of cheap beer, rather—before he had to go and get himself shot. If he'd just died quietly in his home, Kole would not have been called to the scene, which means he wouldn't be forced to investigate the homicide of his ex-girlfriend's husband.

Ex-husband.

For the record, Hazel and Tommy had been on the outs before Kole ever entered the picture. From what little she'd told him, it seemed they were just two high-school sweethearts who grew up and grew apart, but there were moments when he wondered if something more sinister hadn't gone on behind closed doors. Hazel harbored a visceral fear of Tommy—a realization that reared its thorny head only after she left Black Harbor, when the dust settled and he was alone with his thoughts. He hadn't picked up on it earlier because he hadn't wanted to.

We see what we want to see.

He told her that once, upon explaining why police don't usually put too much stock into eyewitness statements. And yet as it turned out, he was guilty of that himself.

There were other behaviors that supported his suspicion. She was a piss-poor decision-maker, for one thing; it seemed like she was always waiting for someone else to orchestrate her next move. And once, in a vulnerable moment, she mentioned the agonizing pain of sex—that whenever she had intercourse with her husband, it felt like being stabbed with a hot poker. *But not with you,* she said, as though amazed at the discovery. *You feel so fucking good.*

He isn't a therapist, but he knows from working with victims of abuse that somatic symptom disorder is a physical manifestation of intense emotional distress. He researched it after she left, in an effort to better understand, and it broke his heart. How afraid does a person have to be to live as tense as a balled-up fist, always ready to fight or flee? Hazel was a runner, not a fighter. And she ran far away from Black Harbor as soon as opportunity knocked.

An hour later, Tommy's organs are separated into metal trays and blood samples have been collected. "I'm gonna peel his face off his face now," Liz warns. "Are you ready?"

Kole takes a fortifying breath. "Do your thing, Liz."

The forensic pathologist looks almost giddy when she moves toward the head.

"So what do you make of the bleach?" Kole asks. He diverts his gaze as she slices the scalp from ear to ear.

"Bleach?"

"Yeah, that was poured all over him."

"Ah." Liz is an artist, making meticulous lines on her body of work. She doesn't look up. "I think it was a shitty Plan B." She pauses, her tongue sliding between her lips as she makes a long incision. "Order of operations: they got him liquored up, they followed him into the bathroom, they shot him and then shot him some more, then they wrapped the body in garbage bags and poured bleach on it."

"Yes," says Kole, mentally ticking off each action as she says it, as if they're items on a grocery list. "My guess is that their Plan A was to dump the body somewhere. But they heard the police coming, so they poured bleach on the body to try to erase their fingerprints."

Liz snorts. "Come on, Nik. You can do better than that."

He flinches slightly.

"Not just *somewhere*. Where does everything get dumped in Black Harbor?"

The answer is obvious. Once he sees it, he can't understand how he didn't see it before. "The river."

With one hand still wielding the scalpel, Liz snaps her fingers for applause. The sound is immediately swallowed by the exhaust fan. She starts to peel, then, which prompts Kole to wander across the room, where a paper bag slumps on a stainless-steel table, its top folded down so it resembles an oversized sack lunch. Tommy's clothes are in it, along with whatever Liz took out of his pockets.

He checks inside and, one by one, extracts a bloody, cream-colored T-shirt that's riddled with bullet holes, and a pair of shorts, their khaki material mottled with bleach. The pockets are all empty; whatever contents they held are in a separate smaller paper bag.

He dumps it out to discover Tommy's wallet and some loose change. Nothing to write home about, until—

Kole stops breathing when he sees it. When he finally exhales, his breath fogs his face shield. He pushes it back so he can study the thing clearly, this bright-yellow paper that's pinched between his fingers. It's a scratch-off ticket. The words KA$H KA-CHING flash at him in red. He drags his gaze down to the scratch portion of the cardstock and reads the numbers all in a row: 0-5-3-7-3.

"Oh yeah, I found that in his back pocket." Liz's voice forces him to snap to. "I know a scratch-off probably isn't going to help you, but one lead I can give you is that he's not indigent."

"He's not what?" he repeats, but he heard her. His body is on autopilot while his mind whirs on overdrive. "Indigent" refers to bodies that have either no money, no one to claim them, or both. Unless a girlfriend comes out of the woodwork, Tommy's got no next of kin. Not around, anyway. According to Kole's research, both parents died in the past couple years and his sister lives overseas.

"Someone claimed him," says Liz. "Streuthers Funeral Home called me and arranged a pickup."

"Any idea who?"

Liz makes another careful cut. "My investigation's in here. Yours is out there. Call Streuthers if you're so curious. See who this guy belongs to."

7
HAZEL

The tendons in my arms threaten to snap as I grapple with the dozen or so plastic grocery bags deposited on the concrete stoop. I ordered them just over an hour ago so I wouldn't have to take a bus to the store, then spent the past twenty minutes in the lobby, watching like a hawk so if any of my temporary neighbors had half a mind to steal my food, they wouldn't have half a chance.

I punch the button to the elevator with my elbow. Refusing to take more than one trip is my fatal flaw. Thankfully, the car is already down here. It's outfitted with what must be the original black gate. Stepping inside feels like walking into a jail cell or a cage. Above, the dome light flickers, shining a strobe on the colonies of cobwebs in the ceiling.

Setting down one armful of bags, I hit the *2* button.

"Hold the door!"

Fuck.

I press the DOOR CLOSE button once, twice, three times. Finally, the gate drags across the platform. The toe of a shoe keeps it from going any farther.

Double fuck.

"Oh, sorry about that," I say, sounding breathless and almost sincere. I shrug and gesture vaguely to my groceries as if to prove I was preoccupied.

"It's all good." A man steps into the cage that was claustrophobic enough without him in it. He isn't terribly large and yet he seems to swallow up whatever space remains. I recognize him as Robbie, the building manager I met last night. His face is flushed and shining with sweat.

"Just out doing some repairs," he says. He tosses up his hands to reveal palms blackened with grease and grime.

Now I flush, because he obviously noticed me noticing him. "No rest for the weary."

"You can say that again." He huffs out a breath and removes his hat to scratch at his scalp. He has white-blond hair that's so light it all but disappears. His eyebrows are the same, barely existent.

"What floor?" I ask. Now that he's along for the ride, it won't kill me to be polite.

"Same." He nods at the illuminated 2.

The elevator is painstakingly slow.

He drips sweat onto the scuffed floor, each plink the tick of a metronome. I feel his stare pinning me to the wall. I don't dare match it. Avoiding eye contact isn't so much a Black Harbor thing as it is simply, sadly, a woman thing.

My skin prickles. My palms sweat. Finally, the car lurches, having arrived at my floor. I offer a parting smile, because not doing so has its own dangers, and step off the platform. "Let me help you," he says. It's a command, not an offer.

"Uh—" Before I can protest, he takes several of my bags and falls in step behind me. "Okay, just . . . this way," I say dumbly. Of course he knows where I'm going. He's the one who rented me the place. My heart jumps into my throat. *You're just being paranoid*, I tell myself as the door to my unit grows larger. *Not everyone is out to kill you.*

Still, no one's out to be my friend, either, that's for damn sure.

"Thank you," I say, relieved to be at my door. "You can just set them on the floor."

"You sure?" he asks.

I nod, not wanting to key my way inside with him so near. He might take it as an invitation. And then what? I'd be trapped.

He relinquishes the bags. A package of ground coffee tumbles out.

He catches it with his foot and bends down to stuff it back in. Still, he doesn't leave. "Sleep well?" he asks.

I'm caught off guard. "Um . . . yeah." I force a smile as if that's proof enough of a restful night. The truth is, I endured my eight hours of darkness all twisted up in the sheets and wishing I'd rented a place with central air.

"So, you're here for business, I assume."

I turn toward the door, hoping he will get the hint to leave already. Funny, he was in such a hurry to get in the elevator with me and now he seems to have all the time in the world. I nod. "Why would you assume that?" I ask, although in all honesty, he could assume worse things about me.

"Black Harbor's not exactly a vacation destination, sweetheart." His words are slick, dripping with condescension. He seems pleased with himself, as if he knows something I don't.

I clench my jaw, forcing my tongue to stay inside. Now isn't the time to regale him with tales of my tenure. I have as much right to be here as anyone else, present company included. "And yet you started an Airbnb."

His barely there eyebrows dance as his face splits into a grin and I hear the word he doesn't say. *Touché.*

"What kind of business?" he wants to know.

None of yours. "Writing."

"Like a journalist?"

Slowly, I nod.

"You're here for that murder, aren't you? The one that happened at the Mineshaft."

"Uhh . . . no," I lie. "Although is that something I should know about? Since I'm staying here and all?"

Robbie straightens his spine. His chest puffs out with an air of self-importance, and I get the feeling he fancies himself a Black Harbor tour guide for any women who rent one of his units.

"Not much to tell at the moment," he says. "Just a guy was found shot and wrapped in garbage bags, bleach poured on him, and left to rot in the bathroom of this old clubhouse. Only the worst of the worst go to that place, so I'm sure he was up to no good."

I flinch at the description. Despite the fact that I've been digging into as many sparse details as I can surrounding Tommy's recent demise, hearing about it so bluntly is unpleasant, to say the least. Tommy didn't deserve to die like that.

Or did he?

"Have you ever been there?" I ask.

A strip of his teeth is visible as he smiles. Unfortunately, he seems to take my honest question for flirting. "You think I'm the worst of the worst?"

"I hope not," I reply. When he leans in ever closer, I say: "I need to get back to work."

He gives me one last look up and down. "No rest for the weary," he echoes, and I can tell he thinks he's clever with how he's bookended our conversation. Down the hall, a door creaks open and someone steps out. The tension eases as the space is charged with one other person's molecules. I won't exhale until I'm back inside, though. Alone.

Robbie's gaze slides toward the sound. He flicks a nod at the tenant and turns back to me. "Look, if you need anything, I stay in the other wing," he says, jabbing his thumb over his left shoulder. "I'm literally in the unit right across from you."

"Thanks," I say, and I hate how brittle my voice sounds. Then, finally, he turns to go. I wait until he disappears around the corner to unlock my door. First, I have to dislodge the key that I've been holding like a blade between my knuckles.

8
KOLE

The house at which they arrive is squatty, the grass crispy and overgrown. A push lawnmower is parked in the front lawn as though it stalled out and stayed there. Kole parks his Impala beneath the shade of a maple tree and gets out. Axel joins him on a sidewalk covered in chalk drawings. He smiles, perhaps remembering a time when his own daughter was young enough for chalk art. Kole, on the other hand, frowns as if they are glyphs, each one a clue to solving the mystery at hand.

The sun is so bright it hurts, especially after three hours in the morgue. They both wear aviators as they approach the house and even though they're not in uniform, they couldn't look more like cops if they tried.

Kole knocks on the front door and steps back. He watches for movement, then—a shiver of blinds behind the picture window—and listens. It's eerily quiet; not just in this neighborhood but everywhere. Then he hears the clamor of a dog barking and footsteps padding toward him. The door falls away and it feels like they're standing in front of a walk-in beer cooler. Curls of air-conditioning leak out of the house. A woman stands on the threshold wearing a stinging red tank top stained with what he surmises to be formula, judging by the baby bouncing on her hip. Her eyebrow piercing glints. The look that flashes across her face tells him she knows who they are and why they're here.

"Mrs. Jeske? Is your—"

"Cam!" She leans back and shouts into the house, cutting him off. "The cops are here!"

More footsteps and then in a seamless transition, the woman and the baby melt away, replaced by a large, ruddy-faced man. The logo on his shirt is that of the water treatment plant, where Jeske works. It's the same place Tommy Greenlee worked up until Friday afternoon.

Kole made contact with his supervisor before coming out here. According to his time sheet, as of Friday at 1602 hours, Tommy Greenlee was employed with the City of Black Harbor as an aquatic ecologist. His criminal history was clean—not so much as a speeding ticket. While that didn't necessarily mean he was a law-abiding citizen, it did mean that he at least wasn't stupid or careless enough to get caught in bad situations he couldn't get out of.

Kole clears his throat. "Cameron Jeske. I'm Sergeant Nikolai Kole of the Black Harbor Police Department. This is Investigator Axel Winthorp. I just want to say that I'm very sorry for your loss. I understand Tommy Greenlee was a good friend of yours."

Cameron says nothing at first. He squints; his pupils are dilated, each one as small as the bead on a rifle sight. His mouth hangs slack for a moment. His breathing quickens. And for a split second, Kole wonders if he doesn't register his name. Depending on how good of friends they were, there's no chance Greenlee abstained from mentioning the cop who fucked around with his wife.

Unless his pride kept him quiet.

Finally, Cameron cuts his chin over his shoulder and says, "I'll meet you in the backyard."

A champagne-colored minivan is parked in front of the garage. The air is thick and sour back here, the obvious culprit a garbage can overflowing with diapers. A chest-high fence is on their left.

"Guy seems a little cagey," Axel comments under his breath. "You think he knows something?"

"According to their boss, these two knuckleheads spent just about every day on a boat together. He definitely knows something." Per his conversation with Tommy's supervisor, the guy stated that while Tommy was quite opinionated, especially when it came to politics, in the ten years he was employed at the water treatment plant, he worked hard and never missed a day.

So, even if he had been an alcoholic, he'd been a functioning one.

They maneuver around the side of the house, stepping on more chalk drawings, as Axel turns to ask: "Any word from Hazel?"

Kole stiffens. "I haven't had a chance to call her yet."

Axel's eyes squeeze in a way Kole doesn't like. He knows disbelief when he sees it, but it's more than half true. "Oh, I'm sorry. I forgot I have all the time in the world between hunting down stolen guns, going to an autopsy, and getting us here to find out what motivated this motherfucker to pay for our victim's entire funeral to make a phone call." He knows he sounds defensive. He doesn't care. The nerve of Axel. Honestly, the guy has worked enough homicides now to know that there's no real downtime during these cases.

Axel pauses. He actually *chooses* his next words. "I think you're scared."

Kole scoffs. "Of what?"

"That she'll pick up the phone."

Cameron Jeske beats them to the gate from the other side of the fence. He unlatches it, then swings it open to let them in. They join him in the backyard. "Thanks for agreeing to speak with us, Mr. Jeske," says Axel, taking the lead.

"Call me Cam. And I haven't agreed to anything yet." His eyes dart back and forth, checking for eavesdroppers.

Kole and Axel exchange a look. Cam's right; he hasn't agreed to anything. But he let them on his turf. Which means he wants to talk. Whether for his own pride or for Tommy, he just has to put up a tough-guy front first. It's clear, however, that he doesn't want to talk to Kole. Reading the situation correctly, Axel speaks. "I'm sure this is very difficult for you, Cam. Tommy must have been a true friend, for you to make all those funeral arrangements."

Cam stares at the ground. A piece of straw-colored hair falls in front of his caveman brow. He sniffs. "He would'a done it for me. Besides, a bunch of us at work all chipped in." Emotion gets the better of him, then, and he gives a violent shudder. He jams the heel of his hand under each eye to dam the flood of tears.

"You two were close."

Cam hawks a loogie into the grass and collects himself. "He was 'Uncle Tommy' to my kids." His mouth curves into a severe frown, perhaps at the gravity of using past tense. "I don't know how I'm going to explain it to them."

"Do you know what happened, Cam?" asks Axel. "Did Tommy have enemies? Any reason someone might have wanted him dead?"

Cam is still, but for his pupils pinballing back and forth, giving away his racing thoughts. "He'd hate me for telling you."

"He might if he were alive," says Kole. It's too damn hot to be pussyfooting around. The cold, hard truth is that someone murdered Tommy Greenlee, and Cameron Jeske at least has an idea regarding who and/or why.

Cam shoots him a sharp look.

Kole fights an eye roll. "Listen, I know you think you're betraying your friend, but you're not. Anything you tell us will only help us solve the mystery of his murder."

Silence is an unwanted guest in the backyard. Behind them, in the house, the baby cries. After a moment, Axel asks: "How many kids do you have?"

Cam blanches a little, but softens. "Three."

Axel nods. "I have one. She's seventeen now, but I remember when she was little like yours . . . drawing with chalk, riding her tricycle down the sidewalk. Anyway, someone took her last year." He sets his jaw. Any trace of his gentle smile from before is completely erased. "We got her back, but let me tell you, as a parent, the visceral, relentless fear that grips you when your child is gone and you have no idea if she's dead or alive"—his eyebrow arches up into his widow's peak—"it's something I wouldn't wish on my worst enemy."

Cam shifts uncomfortably. His facade is starting to crack. Axel hit him where he knew it would hurt the most: his kids. "Are you saying that whoever . . . killed . . . Tommy . . . is coming for my family?"

"Don't tell us it hasn't crossed your mind," says Kole.

Silence starts to settle again, but Axel breaks it with a question. "Did you know about the guns?"

"The guns?"

"The arsenal in Tommy's house," says Kole.

"Oh." Cam rakes a hand through his hair. "Yeah. He's . . . a prepper."

"A what?"

Cam blows out a breath as if he cannot believe he has to explain something so rudimentary. "A doomsdayer. Someone who prepares for the end of the world."

"Like Reba McEntire in the movie *Tremors*," offers Axel.

"Exactly," says Cam.

Kole fights another eye roll. He knows guys like Tommy Greenlee. Guys who crawl out of their respective basements to show up to the gun range with their paper targets and extended magazines, slinging their canvas satchels so they can collect their empty casings and reload them later, while they daydream about the day the government falls to utter shit, so society can look to them and simply say *Well, by golly, that crazy son of a bitch was right all along.* "You think it's possible someone could have killed him for his guns?"

Cam looks nonplussed. "Were they all taken?"

"Yep," Kole and Axel say in unison.

Cam's mouth pulls into a tight line. "That's not good."

"No, it really isn't," says Kole. It's the first thing he and Cam agree on. "Imagine our predicament. Not only is there a murderer at large, but now he's armed to the teeth, thanks to your friend's—"

"Whoa, whoa." Axel steps between Kole and Cam, whose face has turned tomato-red, and shoots them each a warning look.

To Kole's surprise, Cam crumbles. "He's right," he admits, and Axel lets his arms fall to his sides. All three men relax. "I was worried about him."

"Why?" Kole moves in.

"He got . . . antsy."

Kole and Axel exchange a glance. "In what way?" asks Kole.

"He started keeping to himself a lot. I used to think the prepper thing was kinda fun. We'd go backpacking, take these long-ass hikes, build fires from just sticks."

"But it intensified? Beyond a hobby or however you might have classified it before?"

"Very much," says Cam, now eager to spill what he knows, and Kole wonders if perhaps Cam hasn't been harboring his own suspicions or misgivings about "Uncle Tommy." Perhaps he saw the change in his friend as a potential threat to his family, but didn't know how to broach the subject. Perhaps he was even afraid.

"My wife asked me to stop hanging out with him."

There it is. They've got him up against the fence now. "Why?" presses Kole.

"She just thought he was losing it." Cam throws a glance at the back of the house, as if he half expects his wife to be standing on the stoop, listening. She isn't. "There was that one time a few years ago, I visited him with our oldest, Grayson, who was twelve at the time. Wasn't two seconds after we walked back into the house that the boy was raiding the junk drawer for things to make a pen bomb." He shakes his head. "Last Christmas, he got 'em all bug-out bags. Even the baby."

"Bug-out bags?" Axel leans forward to better hear.

"Tactical backpacks filled with survival supplies. In case you ever need to—"

"Bug out?" Kole offers.

"Yeah," says Cam. "Anyway, after the whole pen-bomb incident, I stopped havin' him around the kids so much. And then life got busy and naturally we just didn't hang out a whole lot. He seemed normal enough at work. So normal, actually, that I thought he might'a dropped the whole doomsday thing and got a life. Started seeing someone, maybe."

"Did he?" asks Axel. "Start seeing someone, I mean."

Cam shakes his head. "I don't know. I never got to ask him, 'cause that's when . . ." He trails off. Kole watches the blood recede beneath his skin like a tide ebbing from the shore. His face goes wan. He wants to tell them. It's right there, on the tip of his tongue.

"That's when what?" Kole prods. He can practically hear his scalp sizzling. His entire body is coated in a sheen of sweat. He has half a mind to slap Cam upside the head and make him spit it out so they can all go their respective ways and find some air-conditioning.

Finally, Cam drinks in a deep breath, and then he gives them the piece of information they came here for. "We found something in the water." He goes on to explain, then, that a few weeks ago, he and Tommy were out on the boat, trawling for zebra mussels that have been clogging pipelines, when they discovered something white floating in the water. "Drugs. White powder, looked like. A couple bricks, just like in the movies. I never messed with the stuff, so I don't really know what it was, if it was cocaine or fentanyl . . ."

Axel's brows have practically disappeared into his hairline. "Bricks? Must've been kilos, yeah?" He checks with Kole, then looks up, as if the answer is being calculated in the clouds.

"How many is a couple?" asks Kole.

"Three," says Cam.

"That'd be about six and a half pounds," says Kole, assuming each brick was the standard 2.2 pounds. "Powder cocaine, street value, you're looking at about a quarter of a million dollars. For the pure stuff. If it's cut with fentanyl . . ." He'd have to talk to one of the Drug Unit guys about the going rate these days. The conversation he had with Malcolm yesterday rears its thorny head. If it was Xombie, they could be staring down the barrel of a mass overdose.

He rakes his hands in his hair, his palms coming away wet. They're finally getting somewhere. Cam might have been a pill at first, but now that they've cracked him open, he's spilling all the good stuff.

"Why didn't you call the police?" Axel plucks the low-hanging question.

Ruefully, Cam shakes his head. "No offense, but Tommy hated cops. Didn't trust 'em."

Kole and Axel are both unfazed. If they gave a fuck for how often they heard that, they'd be all out of fucks. And they have to hang on to at least one fuck now and again to work their cases.

It was nearing the end of the workday when they fished the drugs out of Lake Michigan, and Cam had to pick his daughter up from school. "Our supervisor was on vacation—not that he would'a known what to do with 'em anyway except call the cops. Tommy offered to surrender them at the pharmacy, the one over by the hospital. It was on his way home."

"Did he?" asks Axel.

"He said he did. I never had a reason not to believe him." Cam's eyes have gone blank. He stares beyond both of them, gaze fixed on something in the middle distance. "We never talked about it again."

"You said you don't mess around with drugs," says Kole, "but what about Tommy? You mentioned he'd been acting differently since you guys found that brick."

"Tommy wasn't into that. I know he might'a looked tough 'n all, but he was kind of square. If it threatened his freedom to own firearms, he steered clear. Which is why it's so bewildering to me that he ended up at the Mineshaft," he adds, reading Kole's mind. If a guy didn't want to be slapped with felony charges resulting in him losing the right to own guns, the Mineshaft was absolutely the wrong place to be.

"Any vices besides alcohol?" Kole asks. "Smoking, gambling?"

Cam shakes his head.

"None? Not so much as a scratch-off ticket?" Kole persists.

Cam's brows cinch together. "Not that I recall, but . . ." He looks to Axel as if to say *What's with this guy?* but Axel can't help him. This is the first time Kole is mentioning the yellow ticket he found with Tommy's clothes.

Kole takes out his phone and shows Cam a photo of the ticket. Axel leans in to check it out, too. Cam shakes his head. "He had this on him when they . . . ?"

Kole nods.

"I can't say I've ever seen him with a scratch-off before, but I don't know what that's got to do with all this, do you?"

No, and therein lies the problem. Normally, a clue like the scratch-off ticket would excite Kole. But this one sends a barrage of paralyzing, fear-laced shrapnel.

Axel regards Kole curiously for a second, before posing to Cam for the second time: "Did Tommy have any enemies?"

Cam snorts. It pulls his face into a grimace, makes him look ugly, almost menacing. There's nothing to distract from his pinprick pupils and the way they stab Kole when he says, "You mean besides his ex-wife?"

TUESDAY, JULY 2

9
HAZEL

I wake drenched in sweat for the second night in a row. The sheets are tangled around my legs. Remnants of a nightmare keep me still. Only my eyes move, darting to each corner of the room that isn't mine as I brace myself, half expecting to see Tommy standing in the doorway.

He isn't here, though. I'm alone.

Moonlight stripes the blankets through the blinds. I clutch a fistful of fabric and hug it to my chest.

Tommy is dead. He can't hurt you. Tommy is dead. He can't hurt you. Tommy is dead.

Tommy.

Is.

Dead.

Those three words slam into me with the finality of nails being pounded into a coffin. Tommy is dead and it's more than a little bit my fault.

I abandoned him to Black Harbor.

I let it swallow him up and I walked away. No, I ran.

And I am so goddamn tired of running.

Ever since I found that stupid house key a few months ago, all I've thought about is coming back and I don't know why. To face my demons, maybe. To prove to myself that I triumphed once, I could do so again. The therapist I've seen a few times online attributed my recent anxiety and panic attacks to post-traumatic growth, a delayed response to my life before. Logically, I recognize that I'm in a safe place now—or at least I was—and yet, there are parts of me that haven't caught up. Parts of me are stuck in the past, returning to their primitive programming of fight-or-flight mode whenever I perceive a threat.

Tommy is dead. He can't hurt you.

And yet, he is everywhere.

He's in New York. Slumped in a seat on the subway. Careening toward me in the bike lane. Walking next to me beneath scaffolding. Spying on me behind bookshelves. Jogging over the Brooklyn Bridge.

Those are the moments when fear takes over and I run. I run away from my perceived danger into potentially very real danger—traffic, other people. Once, when I thought I saw his blue-and-brown-plaid jacket, his mop of dark hair, I bolted so suddenly and without any regard for my surroundings, I almost fell off the subway platform. That's when I started talking to the therapist, because I realized that my fear is negatively affecting my life. Worse, it keeps getting worse.

I am not in control of my body's responses.

It's a terrifying realization to come to.

The only way I can regain control, I hope, is to find out what happened and what part I played in it so I can start packing up all those problems into their respective boxes and move on.

Bleary-eyed, I turn over and tap my phone on the nightstand. The screen glows to life.

It's 4:18 A.M.

No new messages. No one wondering where I am.

After a silent debate with myself, I get up and use the bathroom. On my way back to bed, I pause in the dinette and peer into the apartment across the way—Robbie's apartment. The blinds are only half lowered. A dim light shines on what appears to be a dining room table. A ceramic mug is set next to it. He must be getting shit done already—the glamorous life of a building manager.

Feeling guilty, my gaze drifts to my laptop. I could get shit done, too. I could write what I'm feeling, channel this sleepless night and these negative emotions into something enlightening. Grabbing a blanket off the back of a chair, I burrito myself in it and sit. A blank Word document stares back at me, cursor blinking. I stare back for a moment before pulling up a fresh tab and instead of writing, begin scouring for updates on the case.

The funeral is today, I learn. I won't go. I can't risk running into people from my past—Cam, most of all. He and Tommy were thick as thieves when I left. I can only imagine the words he's weaponized for me. But that isn't the only reason I'm staying away. A funeral is meant for people to pay their respects, and I simply have none to pay.

I click around, scrolling through one article after another. They all say the same thing. That Tommy was shot five times in the back of a club. *Investigation to continue*. I zoom in on a picture of the establishment. The Mineshaft. It doesn't seem like a place Tommy would go, but then, I stopped knowing him a long time ago.

I inch my way down the article when suddenly, I stop mid-scroll where it mentions a handful of shells being collected from the toilet.

Smith & Wesson .38 Special. It isn't a rare caliber, but it isn't exactly common. Unfortunately, it fits a gun I stashed away in the hopes that Tommy would never find it.

I clutch a fistful of my pajama shirt, then lean in to peer closer until the screen burns my eyes. I feel myself breaking out into a cold sweat again. This doesn't look good. I can see the headlines now, the way the media will not hesitate to point fingers at the "vengeful ex-wife" who finally got even.

No. I can prove it with my plane tickets. I didn't arrive in Black Harbor until the day after Tommy's murder. Still, they could claim I orchestrated his death from a distance. My fingerprints will be on the gun. They'll know it's mine. And while it may not be enough to condemn me, it will be enough to cause problems. Try locking in a new publishing contract when you're suspected of murder.

A noise in the hall makes me jump out of my skin. The chair scrapes across the floor as I stand and back up against the wall. The stucco scratches my bare shoulders.

I hear shuffling. Then what sounds like a key about to turn a lock. Heart racing, I creep toward the door. Framed in the fish-eye lens of the peephole is Robbie. Cursing myself for ever letting him follow me, I open the door a crack. The chain rattles softly.

"Hey," I whisper. "Is something wrong?"

He smiles apologetically. He's wearing a grey T-shirt and terry-cloth sleep shorts. "I'm sorry, but I saw you were up and I was wondering if you might be able to spare a coffee filter? I went to make some just now and . . ." He tosses his hands up.

"A coffee filter?" I bite the inside of my cheek. There's no sense lying; he would have no doubt seen them amidst my groceries yesterday. "Sure," I say, trying my best to adopt a helpful tone. "Just one?"

"You'd be my savior, thanks."

"Okay, I'll be right back." Shaking, I close the door. It clicks when it connects with the frame and I have half a mind to keep it closed and turn the lock. But I'm hopeful the coffee filter will send him on his way, just as I'm hopeful the chain is enough to stop him from forcing entry.

Every muscle in my body pulls taut as I go to the counter and unsheathe a paper filter from the stack. But as I reapproach the door, I pause. It's quiet in the hall, so quiet I could be convinced he's gone. I hold my breath and tiptoe closer, when slowly, the doorknob turns once . . . twice.

He's trying to let himself in.

10
KOLE

"Any word on Pitts?" He lobs the question at Riley the second she appears in the doorway.

"Good morning to you, too," she says, slinging her purse over the back of her chair. "I mean, he didn't deliver himself to my doorstep or anything like that, if that's what you're asking. You look like shit, by the way." She moves to the far wall and hangs a black pantsuit on the pipe they use for a makeshift clothing rack.

"I slept like shit." He doesn't recall exactly what time, but it was late when he fell asleep in his recliner. The truth is, he was troubled by something Cameron Jeske said yesterday while he and Axel fried in his backyard: "Hell hath no fury, I s'pose. She ripped him apart pretty good in her book."

"Tommy's ex-wife wrote a book?" Axel feigned ignorance. Everyone knew about Hazel's book. It put Black Harbor on the map as the Gotham City of the Midwest—sans Batman.

"Aubrey and all her friends read it," Cam went on. "They loved it, but I think she started lookin' at Tommy differently after. Like she believed all the bad things that book had to say about him."

Afterward, Kole made a mental note to speak with Aubrey Jeske. She seemed less apt to protect Tommy than her husband. Or "Uncle Tommy," rather. Still, the matter of Hazel remains. Would she have returned to Black Harbor to kill her ex-husband?

She escaped him, but he knows from witnessing it firsthand that trauma can take years to break the surface. Maybe she finally realized the hell he put her through and she decided to get retribution.

It wasn't her. Kole said the mantra to himself over and over last night until he believed it, and yet, there was the matter of the missing gun, the .38 Special registered in Hazel's name. Now overtired and irritable, he watches Riley take a sip from her thermos and he wonders where her head is thus far in the investigation.

"What'd you find out about Big House? Is he really on a fishing trip?"

She nods. "Yeah, his alibi checks out, unfortunately."

An umbra falls over them as they both realize what this means. If a guy like Big House, who's not only the owner of the Mineshaft but also the muscle behind a lot of the city's violent crime, didn't kill Tommy, then this is a legitimate whodunnit. In a place like Black Harbor, the list of who couldn't have done it is much shorter.

"Yeah." She smacks her lips. "Axel gave me the CliffsNotes of your convo with . . . Tommy's coworker . . . was it?"

"His best friend, allegedly. Cameron Jeske."

"He's the guy footing the bill for the funeral?"

"He crowdfunded it, but yeah."

"Not open casket, I hope."

Kole lets the statement hang there. Maybe it should be, he thinks to himself. Let Greenlee's fate be a warning to anyone who looks upon him that this is what happens when you play stupid games.

You win stupid prizes.

Axel arrives next, Fletcher on his heels. All together now, the VCTF catches one another up. So far, there's neither hide nor hair of Robert Pitts, the Mineshaft member who brought Darren Hogan—a nonmember—the night of Tommy Greenlee's murder. According to the complainant, Hogan has since returned to Chicago. He does not have a working phone—Kole calls bullshit—and she does not know where he stays. Which is probably also bullshit.

Cameron Jeske—best friend and coworker of Tommy Greenlee—

confessed to himself and Greenlee finding three bricks of drugs floating in Lake Michigan. Tommy offered to surrender them at a pharmacy, but didn't. Whether something interfered with that or Tommy decided not to all on his own is on them to find out.

"Sounds like they intercepted a drop-off," Riley notes when he's finished. "Maybe the coasties saw something."

Kole nods. "I was hoping you'd go over there this morning and ask around. See if they had cause to board any vessels in the past two weeks."

Beside her, Fletcher snorts. "Probably only about a thousand."

Kole ignores him. He knows as well as any of them that the coast guard has the right to stop and board vessels in order to check for compliance with federal and state laws. This time of year, with its promise of fun in the sun, Lake Michigan is teeming with more boats and bodies than ever. If someone's transporting drugs across the water, that means they could be coming from any of the lake's bordering states.

"On it," says Riley. She grabs her keys as Axel adds: "Regardless, Tommy Greenlee was the last known person to touch those drugs."

"You think he might have sold them?" asks Fletcher.

"Anything's possible," says Kole. "The funeral's at noon. I hope you all got my text about bringing your court costumes." He nods at Riley's jumpsuit, which hangs from the rack, lifeless as a garbage bag.

Fletcher groans and he ignores it. The guy is always balking whenever he can't wear jeans and a T-shirt.

"It's a good opportunity to canvass," says Kole. "See what Tommy's acquaintances have to say about him. According to his supervisor, he wasn't universally liked. I think 'polarizing' was the word he used. Dig up some dirt on him while you're there. And talk to Aubrey Jeske." He looks pointedly at Axel. "I'm curious to learn what she really thought of 'Uncle Tommy.'"

"On it," says Fletcher, mimicking Riley, who flicks a glance at him, then adds: "Wait, while *we're* there? Aren't you going?"

Kole laughs. "I think it's in everyone's best interest if I sit this one out."

When Fletcher looks nonplussed, Riley elbows him and whispers, though not quietly enough for him not to hear, "Dude fucked the dead guy's wife."

Fletcher's head falls slowly back. "Yeah, probably a good idea."

Kole hides his grimace. What he had with Hazel was more than sex, and yet, what good does it do to argue? It's over. His gaze shifts to the clock on the wall. They've got just over three hours to lay some more groundwork for their case. Shifting gears, he heads over to the giant whiteboard where he's already tacked up pictures of Tommy Greenlee, Cameron Jeske, Robert Pitts, and a blank silhouette with a question mark for Darren Hogan. A red dry-erase line connects Tommy and Cam, the label COWORKERS severing the middle of it. Another red line connects Darren Hogan to Robert Pitts, who Kole noted is being worked by Dirty Harriet, Malcolm Jimenez's informant, along with the note "(GHOSTED)." Next to Pitts is Joseph Orien, aka Big House. His rap sheet is stapled into a packet and taped to the right of his photo, its four pages fluttering languidly in the fan's oscillating breeze. Kole writes "MIA—ALIBI ✓."

He circles Dirty Harriet's name now and points his marker at Axel and Riley. "Try and get in touch with her after the funeral. Find out if she's had any interaction with Pitts since her last controlled purchase with him. Who knows, maybe he even mentioned something about poppin' some sucker at the Mineshaft. And Fletcher." He tosses Tommy's logbook across the office. The cover still bears smudges from fingerprint dust. If there was any DNA to be collected from it, they got it. "His guns are all in there, listed by make, model, and serial number. From now until this case is over, this is your Bible. Take it to the shooting range and every pawnshop you can think of. See if they can match any of their inventory to the ones stolen from Tommy's collection. Maybe we'll get lucky."

Fletcher tightens his grip on the journal in his hands. Disappointment over having to wear a suit gives way to determination. "And what about you?" he asks. "What are you gonna do while we're canvassing at the funeral?"

Kole looks down at the floor and shakes his head. This guy is something else. "I've got some phone calls to make," he says.

"To Hazel?" This time the offender is Axel.

"I left a message." The metallic taste of blood hits his tongue when he bites the inside of his cheek. It's his tell, he knows, but at least it's an invisible one. Not like Riley, who runs her tongue along her teeth or Axel, whose ears glow red. Fletcher has a vein that bulges in the middle of his forehead whenever he lies.

"I'm gonna subpoena some phone companies, see if Tommy's phone is possibly alive—who knows, maybe whoever killed him took it and plugged it into a charger. Or they pawned it and I can get a positive ID." Another lie. Tommy's phone is dead. He had Dispatch ping it last night. He could have done it himself, but that would have taken days by the time he subpoenaed the phone company and retrieved the records.

When his detectives depart for their respective assignments, Kole moves toward the persons-of-interest board. He stares at it, challenging the empty space where even he is tempted to place Hazel's photo.

11

HAZEL

The camera is tiny, about the size of a pencil eraser. It was on the doorknob, fitted into the little alcove where a single screw holds the metal plate in place. At first, I squinted at it in disbelief, only for fear to set in as I realized that someone was probably watching my reaction in real time.

Robbie.

That was the reason he came by last night. Not for coffee filters. I gave him three and sent him on his way, so he'll have to think up a new lie if he decides to lurk outside my door again tonight.

Tonight.

The word is a looming threat. I don't want to think about him coming back, in the dark, especially when it seems the building is all but empty. Besides the tenant in the hall yesterday, I've hardly seen another soul. Maybe they all live on the other floors, or maybe the creepy apartment manager has scared them off.

I know now, though, that the knob turned when he was fitting the camera in place. Judging by its location, it must be to monitor anyone coming or going from my unit. The question of *why* prickles the back of my neck, long after I promptly pulled the camera from its mount and tossed it down the garbage chute. Now, the uneasy feeling of being watched sticks to me tight as a shadow as I skulk around my old neighborhood in broad daylight.

If the need to recover my old revolver was a seed that took root in my head last night, today it's a jungle invading every inch of my mental space. I need to get that gun. Besides the fact that it's registered in my name, my prints are on it, which means that if police find it, they'll want to find me.

If they don't already.

I stand on the sidewalk across from the duplex, engaged in a silent showdown. My throat itches. I force a cough and spit in the scorched yard, right into the rosebushes I planted practically a decade ago, when I was naïve and full of hope that this city on the lake could be our fresh start. The fact that they're alive is surprising, and yet, "alive" might be too generous a term. The blossoms are shriveled into scabs, petals pulverized into dust.

Shingles are missing from the roof and the porch stairs mimic a broken jaw—all cockeyed and splintered—cordoned off with slashes of yellow caution tape, the ends of which waver in the scant breeze, fingers bending, beckoning me to come on in.

I obey.

The door is closed but not locked. The dead bolts on the other side of it are just dead weight. Remembering how religious Tommy had been about locking this door, it seems counterintuitive when he clearly wanted someone to trespass. He craved a reason to kill another human being and be absolved through self-defense. I could smell it on him, that want.

The stairs creak beneath my weight. Holding my breath, I peel away the yellow barricade tape, ignoring its warning of CRIME SCENE DO NOT CROSS. My eyes scan the porch: for the broken flowerpot filled with our neighbor's cigarette butts, the faded newspaper that was basically fossilized in front of the door. But they're gone now. To the right, just off the driveway, a recycling bin overflows with beer cans and pizza boxes. The windows to both units are dark. I exhale. No one's here but me and the memories that wait inside.

I reach and close my hand over the doorknob. For the first time ever, the door just falls away. The house is a horror show. Dead animals stare at me from their mounts, their gazes empty and pitying, as if they know something that I don't. *What did they see?* I wonder.

The couch is flipped over on its back, gauzy kerchiefs of dust clinging to its legs. The mesh on the bottom is slashed apart. Cushions are thrown across the room and eviscerated, spilling entrails of stuffing. A lawn chair sits in the middle of it all, a director's chair for the invisible intruder to survey their handiwork.

The cops have obviously conducted their search by now, but this mess isn't their doing. Someone ransacked the place, probably to steal all the guns and sell them on the black market.

Not all, I hope.

I continue moving through the house. To my left is the dining room table, the same one on which he used to set his handgun and make sure it was always pointing in my direction. The gun is gone. In its place, I imagine a pale print, like when you move furniture away from a wall. Still, I don't go near it.

On my way to the stairs, I catch my reflection in a full-length mirror on the inside of the hall closet door that's been left ajar. Here I am in a blue tank top, arm holes gouged down to the dip in my waist to expose my sports bra underneath, spandex shorts, bare legs. I might as well have wandered in here naked for all the protection my clothes afford me.

The stairs unfurl like a tongue. I look away from them, down at the register. My blood isn't there anymore. *You'll never leave Black Harbor.* The memory of his words envelops me, tight as a straitjacket, and I'm suddenly transported back to that moment eight years ago when I'd fallen down the stairs. I was on my knees, trying to pick up my things, when he grabbed the back of my head and ruined me in a way I couldn't come back from.

I blocked that part out for a long time. Until one day, it became the only thing I remembered. The only thing I could think of. It consumed me. And as much as I hate to admit it, it crippled me.

Sometimes I'm convinced my life is a novel that someone else is writing, and, just like in a novel, there are tent poles—key plot points when things took a turn for better or for worse. That was one of them, where I learned that as but a character in my own story and not the author of it, I have no free will. If I did, I would have fought back.

I didn't even run.

And that has been the hardest thing to accept.

Eyes burning, I climb the carpeted stairs. At the top of the landing, the floor plan splits off to a bathroom that's clearly fallen into disrepair, the master bedroom, and a guest room that Tommy transformed into a reloading room. His press is still there, parked in front of the TV. If he still had a video game system, someone stole it. There's a bug-out bag in the corner, next to a pile of porn magazines and crumpled tissues. I cringe. He used to make me pick them up, reasoning that it was my fault that he had to masturbate in the first place.

The master bedroom is spartan. An unmade bed butts up against the wall, facing two dressers. The only clothes in the closet appear to belong to him. There is nothing to indicate a woman lives here.

I skirt past the bed and crouch next to my old dresser. Tear out the bottom drawer. It's been infiltrated by his things now—camouflage pants and jackets. I toss them out. My heart pounds in my temples. This is it. If my gun isn't here, I'm fucked. Not only because it could be the same one that killed Tommy, but because nowhere in this city is safe. I don't know what Robbie wants from me, but I'm willing to bet it isn't coffee filters.

The panel is stained slightly darker than the rest of the dresser. A shot of relief flows through my veins. I painted it to match. It isn't perfect, but it was enough to get past Tommy. Sliding my fingers under its edges, I lift and—

My ears prick to the sound of a gun sliding from a holster as a serrated voice warns: "Don't fucking move."

12
KOLE

Twenty-three years in law enforcement and he's never had to shoot anyone. Of course today would be the day, when he's technically trespassing. He should have just jumped through the hoops and gotten the damn warrant.

The person is on the floor, kneeling in front of the dresser. It's a woman wearing a blue racerback tank top. A dark ponytail cascades past her shoulders, down her spine. He watches the muscles in her back work as she reaches for something.

He told her not to move, but before he could even finish the command, she turned around and now he's staring down the short bridge of a revolver. Not just any revolver. A .38 Special. Kole leans forward, his Glock pointed at her chest, finger on the trigger when suddenly, his eyes lock on hers and recognition sets in.

No one named Hazel has a right to have eyes this blue. He remembers saying it to her once, when they lay together, fingers entwined, telling two truths for every lie.

"Nik," she breathes, but she doesn't lower the gun, and he can't deny that even though they're finally in the same crime-ridden city, in the same tiny bedroom, it feels as if the whole world stands between them.

He holsters his gun. "You don't write. You don't text or call. You know, there are easier ways than committing a felony to get my attention."

Slowly and with what looks like a great deal of uncertainty, she lowers the pistol to her side. "You never called either."

"I didn't show up in your city."

"Black Harbor doesn't belong to you."

"Are you sure about that?" He feels the corner of his mouth tick upward and he wishes, for a split second, that he didn't have to be such a smartass all the time. But it's worked for him all these years. It's how he rocks people, by challenging what they have to say and holding his own. Even when they're right.

Black Harbor does not belong to him.

It's part of him.

"Find what you came for?" He tips his chin toward the gun she's got in a death grip. He can't help but notice, though, how she holds it away from her body, like it might bite.

"It's mine," she says defensively. "Tommy bought it for me, like, ten years ago. As a birthday present."

"I could give a fuck." Kole takes one step toward her. He hears her suck in a breath. "What I do care about is the fact that you're trespassing."

"Trespassing? I used to live here." He hears the bitterness of the confession.

The silence of the house echoes around them.

"'Used to,'" he repeats. "Words matter, Hazel. You taught me that." Slowly, he takes another step. And another. He's bluffing, but she doesn't need to know that. He has as much clearance as she does to be here, which is zero. However, if someone were to catch him now, he would simply say he was driving past and noticed a burglary-in-progress.

"Everybody lies, Nik. You taught me that." Albeit quiet, her voice has an edge. She is harder than when he saw her last. All sharp angles and negative spaces. He could reach out and touch her now if he wanted to, to see what she's made of. He does want to and yet, he fights the urge to caress the smooth line of her neck, the bow of her lips. To press his mouth to hers and inhale every secret she's keeping inside. It would be less wrong than it was when they first got together. She isn't married—he doesn't think so, at least—although the absence of a wedding ring could simply mean she took it off before she went for a run. That's what she's dressed for anyway, wearing a blue slip of a tank top, the fabric so thin it's translucent, and shorts that might as well be painted on.

In another life, she would have let him peel them off and they would have found some unsullied piece of furniture to fuck on or against.

This is not that life.

They are not those people anymore.

As much as he hates it, it's for the better. They were almost the end of each other last time. In more ways than one.

"I wager you're not back in town because you missed me," he says. There's no sense in sugarcoating it. "So did you come back for Tommy or for the gun that shot him?"

Her face twists into a hurt expression before revulsion takes over. She bites her lip.

"Your husband was killed early Sunday morning," he says, needling her. "Shot five times with .38 Special rounds and left for dead in the back of the Mineshaft. But you knew that."

She's shaking her head, and it doesn't seem that she's disputing his claim as much as she seems to be malfunctioning.

"When did you get back in town, Hazel?"

She says nothing at first. Just stares at the gun she's still holding as though checking for telltale signs of murder. Blood. Powder residue. Fingerprints. Her own are on it now, if they weren't already. And then after a moment, her lips part and the weakest sound comes out. "*Ex*-husband," she says, and again, more seething: "He's not my husband."

"Semantics," Kole says in lieu of an apology. "So, how long have you been here?"

"Two days."

"Can you prove it?"

Her eyes flash to him. Wild and bright, they're almost too large for her face, as if she's some crepuscular creature crawling around in the daylight. She's out of her element here; she will not beat him at his own game. "Are you for real, Nik? I didn't fucking kill him."

"I'm gonna need to ask you a few questions."

"I thought that's what we've been doing."

"Come with me." He reaches vaguely for her, as if to usher her out of the bedroom.

"I'm not going anywhere with you." She bends at the knees, lowering her center of gravity. She's got nowhere to run. Her back's literally against the wall. He remembers having picked her up years ago; he grabbed her from off the bridge and slung her over his shoulder as she hurled punches into his kidneys. He's better off not trying it again. She looks half-crazed, like she might actually put up a real fight this time.

"I'm not going to arrest you."

"You're lying."

He stifles a derisive laugh. What are they doing? They're two grown adults who loved each other once—at least he thought that's what it was—and now they're pointing guns and threatening each other. She takes a step toward him, and another, and then she's past him.

"Yeah, leave. You're good at that." He shouldn't have said it, but there it is.

She pauses for a moment at the top of the landing. The muscles in her back pull tight. Then, she goes down the stairs.

He follows her. "You're not taking that gun, Hazel."

"It's mine."

"It's evidence."

"You don't know that." She's on the main floor again. She marches into the living room on a mission to leave this house. He can't let her.

"But I don't know that it isn't. And now that your fingerprints are all over the damn thing, I can't exclude you." He reaches for her at the same time she whirls around.

"Are you serious, Nik? I didn't do it. I wasn't here. I've got a fucking plane ticket to prove it." Her face falls as she no doubt realizes how guilty that sounds.

"Just, please, give me the gun. You don't even know how to shoot it." As soon as he says it, he knows he overstepped. Fury blazes in her eyes. In one fluid motion, she pivots toward the far right corner, raises the revolver so that it's pointing at a deer mount, and squeezes the trigger. The shot is deafening. He jumps back, his hands clamped over his ears.

"Jesus, Hazel!" he yells, but stops. She looks just as surprised by her actions as he is. Shaking, she staggers a few steps and lays the revolver down on the side of an overturned gun safe.

"Oh my God," she breathes, her fingers crawling toward her mouth.

Oh my God is right. Kole's gaze is fixed on the far wall, where from the throat of the taxidermied deer pours a steady stream of white powder. Careful not to touch it with his bare hands, he stands on his toes and yanks the deer head from the wall. He turns it over so the deer is face down on the floor, then, taking his knife out of his back pocket, stabs it into the back of the mount. Lying in the hollow of the beast's neck is the reason why Tommy Greenlee was murdered.

Kole takes in a breath. His hand hovers over the half-disintegrated kilo, and just as there isn't a shadow of doubt in his mind that this is what Tommy fished out of the water, he also knows that whoever it belongs to will stop at nothing to get it back.

13
HAZEL

I run.

The duplex and Nikolai Kole shrink behind me. It feels as if the trees on my left are closing in. One wrong step and I'll end up in their teeth and be dragged down the steep hill with my face planted in the creek. If it hasn't dried up, that is. It's so stiflingly hot, I imagine I'm running on a conveyor belt into an incinerator. But I can't stop now. Not until I'm safe inside, hidden away.

Safe. That's a novel concept for here.

I didn't tell Kole the other reason I'd come for the gun. Because it was mine, yes, but also to have it in case I need it, for protection. I don't know what Robbie's deal is, but returning empty-handed to the apartment where he has a master key to every unit feels incredibly cavalier.

Had we not accidentally discovered the drugs stashed in that deer head, Kole would have pressed me harder about why I'd come and where I was staying. Instead, he let me go. Chivalry isn't abysmally dead, I learned in the moment he walked me out of the duplex and we stood, barely inches apart on the porch. I felt it then—that spark that could raze everything to the ground—which is why I can no longer deny the fact that I've been lying.

To myself, of all people.

The same as with the gun, I've been omitting one key part as to why I've returned, not just to this duplex but to this whole crime-ridden city.

Needing to solve Tommy's murder was enough to get me here. Seeing where things could go with Nikolai Kole could be enough to get me to stay.

What is the frisson that flows through my veins when I'm near him? The sudden impulse to kiss him and breathe in every atom that he is. Is it love, or am I an addict, eight years sober, and he's my vice?

He kept the gun. Said it needs to be photographed and collected as evidence. Surely it cannot be the same one that shot Tommy, but they need to rule it out.

"But my fingerprints." We stood on the porch when a flash of copper-red hair caught my eye as a woman ambled down the sidewalk. I locked eyes with her so fleetingly I might have imagined it, then she turned to appraise a ratty old couch slouched on the curb.

"The gun is yours, right?" said Kole. "So, why wouldn't your prints be on it?" His tone was different out here than it had been inside. Compassionate. Reassuring.

Tears of relief welled in my eyes. "I'm not a . . ." I couldn't even finish the sentence.

"A suspect?" He shook his head. "But the fact that the victim is your ex-husband, and now after eight years you're suddenly back in town, sneaking around his residence after he's been murdered, only to be caught red-handed with the same make and model of the gun that shot him . . . it's circumstantial, I'll admit, but there are too many connections to ignore."

Talk of the gun threw me back into a memory. One I'd tamped down and tried to erase from years ago when Tommy and I went to the shooting range, the last time I ever touched that stupid thing, until today. It was spring, just a few days after my birthday. The air was wet. Shallow puddles reflected the lights of Alpha's giant neon bull's-eye that can be seen from the highway. I always imagined it to be a beacon for Tommy's kind—doomsdayers whose hobby only paid off if an apocalypse came about.

I never understood why someone would want to live like that—betting against humanity, hoping for the end of the world. But my husband did.

He fantasized about it the way most people fantasize about winning the lottery or taking a dream vacation.

I'll admit, I didn't hate it at first. It was a bit like living a real-life video game. Hunting, gathering, rationing. *Leveling up,* Tommy called it whenever we learned a new skill or broke a previous record, like during power fasts when he'd cut the power for twenty-four, thirty-six, or up to forty-eight hours until I begged him to turn it on so I could shower and go to work. He said we were building up our tolerance for when the power grid eventually, inevitably, went to hell. I think he just wanted to shave a few bucks off the electric bill.

Disenchantment set in after a few months of entertaining his antics. But I put up with it for a year, during which time he seemed to worsen. Our pantry boasted only shelf-stable canned goods, cereal, and MREs he bought from the army surplus store. Our fridge became cold storage for the carcasses of fish and mourning doves, and a case of beer. Guns stood sentry in every corner and shadowy space of the duplex.

Alpha was Tommy's church, firearms his religion. He rarely brought me except for tournaments. He'd even stopped inviting me for the most part, well aware that I would rather spend my time writing or doing literally anything else than standing against a concrete wall and watch him punch bullet holes into paper targets.

There was no tournament going on this day. Still, Tommy led me through the storefront area with guns under glass cases and T-shirts tacked up on shiplap walls. We skirted past guys in canvas jackets, through the vending machine room with cheap Formica tables, its stale air filmy with the smell of lead and burnt coffee, and out into the range area. The shooting partition reminded me of a voting booth, with flimsy walls on both sides. Tommy chucked up the first paper target and sent it whizzing back twenty yards on the wire. Then, he unlatched the black plastic case to reveal my birthday present—a handgun.

"It's a revolver," he explained to me, giddy with excitement when I opened the thing. "Which means it won't jam. You've got five shots at stopping an intruder or some guy who comes at you on the street." He put it in my hand. "How does it feel?"

"Cold," I said.

His face tightened. I was disappointing him already, lack of enthusiasm and whatnot. I sighed and added: "It's lightweight, though. Comfortable." The gun was neither of those things to me. Still, he brightened at the words he wanted to hear.

He stood behind me, his chest pressed to my back as he puppeteered me into the correct shooting stance. Feet shoulders'-width apart, knees slightly bent, leaning forward, arms extended, a slight bend at the elbows. "Keep both eyes open," he reminded me. His voice was muffled by my hearing protection. I breathed in, then let half of it out as he'd taught me before. My index finger squeezed the trigger. The short barrel exploded, pitching upward and jarring my wrist. An electric current surged through my arm. My heart pounded. I hated it.

When he'd breezed through all the features, he forgot to mention one crucial detail: the smaller the gun, the larger the recoil. My shoulder screamed. My heart catapulted into a chaotic rhythm.

"A little left," coached Tommy. "Shoot again."

Gathering my resolve, I did. I shot again, and again, telling myself that I would just suck it up and finish the five rounds and be done. It wasn't as if I ever planned to shoot after this anyway. As far as I was concerned, Tommy had bought himself a present.

The last round careened down the aisle, zipping through the paper target. I didn't see where they'd all hit; I didn't care. I just wanted to leave. My whole body shook as I set the gun back in its case on its bed of foam.

"What are you doing?" he asked as he pressed the button to bring the target back in and swap it out for another.

"You can shoot," I said. "I'm good."

He narrowed his eyes. "I spent four hundred dollars on this and you're not going to fucking shoot it?"

"Four hundred dollars, Tommy? That's—" I was at a loss for words. I hadn't been able to go grocery shopping for a month and we were late on the water bill. Now I knew why.

He loaded it and thrust the gun back in my hand, crumpling my fingers over its grip. "Shoot," he said.

I shook my head. "I said I'm good."

"You're not good. You've got a spread a mile wide." He put his arms around me in a bear hug and walked me back to the opening. My nerves prickled. I wanted to tear away from him but couldn't. His breath was hot on my neck. I closed my eyes, wishing I wasn't there.

"Breathe in," Tommy instructed. "Now exhale just halfway."

I obeyed, and hated myself for it. Then he rested his index finger over mine and made me pull the trigger.

Pop!

The barrel exploded again, and again, my palm absorbed 70 percent of the recoil, the rest of it traveling as a shock wave up my arm and pummeling my shoulder.

Pop! Pop!

"Okay!" I shouted. "Enough, Tommy, I'm done!"

The paper target was a blur. Tears streamed down my face. But we didn't stop. Not until all three boxes of bullets had been shot and my palm was black and blue.

I couldn't write for a week after that and I never touched that gun again except to stash it away somewhere I hoped he would never find it.

And he never did. In fact, it proved to be such an inconspicuous little cache that both the police and the looters had missed it. But it seems Tommy, himself, had found an equally effective hiding spot by stuffing that brick of powder into the deer mount. It has to be the reason he's dead. Why else would anyone want to kill him?

Tommy, what did you do?

14
KOLE

"Well, Greenlee's in the ground." Fletcher plunks down at his workstation. He's down to his undershirt. Kole bets he didn't keep himself together for two minutes once they peeled out of the cemetery. His button-down is a shed skin, draped over the back of his chair.

"And?" Kole arches his brow. He beat his detectives back to the lighthouse by a good hour, even after calling an evidence tech to come photograph and collect the controlled substances and the gun. The white powder is now being field-tested—for fentanyl, cocaine, baby powder, what-have-you—and he inventoried the gun as evidence.

"Most people were appropriately distraught," says Axel.

"Most people?"

Axel, Fletcher, and Riley all share looks before Axel offers: "Aubrey Jeske had a few beers at the . . . luncheon."

"*Afterparty* would be more accurate," clarifies Riley.

"You can always tell when parents get a babysitter for the first time in a while. Doesn't matter the circumstances, festival or funeral, they're gonna throw a few back." Fletcher has four kids of his own, Kole knows, which means that out of everyone on the task force, he can probably empathize with Cam and Aubrey Jeske the most.

While turning a funeral into a bender isn't a crime, it is frowned upon, like driving naked or marrying your stepsister. "Sounds like

Tommy's kind of funeral, to be honest," says Kole. "So, Aubrey spilled some tea?"

"The whole pot," says Riley, pulling up her chair.

"Well, should we all change into our pajamas and put on face masks, or do you wanna just tell me now?"

Axel pushes his sleeves up to his elbows. "There's no love lost between her and Tommy, that's for sure."

"If you ask her—and we did, eventually," Riley chimes in, "she's glad he's gone and good riddance. Her words."

Kole winces. "That's a glowing send-off. You find out the reason for her animosity? Or *reasons*, I suppose."

"Just a bad influence, seems like." Riley is shaking her head now. "Especially with her oldest son, Grayson. Axel and I sat her down and chatted with her while Fletch kept Cam away."

"Smart," Kole acknowledges.

"Guy knows a lot about fly-fishing." Fletcher lets his head fall back, as though he's still bored to death by the conversation.

"So what was the deal with Tommy and this kid? How old is he now?" Kole asks, remembering the conversation in Cam's backyard.

"Sixteen. Tommy was a pseudo 'uncle' to him," says Riley, making air quotes. "They played video games together. He'd take him fishing or to the gun range."

Kole shrugs. "No harm in that, yeah?"

"No," Axel agrees after exchanging a glance with Riley. "But she said she started getting concerned about Grayson last year or so. He was becoming more withdrawn, opting to hang out with Tommy instead of his friends. He started to share in Tommy's obsession for prepping, like for the end of the world. He even begged his parents for a gun for his last birthday. They said no, but, eventually, Aubrey found out that Tommy bought him one and kept it at his house for him."

"Super illegal." Kole sniffs. "How'd she find out about it?"

"He confessed," says Riley.

"Tommy?"

"Grayson." Riley goes on to relay what Aubrey Jeske shared with her and Axel at the funeral, which is that a few months ago in the spring, her son had come home in tears. According to Grayson, Tommy had texted him about a surprise and that he should come over after school. He then took Grayson to a spot in the woods across the street and revealed his gift: a box of feral kittens he'd discovered near a dumpster. The kittens mewled and clawed at the cardboard. They couldn't have been more than eight weeks old. Grayson crouched to pick them up, when Tommy stopped him and shoved his gun at him. "Target practice," he said, and proceeded to dump the kittens out onto the marshy earth.

"He didn't let Grayson go until he'd shot every last kitten." A heavy silence falls as Riley finishes.

"Jesus," says Kole. "What a—"

"—fucked-up piece of shit," Fletcher ad-libs.

No one disagrees. They sit quietly for a while, and Kole can't say whether it's the suffocating heat or the thoughts racing through his mind, but he feels dizzy. Casting a surreptitious glance at each of his detectives, he thinks of how none of them know that Hazel is back in town. He doesn't plan on telling them. Not yet, anyway.

He'd escorted her down the stairs and out to the porch. He needed to watch her disappear, to see for himself that she listened to him for once and got out of there. It's for her own good. She won't go too far, he knows. She's got too much invested in this case to ditch Black Harbor so soon.

He stood in the doorway, blocking her from reentering. "You know, you're not off the hook. Trespassing's a crime."

She paused and turned toward him. Sweat dripped from her hairline, carving a trail down her smooth, lightly tanned skin. "Add it to my rap sheet." Her lips moved slowly, enunciating each syllable. Even though she spoke in a whisper, he heard her loud and clear. She had come here for answers, and she wasn't leaving until she got them. Then, she rocked back on her heels and made to leave.

"Hazel, wait."

She paused again. If he'd kissed her then, would she have let him? If he'd told her he missed her, would she have believed him? "Are you in danger?" he asked.

She said nothing, just stared at him as if he'd posed the dumbest question in the world, and in the seconds that followed, he realized that he had not entirely lost the ability to read her. He knew what she was thinking: to be in Black Harbor was to be in danger.

He'll see her again soon enough. In the meantime, he checks on the tasks he assigned this morning. "What'd the coasties have to say?" The question is directed at Axel and Riley.

"Business as usual, for the most part," states Riley. "Pulling people over in no-wake zones and for operating under the influence."

"What's the other part?" asks Kole.

"Chicago cops visited them a few weeks ago, wanting to know if they'd seen anything. Apparently, they suspect a Mexican cartel has a satellite location set up somewhere in Chicago and it's possible they're using Lake Michigan as a water route to ferry drugs across."

"Drugs like Xombie?"

"Among others, yeah."

"They contacted the coast guard and not us?" Kole's irritated but not surprised.

Riley raises her hands, palms facing out. "Don't shoot the messenger. Anyway, the coasties told me what they allegedly told Chicago PD: they haven't seen anything, but they'll keep a lookout."

Kole pivots from her to the matter of the stolen guns. "Any luck at the pawnshops?"

"Not yet. We've been doing some recon online," says Fletcher, and Kole knows that "we" refers to him and the ATF agent he's partnered with. "I think it's time to start going door-to-door, though, see what's come into the pawnshops lately. Or give them an alert in case one of Tommy's guns does show up."

"Yes. And head over to Alpha—"

"Already done."

"And?"

Fletcher gives them all the CliffsNotes version of his visit to the shooting range where Tommy spent most of his free time. "The old guy who runs the place described him as being 'on edge' the last couple of weeks. But what really piqued my interest is the fact that, the last time he was there, Tommy paid off his tab."

"How much?" asks Kole.

"Six hundred thirty-seven dollars and forty-two cents."

Riley whistles, impressed.

"What's unusual about that?" challenges Axel. "Maybe they strong-armed him. Banned him from the range until he paid."

"They didn't," says Fletcher. "I asked. According to the owner, Tommy just bellied up to the bar one day and paid up."

Kole chews on this new morsel of information. Fletcher is right to take note of it. He will confirm with Hazel, but from what little he knows about Tommy, the guy was pretty miserly with his money.

"What'd you hear from the phone companies?" Fletcher asks, changing the subject, and Kole suddenly remembers his excuse for not attending the funeral.

"Dead," he says, in reference to Tommy's phone.

"What about Hazel?" asks Axel. "You get ahold of her yet?"

He can see it in their eyes that they don't believe him about leaving her a message. Good thing he's got a proverbial flash-bang to toss so he can divert their attention elsewhere. "There's something I need to tell you guys."

They lean in. The room feels smaller.

"I went back to Tommy's residence. Pursuant to our discussion with Cam about the drugs they found in the lake, I thought I'd take another look around while most of Tommy's acquaintances were at the funeral."

"You got another warrant?" asks Axel.

"No. Who's gonna contest the search? A dead guy?"

"What'd you find?" asks Riley.

"A gun. Probably not *the* gun, but . . . remember Hazel's 'missing' revolver? The .38 Special? It was hidden beneath a panel in the dresser in the upstairs bedroom."

"Shit," muses Riley, no doubt saying what's on everyone else's minds.

"How do you know it's not *the* gun?" challenges Fletcher. "If there's one thing the entry point of Tommy's residence tells us, it's that he either knew his attackers and he let them in, at which time they ransacked his place and brought him to the Mineshaft against his will. Or . . . they let themselves in. Someone who had a key. Now, who's to say the scorned ex-wife didn't return to Black Harbor, take care of Tommy, and hide the murder weapon?"

Kole would have to be a fool not to have run through this same scenario. It's plausible; of course it is. But it isn't probable. The looming question being: What motive would Hazel have to murder Tommy after all this time? Unless—

She ripped him apart pretty good in her book, didn't she? Hell hath no fury . . .

Cam's words float back to him on a current of dread. Kole disagreed with the man at that moment, but kept his mouth shut. From what he'd read, Hazel had been kind to Tommy; for as much as she'd disclosed, he sensed there was a lot more that she'd kept off the page. Being in Tommy's place all but confirmed it. It wasn't just the taxidermied animals. This is Wisconsin—a decapitated deer head above the mantel is a lot of people's idea of interior decorating. It was the stillness, the palpable hush that permeated every atom of air, as though the walls were holding their breath. He's been in enough places where bad things have happened to know it when he feels it, the needling sensation that something untoward has occurred.

"Because," he says, "whoever killed Tommy, killed him over this." Pulling up the photo of the brick, he lays his phone faceup on the desk.

"Is this . . ." starts Axel. His mouth falls open and stays that way.

Fletcher's brows are pulled tight. "Why's it look like it's been shot to hell? Where did you find this?"

"He shoved it in a taxidermied deer head," answers Kole, skipping the first question. "Or someone did."

Those last three words steal every last molecule of oxygen from the room. *Someone*, indeed.

"Tommy was on his way out," Fletcher says with confidence. "All packed and paid up. Why would he want to bring something like that with him? It'd be like carrying around a grenade without a pin in it. Besides, the market's here."

Kole nods along as it tracks with everything he's been thinking.

"So, why would he keep it in his house?" asks Riley.

"Because he didn't know it was there," offers Axel.

The more Kole sits with that theory, the more it feels right. Maybe he can confirm it with Hazel later, the resident Tommy Greenlee expert.

"What's that?" Axel pinches the screen to zoom in. They all crowd around the phone to better observe what Kole has already seen in person. He swipes to reveal a more close-up image of a distinct imprint pressed into the brick. It appears to be a rabbit missing a foot. Oftentimes, drug dealers will brand the packaging or the kilo itself as a way to track their controlled substances and ensure they haven't been cut and re-rocked. The fact that this imprint is here, on a brick that was fully intact until Hazel put a bullet through it, means whatever this substance is, it's premium.

Fatal.

He's already sent an email to SIU, inquiring if anyone's seen this particular imprint. Identifying exactly what kind of drugs Tommy intercepted could give them a new thread to pull on in the hunt for his murderer. But it could also open a Pandora's box. They may not want to know what trouble is headed for Black Harbor.

Or what trouble is already knocking at their door.

"Hoodoo?" suggests Riley.

"Voodoo?" says Kole.

She shakes her head. "Hoodoo. Black magic. It's African American spiritual work. Started with slaves in the Southern states."

"Black magic?" repeats Fletcher. "So, it's evil."

"It can be. Anyway, within hoodoo are strong beliefs in luck and omens."

Black magic, the final ingredient for this recipe of disaster. Kole jams the heels of his hands into his eyes as this investigation transmogrifies by the minute.

Axel, especially, seems unsettled. Or lost in thought, perhaps. He stares out the window, fixated on the illusory point where the blue of Lake Michigan meets the blue of the sky. When Kole asks him what's wrong, Axel gives him a look that makes his skin break out into goose bumps.

"Check the signature on the back of that mount," he says, flicking his eyes to Kole's phone again. Kole scrolls to the photo of the kilo, now split open, shoved into the buck's hollow neck cavity. His eyes move to the handwriting in black marker, at the name he carved down the middle with his knife: *Deschane's Taxidermy*.

15

HAZEL

In the bathroom, peeling off my sweat-soaked clothes, my hand trails up the side of my thigh, fingertips grazing the ugly serrated scar that runs past my knee. That's Black Harbor for you. If you ever dare to forget that you're a fish out of water, someone will try to filet you like one.

Speaking of filet, there's a kitchen knife on the pedestal sink. I set it there in case Robbie gets brave before I step naked into the porcelain tub, yanking the see-through plastic curtain across. The sound of the shower is calming, the smell less pleasant. A hint of rotten eggs wafts with the steam and a rust-colored ring around the drain tells of high iron content. Closing my eyes, I tip my head back and let the water gently pummel my scalp. It feels good, like a massage, and for a moment I can almost forget about the fact that I'm a person of interest in my ex-husband's murder.

I'm not a suspect. But . . . I'm not *not* a suspect, either.

Staring at the stains on the bottom of the tub, I read them like shapes in a Rorschach test. In them, I see Kole, because the truth is he has haunted me every bit as much as Tommy has. For years since I left, I've created the moment of seeing him again in my mind ten thousand times, ten thousand different ways. No matter what was going on, whether I was launching a book or sitting alone in my apartment or at a rooftop cocktail party, I allowed myself the small indulgence of imagining us meeting again.

He was anywhere and everywhere.

On the subway, I'd peer over the pages of whatever book I was reading and catch him watching me.

In Central Park, I'd be walking with girlfriends and notice him standing at Bethesda Fountain, as if we'd subconsciously agreed to meet there.

When I worked from cafés, I'd look up over my screen and conjure him sitting alone at a table, drinking a hot chocolate because he detests coffee. It was no small miracle I remembered such details; I remember everything about him, from the circumflex scar beneath his right eye to the mesmerizing way in which he pronounces my name, replacing that sleepy *z* with a sibilant *s*. How he made me come to life with just those two syllables, as though my name was a secret spoken only between us.

Tell me something confidential.

I was his something confidential once. And he was mine.

But what are we now? And who? Because I am not the same broken person I was when we met, and I cannot expect him to be the same either.

As I tally up the time I've spent daydreaming about being back in his orbit, I realize it wasn't a small indulgence at all, but an obsession. In eight years, I cannot effectively say that I ever stopped thinking about Nikolai Kole. And always in my imagination, when we saw each other again, it was as if hardly any time had passed at all. Always, he cradled the back of my head and kissed me. Always, I kissed him back.

Never did I imagine the two of us would reunite in that old half-dilapidated duplex with guns drawn on each other.

"The way I see it, we have two options," he said when we stood on the sinking porch. "Either I can arrest you on felony charges . . . or you can meet me at Beck's tonight to tell me everything you know."

My eyes lifted to meet his. I held on him as if my stare alone had the power to keep him in place, standing in that doorframe, a barrier between me and the life I left behind. Beyond him, the interior of the duplex was a black hole, threatening to suck me back in. I bit my lip as I considered his proposition.

Kole knew what he was doing.

He wasn't giving me an option. It was an ultimatum.

16
KOLE

Deschane's Taxidermy shop has been around since the Middle Ages. Generation after generation of old, bearded men have stuffed every dead animal this side of I-94 for literal centuries. While it wasn't a shock to see *Deschane's Taxidermy* scrawled on the back of the mount, it might be a lead. He and Axel hope to prove it one way or the other as they approach the building, which, like most buildings in Black Harbor, is faded and falling apart. Kole touches a panel of cedar and it comes free like a loose tooth. Axel doles him a scolding look and opens the door.

It's dim inside, the main light source coming from a workstation behind the counter. The smell of sawdust tickles Kole's nose. He tries to stifle a sneeze and fails.

"Gesundheit," a gruff voice offers.

"Thanks," Kole mutters. He looks around. His eyes are already itchy. He should have sent Riley, but she's over at the Jeskes' house, trying to set up an interview with Grayson. Who knows, for as much time as that boy spent with Tommy, maybe he met some seedy characters Tommy was fraternizing with in the weeks or months leading up to his death. It's also possible that Tommy confided something to him—something he didn't tell anyone else.

Deschane comes around to meet them. He's a bear of a man, with baseball mitt–sized hands. It's a wonder he can work so deftly, make all those small, careful cuts on his specimens. They're here to rule him out more than anything else. Kole knows that. Axel knows that, too, or at least he should. Now it's Kole who fixes Axel with a warning look. He better not say anything stupid.

The problem with Black Harbor—and there are a few—is that it's not all that big of a city. Every time they take a case, they play a game of Russian roulette to decide whether or not the case will be personal to one of them. If he excluded his detectives from working every investigation they had a connection to, there'd be a lot more cold cases. With a solve rate nearing 95 percent, no one can really balk at his methods.

While Axel isn't personally connected to the case at hand, there is unresolved animosity between him and Deschane. The taxidermist cropped up as a person of interest last year when Axel's daughter was abducted at the same time a couple of her classmates were murdered and missing pieces. He was absolved, although as far as Axel is concerned, while Deschane didn't necessarily get away with murder, he got away with something. It's that *something* he hasn't been able to put his finger on that drives him up the wall. Axel isn't unique. They all have unanswered questions, unsolved mysteries that haunt the quiet hours. Kole's has everything to do with that scratch-off ticket he found in Tommy's pocket this morning, and it's connected to the kilo of Xombie stuffed in that deer head.

Tommy wasn't a dealer, at least to his knowledge. He didn't do drugs, according to his autopsy. Which means that brick wasn't his. If they find out who it belongs to, however, they'll find out who killed him.

That's why they're here.

"The body's in the back." Deschane jerks a thumb over his shoulder, then cracks a smile as he wipes what looks like oil off of his hands. He threads the red microfiber rag through his belt loop where Kole notices a keychain, on the end of which hangs a lucky rabbit's foot. "I assume you're here to pin another murder on me, yeah?" Dale Deschane is a Neanderthal, his size rivaling that of the stuffed black bear standing guard by the entrance. He straightens his spine, drawing himself to his full height.

Axel sets his jaw. "It's just part of our canvass, Dale. We're hoping you can help us."

The fiberoptic hairs on Deschane's chin bristle as he sniffs. "You're asking around about that guy in the Mineshaft."

"Did you know him?" asks Kole. What Deschane says here will be telling. Tommy had too many animal mounts for them not to know each other. If Deschane lies about this, what else would he lie about?

"Yeah, I knew him," he says. "Stuffed some critters for him here and there."

"When was the last time you saw him, do you think?" asks Axel.

"Last huntin' season, I reckon. Brought in a buck. Ten-pointer."

The deer Hazel shot off the wall this morning has twelve tines, Kole recalls.

"About how many deer mounts have you done for him?" Axel again.

Deschane sucks his tobacco-stained teeth. "A few. Over the years."

Kole moves away from the counter and makes a show of perusing Deschane's menagerie of coarse hair and claws and marble eyes. He touches the stark white teeth of a beaver. "Are the teeth always fake?" he wonders out loud.

"Yeah," says Deschane. "Real teeth will dry out. So we use artificial jaw sets."

Kole knew that, having read through a forum before coming here, just like he knows the answer to the next question he's about to walk into. He pinches the cottontail of a rabbit, then picks up the whole creature. "It's light," he says.

Deschane is nodding as if he gets that particular compliment all the time. Still, it doesn't stop him from reveling in it. "My grandfather introduced the hollow-fill method in the sixties. My dad perfected it and I've been using it ever since."

"I'd say you got it down to a science," Kole marvels as he shifts the rabbit from one hand to the other. Deschane's use of this particular method all but erases the possibility of someone having just forged his name on the mount. He taxidermied that deer head for Tommy, but long before that kilo of Xombie made its way into Tommy's house, which brings them back to his original theory: either Tommy hid the drugs there or someone he let into his house did. "That's unusual, isn't it?" Kole says, stoking the conversation. "I've heard of it being done with fish, but . . . is it messy, to do with larger animals? I've read that the sawdust gets everywhere."

Deschane shrugs. "If you don't do it right, sure. But measure twice, cut once, that's what I always say." His gaze narrows. "You know quite a bit about taxidermy for a cop."

Kole sets the rabbit back down. "I'll admit, after the whole thing last October, it sparked an interest for me." He cuts his chin toward Axel, having just brought up the elephant in the room.

Deschane's hard exterior softens. "How's your girl?" he asks.

"She's good," Axel offers curtly.

Deschane nods, and that's the end of it.

"So, the last time you did any business with Tommy Greenlee was sometime last fall?" Axel recaps, and Kole knows the thread that's running through his mind, which is that, according to Cam, he and Tommy discovered the drugs a few weeks ago. If Tommy hasn't brought Deschane anything to stuff or doctor up since the fall, then it's highly likely Deschane has no idea about the kilo that Kole and Hazel discovered in the mount.

He didn't put it there, at the very least.

"That's right," says Deschane.

"I know it was a while ago," says Axel, "but do you recall if he mentioned anything about the Mineshaft, or did he bring up any names? Was he with anyone?"

"Can't say I ever heard him talk about that place. He wouldn't strike me as the type, to be honest."

"Would he strike you as the type to sell drugs?" Kole punches to the point.

"I wouldn't know about that."

"Did he do drugs?" asks Kole.

"Again . . ." Deschane shrugs. "I wouldn't know. We weren't friendly or nothin'."

"You saw him a handful of times," says Kole. "He ever come in here lookin' high or strung out?"

Deschane shakes his head. "I wouldn't know."

"You wouldn't."

"No."

"How old are you, Dale?" asks Kole.

Deschane's brows knit. His eyes narrow. "Forty-seven."

"You're forty-seven years old, lived in Black Harbor all your life, and you don't know what a high person looks like?"

Deschane scoffs and waves him off. "Look, I just keep my head down and do my work, all right?"

"Did Tommy ever come in here with anyone else?" Axel steps up to the plate.

Deschane holds on Kole for a second, then one bushy eyebrow arches. His eyes move back and forth, rifling through his memory. "I s'pose he used to come in with his wife back in the day. I haven't seen her around much, so I assume she turned tail and ran off."

Silence thickens between them. Kole clears his throat and points vaguely at Deschane. "I notice your lucky rabbit's foot, there. Didn't know they still made those. I had a blue one as a kid."

Deschane's mouth twitches into an almost smile. "That's who I make 'em for. The kids." He glances down at the one on his belt loop. Then, he unhooks two more from a spinner rack and hands them each one. "Here. A souvenir. I'm sorry I couldn't be more helpful, but I've got some errands to run."

Kole stares at the rabbit's foot in his palm. The fur is velvet soft and mostly brown, strewn with black and grey. "You mind if we take a quick look around, Dale? Just to check off some boxes."

Deschane folds in his lips. He looks from Kole to Axel, back to Kole. "Look, I'm not trying to dredge anything up, but I gotta protect myself. After what happened last year, with you guys almost pegging me for killing them little bunnies, I'd rather not. Not without a lawyer present."

Bunnies. That's right. He remembers that's what Deschane called the missing and murdered girls.

Beside him, Axel stiffens. Kole feels the tension in the air, now taut as a garrote. It wasn't a slip of the tongue—Deschane is intentionally rattling him. And now that he just lawyered up, there's no reason for them not to do the same.

"There are three reasons a guy like you wouldn't let us look around," Kole says to Deschane. "You're either hiding drugs, a body, or a gun."

"Or all three," adds Axel.

"Which is it?" presses Kole.

Insulted, Deschane puffs out his chest. "If I catch either of you pigs on my property again, you'd better have a warrant."

"Do *you* sell drugs, Dale?"

"Get the fuck out." Deschane shows them the door.

On the other side of it, now, Kole looks at Axel over the roof of his Impala. "That went well."

Axel drops into the passenger seat and sulks, turning over the morbid souvenir. Ninety-five percent clearance rate or not, there are certainly drawbacks to his detectives working cases they're personally connected to. They work harder, yes, but you have to be careful they don't start making false connections. It's why, in these cases, Kole goes along for the ride, so he can check them on their bullshit.

He isn't surprised that Deschane lawyered up. If the tables were turned, he would do the same. In a place like that, filled with dead animals and sharp objects, who knows what police might find if they poke around. And, if he's being honest with himself, he doesn't have time to poke around anyway. He's got to meet Hazel.

"Look, your kid's fine," Kole says as he pulls out of the lot. "Last I saw her, she wasn't walking around with a set of artificial teeth or glass eyes. She's got all her fingers and toes, and I don't think she's stuffed full of sawdust. We caught our guy and it wasn't Deschane. So either you fucking deal, or you write a warrant, and I'm telling you right now, you don't have enough probable cause to do that."

A muscle in Axel's jaw clenches. As skilled a detective as he is, he doesn't exactly have a spotless record. He rolls down the window and chucks his rabbit's foot out onto the road. "I'll figure it out. I'm getting that warrant."

"Knock yourself out," says Kole, thinking to himself that those are some bold words for a guy who literally just threw his luck out the window.

17
HAZEL

"Hello, Transcriber, this is Investigator Nikolai Kole, payroll number 6186, calling in a supplemental report pursuant to a search warrant that occurred on Friday regarding a suspicious death at 3704 Fulton Street."

The memory of hearing Kole's voice for the first time slams into me now as I walk past the Black Harbor Police Department. I remember the nights I spent here. Alone. Looking back, it was voyeuristic, in a sense, the way I would leave my shoddy homelife behind to punch in, put on a headset, and become a fly on the wall for whatever murder, controlled purchase, fraud, robbery, you-name-it had just occurred. And then, of course, there were the jumpers—people who plummeted to their deaths from Forge Bridge.

I was a faceless entity in those days. The only tangible traces I left of myself were the things I tossed in the river and the initials I typed at the bottom of each report. And they're not even my initials anymore. I reclaimed my maiden name after the divorce. "Greenlee" never felt like mine, anyway. It was a shoe that was a half size too small. A hat with a too-tight brim. A straitjacket.

I am Hazel Rydelle again. The person I was before I married Tommy and moved here to Hell on Earth, and this Hazel has never been to Black Harbor. What fresh horrors will she discover? What happens to darkness when it's exposed to the light?

The same can be said about Nikolai Kole. I don't know him. Not really. And yet, whether it's the way he holds himself or the intensity of his gaze that makes me feel as if I'm the only person in his world, something tells me he hasn't changed. He may be harder, sharper, rougher around the edges. But at his core, he remains steadfastly the same.

I'll admit, when I saw him for the first time earlier today, a piece of my icy exterior melted away. I was tearing into the contents of the dresser when suddenly, he materialized as if he'd walked out of a dream. Blond. Eyes the color of frost. Black T-shirt sticking to him, outlining every edge, every muscle. Too goddamn good-looking for my own good.

Agreeing to meet with him was a mistake.

I knew it even before the word tumbled from my lips, that three-letter combination that has a knack for getting me in trouble.

Yes.

Still, I said it. And still, I returned to the apartment to shower and change. The camera in the doorknob hadn't been replaced, but I had a feeling I was still being watched. I checked the bathroom for other surveillance equipment, and although I didn't find any, I continued to get dressed with a towel half wrapped around me, like how one changes out of a wet swimsuit at the beach. Robbie could have come into the unit and installed them while I was out, or it's entirely possible that was all done before I even checked in.

Does he know who I am? I wondered, remembering how he'd jumped to the conclusion that I had an interest in the murder at the Mineshaft. *A lucky guess, or does Robbie know more than he's letting on?*

While I had half a mind to ask him point-blank when, on my way out, I saw him in the back lot by the dumpsters, the other half just wanted to put as much distance between us as possible. He stared at his phone, but a woman knows when someone's eyes are on her, when they follow her until she turns a corner.

Now, I cross the roundabout. On my right is a patch of gravel where a row of blue apartments once stood, and I can't not think about what happened there, at 3704 Fulton Street, when a boy overdosed on oxycodone and my neighbor confessed to throwing his corpse in the dumpster.

I hid a body.

The message he wrote in the frost on my transcribing window has haunted me ever since. Sometimes when I get out of the shower, I will see it carved into the steam on the mirror. Or I'll re-create it myself by transposing letters on billboards or signs. Most often, though, it's simply scratched into the backs of my eyelids so I read it over and over again as I fall asleep.

That's how it all started between Kole and me. I was too willing to go places I shouldn't and he was all too happy to lead me into darkness. The physical building is gone now, but an eeriness holds its place. Ghosts latch on to me, sewing themselves into the fabric of my clothes, injecting themselves in my veins. They're not just the ghosts of those who have died—they're also the ghosts of Kole and me, when we ventured into that apartment in search of a satchel filled with prescription drugs. He lifted me up onto the pedestal sink and kissed me in the middle of a crime scene. I didn't stop him. Instead, I combed my fingers through his hair and kissed him back, harder.

A familiar ache settles in the pit of my stomach. It never left, not really, this sense of wanting him. But it intensifies now, as I immerse myself in this city of memories and nightmares all the same.

Forge Bridge, a nightmare in and of itself, looms in the not-so-far distance and I swear I hear its siren song, calling to me, beckoning me to tread on its railroad ties again and finish what I started. Which was what, exactly? Eradicating myself? Perhaps that's why I cannot bring myself to go there. Not yet, anyway. Because I have nothing else to give.

The sun is starting to set. It sinks behind the buildings, stunted brick and concrete stalagmites that erupt from the pavement. They're nothing in comparison to New York's skyscrapers. The sky is a painting of periwinkle strewn with neon orange, the same as the sign that glows above Beck's.

I approach the entrance and push my way inside. The air-conditioning is a welcome reprieve from the oppressive July heat.

The place has hardly changed but for new TVs behind the bar on which air baseball, sports updates, *E! News*, and some cheesy game show. Arcade games line the walls. An air-hockey table practically blocks the entrance. I walk around it, my eyes scanning for the Pac-Man game Kole and I used to play. Instead, I find Kole sitting at a high-top table in the same corner as the dartboards. There are two glasses of soda in front of him.

He looks up as I approach. I'm sure he watched me through the window, watched as I entered what used to be our place and searched for him, and I wonder if he reveled in those few seconds when he could see me but I couldn't see him, like how a hunter watches his prey just before he squeezes the trigger.

An easy smile brightens his face and my knees go weak. He stands. His voice is soft and arresting when he says: "Come here."

I want to fall into his arms, but an internal warning stops me. *You don't know this man,* I remind myself, and yet I do. I've memorized every detail of his face, the tactile sensation when he traced the curve of my neck, and the talent he had for getting me to follow him with as few words as possible.

I need you.

Those three little words floating on my phone screen were the end of me once. They can't be again. I can't afford to lose my edge around him. He made me come here for a reason, and I doubt it's so we can get reacquainted. I hope it is a little bit, but still. My ex-husband is dead. I'm back in town after almost a decade of being gone. And Nikolai Kole is hell-bent on finding out why.

18
KOLE

"I'm glad you came," he says when he and Hazel part.

"You threatened me with a felony if I didn't." Effortlessly, she lifts herself onto the tall barstool to sit across from him.

He nudges a sweating glass of soda toward her. "I got you a Diet Pepsi. You can order something else if you want."

She glances down at it. A maraschino cherry bobs at the top. The corner of her mouth twitches in either a silent *thanks* or *fuck you*. He can't discern which. She's tougher to read now than she was before. A closed book.

It's because of her book that Aubrey Jeske seems convinced that Hazel had a hand in offing her ex-husband. Kole doesn't buy it. If he had to guess, right now, it would be that Hazel returned to Black Harbor because Tommy was killed . . . not to kill him. He just needs to find out why she even gives a shit. From what she'd told him before, Tommy was never exactly husband of the year. But for some reason, his death brought her back to the one place she almost died trying to escape. Whether she's getting close to the investigation so she can write another book—it worked for the whole Candy Man clusterfuck—or because Tommy had some kind of hold on her, she's right here with him in the sports bar where they used to play with fire.

He wouldn't mind talking to Aubrey Jeske himself, to ask her what exactly is setting off the alarm bells about Hazel. Perhaps he will find an opportunity tomorrow, when they interview Grayson. Riley filled him in on his way over here. She made contact with Cam, who was the only one home at the time. Aubrey had taken the kids to her parents'. He'd sobered up and wasn't in the mood to socialize anymore. By the looks of it, he was alone in the house, Riley reported. All the lights were off and the TV was on.

"It's still here," he says when he notices Hazel's gaze roaming the room.

"What?"

He tips his head toward the Pac-Man machine. God, she used to drive him crazy when she'd lean over it, pressing her knee up against the coin slot. He could study the curve of her spine for hours, the way it disappeared into her jeans. There was a gap between denim and skin that looked just the right width for him to slide his fingers in and pull her to him. He never did that, as much as he'd wanted to.

A smile flickers and it looks less like the *fuck you* kind than the one before. She takes a sip and sets her drink down. "If you give me a quarter, I'll pummel your ass."

His heart thrums as he digs in his pocket for a coin. A headiness comes over him. Lack of sleep and old flames. She is the only person who's ever had this effect on him. She can make him lose his composure, do things he knows he shouldn't.

His fingertips find the ridges of a coin. It's a nickel. Disappointed, he sighs, but Hazel is already on her way to the bar. She leans forward like she used to, giving him a prime look at her ass in cut-up jean shorts. Her legs are a mile long. There's glitter in her lotion; sparkles catch in the light. She is molten, born of fire, and if he gets too close, she will burn him to ash this time.

He might just let her.

After he figures out why she's here.

Hazel swings by the table again to grab her purse. She doesn't wait for him. He hops off the stool and follows her to the far side of the room, beneath a neon *Leinenkugel's* sign.

"About the felony," he says, grabbing their drinks. "I might have been bluffing."

"I might have figured," she says without turning around.

"And you still came."

She shrugs. "Curiosity and all that." There's a tinkling sound as she sets what looks like five dollars' worth of quarters on the tabletop next to where he set their drinks. The pile of change fills him with naïve hope that they could spend all night here while Black Harbor implodes around them.

That isn't what he wants, though, and he knows it. Twenty-three years ago, he cut his own deal with Black Harbor. The keys to the city in exchange for an early grave. His oath promised him a chance to fulfill a calling—the sentient voice that compels him to help the helpless, give hope to the hopeless—and in return, he will give his life if that's what it asks. While he might be letting naïveté creep in, he isn't an idiot. He knows that if he doesn't die in the line of duty, the job will get him in the end. He had too many friends who retired only to drop dead three months later. It isn't a coincidence that "widowmaker" is a name shared by a heart attack and a career in law enforcement.

And a Porsche. But that's another story.

"Do you want to go first?" Hazel holds out her hand, offering three quarters.

He frowns as he collects them, intensely aware of his fingertips grazing her palm. "Didn't it used to be fifty cents?"

"Inflation."

"I guess." He crouches slightly and inserts the coins into the mouth of the machine. The lights deepen to red and the bubble screen glows to life. The last time he played this game was with her. Luckily, playing Pac-Man is like riding a bicycle. Just try to eat all the dots before the ghosts eat you.

Eat or be eaten. He smirks. If that isn't the age-old ultimatum of the universe.

Silence wedges between them like a third wheel. He plays his round, keeping an eye on her in his peripheral vision. She stares at the screen, as if fully invested in the game. Finally, after several minutes of play, the blue ghost catches up to him and Pac-Man falls into the abyss. Kole slides away from the machine. "Your turn."

"You know if you want to move faster, you should choose a route with fewer dots."

"Thanks, armchair quarterback. Let's see you do better."

The girl has clearly been practicing. Only when she more than doubles his score does she throw a glance over her shoulder to make sure he's still paying attention. As if she doesn't feel his eyes glued to her. "I know you didn't need me to come out here just to beat you at Pac-Man. So what's the deal?"

He takes her question as an invitation to close in a little. "What were you doing in Tommy's residence earlier today?"

"Looking for my gun, obviously. Which you confiscated."

"Why do you need a gun, Hazel?"

"Why does anyone need a gun, Nik? For protection. It's not safe here, in case you haven't noticed."

He rolls his eyes, unsure if that's a dig on his policing or what. She's usually good for one or two of those. *I can protect you,* is what he might've said in the past. He can't say it now. She won't even tell him where she's staying, for one thing. And for another, this Hazel 2.0 doesn't want to be saved. "So you knew the gun was there because you put it there." He reiterates what she told him this afternoon.

Her silence is as good as a *yes* in this case.

"What about the drugs?" The findings of the Nark II test kit confirmed his worst fear. The white powder tested positive for carfentanil, fentanyl, and xylazine.

The three main and deadliest components of Xombie.

"Do you have any idea how Tommy might have come by an illicit substance like that?" He asks even though he knows what her answer will be.

She shakes her head. Her ponytail swishes back and forth, dusting her shoulder blades. Before coming here, he considered whether or not he should tell her about his conversation with Cam Jeske. There's no reason not to. "Apparently, he and a coworker found a brick like that in the water," he shares.

"The same brick that we found in the deer mount?"

"I don't know yet. But probably."

"That tracks," says Hazel, pushing the joystick left, then up. "He was always finding shit in the water. Mostly tampons and condoms, but . . ."

Kole screws up his face. "Never drugs."

"Not to my knowledge."

Hazel goes quiet. She pretends to be even more enmeshed in the game.

Kole tries a new thread. "One of my guys stopped by Alpha this afternoon."

"How'd that go?"

"How was Tommy with money?" he asks instead of answering her question.

"Cheap," she says without hesitation.

"Do you know if he kept a tab at the range?"

"Probably."

"Any idea why he might've suddenly settled up three days before he died?"

She freezes for a fraction of a second. It's so quick, it might be a glitch. He watches her shoulders slowly fall, then, as she exhales. He knows if he would stand in front of her, he'd see her jaw clamped tight as she fights to keep all her secrets inside. But just like the gun safes in Tommy's house, all it takes is the right combination.

"How much was it?" she asks.

"Six hundred thirty-seven dollars and forty-two cents."

She whistles. "I don't think he spent that on all of my Christmas and birthday presents combined." There she is, the bitter ex-wife. Still, the fact that Tommy, a bona fide cheapskate, ponied up and paid off a longstanding debt three days before meeting his maker . . . there's got to be something there. Is it possible that Tommy, in some respects, was an honorable person? Perhaps he wanted to settle his debt before he ditched town, Kole thinks, remembering the bug-out bag in the duplex. Or, there's also the possibility that he knew there was a chance shit could hit the fan, and paying his tab was him tying up loose ends, like people often do before they hang themselves or send a bullet into their brain.

Or jump off Forge Bridge.

Tommy hadn't had a terminal illness, though, which around here is why people kill themselves about 50 percent of the time. He probably didn't even know about the cirrhosis. If he did, he hadn't cared enough to stop drinking, considering how his blood alcohol level was three times the legal limit when he was shot full of lead. The other 50 percent killed themselves because they got themselves into a situation of which death was the only way out.

Except, Tommy's death wasn't a suicide. And yet, paying off his tab hinted at the fact that he knew he was going to die. Or at least that he wasn't going to be around anymore.

Hazel hasn't said anything for three minutes. Something's changed, though. Her body language is more rigid, her shoulders tense. Kole studies how she leans closer to the machine, away from him. She knows something she isn't saying.

Her silence is a grenade. He pulls the pin. "I know you've been in contact with him."

She stops playing. Her hand hovers over the white button. A sheen of sweat glistens on her neck, now. She turns toward him, abandoning the game to the ghosts. He sees now that he was wrong a moment ago; she isn't a safe, but a cage, the secret inside her a wild animal fighting to claw its way out. Her eyes are deep, dark wells of mystery. Her lips part, then, and he can just glimpse a sliver of her tongue, cherry-red, when she says: "I didn't think he'd actually do it."

19
HAZEL

The message came a couple of weeks ago.

I'd just come upstairs from working out in the apartment building's gym and was settled in for the night. I thought I'd get some writing done. I needed to get some writing done. My deadline was—and still is—looming. I had less than three months to write another forty-five thousand words. Good words.

"Normally, I work well under pressure," I tell Kole. We've abandoned the Pac-Man machine for the black leather couch. It sags heavily in the middle, so naturally, gravity pulls us toward each other. "It's actually an important element in my process. I read somewhere that it's something creatives will do, wait until the eleventh hour in order to create a sense of urgency—"

"So, you were procrastinating." Kole's diagnosis cuts deep.

"I was *creating urgency,*" I defend. It's a crucial distinction. Procrastination is the willful delaying of a task, usually due to fear. And I am not afraid of my own writing.

"Okay," he says, unconvinced. "You were *creating urgency* and then what?"

I tell him what happened next, that I typed a few paragraphs that sounded like absolute shit, then loosely sketched out the rest of the chapter to revisit in the morning. When I'd finished, I poured myself a glass of pinot grigio and decided to pivot and get some work done on social media.

"No one works on social media," says Kole.

"Well, writers do. It's basically a requirement." When he raises a brow, I say, "Listen, do I pretend to know how to do your job?"

"Yes."

I can't help it. I laugh for the first time in I don't know how long. He laughs, too, and I feel my heart ache. I've missed that sound. I've missed being near him. Suddenly, all I want is for him to pull me close and promise that we can shut out the world.

Even if it's a lie.

"What happened on social media? Did someone slide into your DMs?"

"I'm getting to that part," I say, and tell him about how I added a selfie to my Instagram story along with the prompt: *Ask me anything*. It's something I do on occasion, whenever I feel the need to boost engagement or I'm simply bored. And if I'm being honest, somewhat lonely. I leave that part out, though.

The messages began flooding in almost instantly, queries running the gamut from asking details about my writing process to advice on getting published to whether or not certain characters will meet again. I answered them as they came in, until one particular question gave me pause.

I must have read it five times before accepting the fact that I hadn't drunk too much wine and imagined it. The inquirer's handle was @deadmann_walking. His question burned on my screen.

> If all you *had* to do was one bad thing, and you could leave Black Harbor behind forever, would you do it?

My mouth went dry as I clicked on his account. There was no profile picture. No posts. He had five whole followers—one of them being Cam—so I knew it was a dummy account. I knew it was Tommy.

"You didn't recognize the handle as something he's used before?" asks Kole.

I shake my head.

"And you didn't block him from your social media?"

I bristle at his accusatory tone. "I did. But all he would have to do is sign in with a different email address and he could find me. My account is public."

I left his profile and, after answering a few more questions that were specific to my books, I returned to the one I'd left unanswered. He only reached out to me to unnerve me. To see if he could pick up where we left off, where he gets to control me. Where I either cower or comply. Or run away. He was asking that question because he knew the answer.

Would I do a bad thing to leave Black Harbor behind forever?

I drained the last of my wine. Then I punched in three little letters.

> Yes.

I sink into the couch now. My back is slick with sweat. I don't realize I'm shaking until Kole wraps his hand around my wrist. In a comforting way, though, not as a constraint. "Is that it?" he asks. He's corrected his tone from before. There isn't the slightest hint of accusation or condescension. He sounds genuinely curious.

Carefully, I nod.

His eyes drill into me. I stare back. There's nothing that makes a person look guilty faster than avoiding eye contact, which raises a fair question: Am I guilty? I condoned whatever behavior it was that got Tommy killed, which likely had something, if not everything, to do with those drugs hidden in the dresser.

"He didn't say anything else after that?" presses Kole.

"No."

"Did he try to contact you again?"

"No."

"Do you remember the exact date of this conversation?"

"Conversation" is a tad generous. It was literally a question and a one-word response. "Thursday, June thirteenth."

He goes somewhere, then; I can see it in his eyes as his brain rewinds through all the clues and dates he's picked up since finding Tommy's body. I'd bet my bottom dollar he's trying to match this date with when Cam told him they'd fished the drugs out of the water.

His phone buzzes. The screen glows with an incoming call from UNKNOWN. It's a cop, then. That's how they always come up on caller ID. "Who's dead now?" Kole answers.

I don't recognize the voice on the other end. It's a male, that much I can tell. I lean closer, not even bothering to be subtle about eavesdropping. He's distressed, whoever he is. There's something guarded, wary about how he rattles off an address and tells Kole to get over there.

I wasn't scared until this moment, as I sit here watching the color slowly ebb from Kole's face. Breath held, I listen. Everyone knows that a picture is worth a thousand words. But most of the time, you can paint a picture in far less than that. Like the ones I hear on the other line: "They went fucking medieval on him."

20

KOLE

"I'm going with you," she says, like this is old times.

"You're not." He's already off the couch, grabbing his keys. "Come on. I'll drop you off."

Hazel is on his heels as he heads toward the exit. "Who's dead now?" she asks, parroting him from a moment ago. His eyes flick between her and the patrons at the bar. He fixes her with a look that begs *Please shut the fuck up*. The air is so thick outside, so humid, he might as well be wading into a pool. His vehicle's just down the block. It's his personal one, but he doesn't have time to switch to his Impala.

"This is me," he says, nodding to the blacked-out four-door Jeep Wrangler.

"Dang," she whispers as she climbs up inside.

"Watch yourself," he warns as he slams the door shut.

He goes around the front, then, and gets behind the wheel. When he slams his door, all is quiet. "What's the address?" He turns the key in the ignition. The vehicle roars to life.

"How should I know? I thought he told you over the phone."

"No, *your* address. Wherever you're staying."

"I'm coming with you."

"Negative, Ghost Rider."

To his utter vexation, she brings the seat belt across and settles in. She stares straight ahead, down the vacant street. He glares, as though a sharp look alone will be enough to needle an address out of her. "I'll bring you back to the duplex, then."

"You won't." At least she's one for two on calling his bluff. She'd fallen for the first one completely. He had no idea she'd been in contact with Tommy. He'd thrown the accusation out as a Hail Mary.

His phone buzzes again. It's Riley replying to his text about rounding up the boys. He's got to go. His jaw clenches as he looks from Hazel to the long, winding street ahead. *Fuck you,* he thinks. *Fuck you all the way back to Brooklyn.* But he keeps the sentiment to himself. Instead, he throws the shifter into gear and rips a U-turn. At least his windows are triple-tinted. Maybe, just maybe she will stay put. If she refuses, he'll handcuff her to her seat.

He blows every red light on the way to the scene.

"I see the traffic laws don't apply to everyone." On his right, Hazel grabs the *oh shit* handle. Her knuckles glow bone white.

"That was orange," he argues.

"Blood orange." So is the next one, and the next three after that. Finally, he turns right onto a street that's flooded with an aurora borealis of red and blue lights, and coasts to a stop behind a police SUV.

"Stay here," he tells her, and to his relief, she doesn't protest. She slinks low, her eyes as round and bright as headlights as she takes in the scene. He wonders if she recognizes the house. He sure as hell does. He was just here.

"Hey," he says, before shutting her in.

She looks at him. Her bottom lip quivers. He knows what she's thinking. She has forgotten how dangerous Black Harbor truly is. She should never have come back.

If she lets him, though, he'll see to it that nothing bad ever happens to her. But she has to trust him. Gripping the steering wheel with his left hand and leaning toward her, he extends his right arm. "Promise you'll stay here? You don't want to see this, trust me."

She considers his hand for a second, then links her pinkie finger with his—something they used to do a lifetime ago.

Four uniformed officers are spaced out around the perimeter to guard against rubberneckers and lookie-loos. He marches toward the garage now. The overhead door is closed on one side, open on the other, with the champagne-colored minivan stopped dead in its tracks halfway across the threshold. That must be when Aubrey Jeske came home and saw the carnage.

Kole veers toward the right. On the asphalt drive, the chalk drawings dance beneath the rotating red and blue lights, and he sees something he hadn't seen before: a primitive, three-pronged crown that's become ubiquitous to all Black Harbor surfaces.

The Nightmare Kings have been here.

"Sanction that off!" he yells to an evidence technician. Weaving through uniforms, he maneuvers quickly around orange traffic cones where there might be blood or footprints—evidence that needs to be photographed. He steps around a garbage bin lying on its side, next to a bag of trash, and enters the garage. While he knows what he's about to walk into, this scene is one he never could have prepared himself for.

The strobe of a camera flash goes off. In that fraction of a second where the whole space is starkly illuminated, he sees the shine of blood. Everywhere.

He finds Sergeant Maldonado and shoulders up next to him. "Where—" He doesn't get the rest of his sentence out before he discovers the body in the empty stall.

Cameron Jeske is slumped forward, chin buried in his chest. His T-shirt is drenched in blood, as is his hair. Black zip ties cut into his wrists, securing him to one of the sun-faded patio chairs Kole recognizes as being from the backyard.

"Jesus Christ," Kole whispers. Beside him, Maldonado just slowly shakes his head.

Medical Examiner Rowan Winthorp arrives. They watch as she maneuvers toward the body and begins her examination. Pressing her gloved hand to his neck, she feels for a pulse. It's a formality, really. Cameron Jeske has as much of a heartbeat as a slab of ground beef. He knows she would normally do other things, like flutter his eyelashes to check for a pupillary response, but his orbital sockets have been smashed to pulp. Automatically, Kole's eyes roam the garage for a blunt weapon left behind.

"Contusions on the skull," Rowan notes. "Consistent with a blunt-force weapon."

"Like a baseball bat?" Maldonado offers.

"Possibly. I examined a body a few years ago of a woman who got bludgeoned to death with a croquet mallet. Looked similar to these." She points to the myriad lacerations on Cam's scalp.

This murder is much more deliberate than the last one, Kole realizes. The killer—or *killers*—weren't rushed or careless, not like dousing Tommy's body in bleach before they had a chance to move it.

They are sending a message.

"Time of death . . . Tuesday, July 2, 21:04 hours." Rowan speaks into her recorder and goes on to dictate the trauma to the maxillofacial region. He doesn't know how she can make much sense of it. The nose is caved all the way in, the cheekbones shattered. There's a split that must be four inches long across the forehead—one of the points of impact. But the mouth is the worst of all. Carefully, Rowan lifts the head. That's when Kole observes the shards of white that speckle Cam's shirt.

His teeth. Or what's left of them, anyway.

"Here, tip his head back, will you?" Rowan says.

Kole grabs hold of Cam's hair—the ends of which are crunchy and wet—and tilts his skull back. His mouth is a ruined cavity. The teeth are broken into pegs, tongue all shredded to hell. Protruding like a cigar is the butt of a lightbulb.

It makes his own mouth hurt just to look at it.

"They really tortured this sorry son of a bitch," Maldonado says. "Looks like they jumped him while he was taking out the trash."

Curiously, Kole pinches a white splinter of blown glass stuck in Cam's tongue. "Then they zip-tied him . . ." he starts, envisioning how it all must have gone down.

"And interrogated him," offers Axel as he enters the arena. The rest of the VCTF is here now. He's right, Kole thinks as he observes one of two overhead lights that would have cast a spotlight on Cam as he sat in the hot seat. The other lightbulb holder is empty. He'd bet money they unscrewed it while it was hot, shoved it in Cam's mouth, and then swung hard. Figuring out how someone was killed is usually easy enough. The hard part is *why*. In this case, however, Kole knows it has everything to do with the Xombie that Cam and Tommy pulled out of the water. He says as much.

"Wait, Xombie's made its way here?" Maldonado's voice all but breaks.

With a captive audience now, Kole gives the abridged version of Tommy and Cam discovering what they now know to have been three kilos of Xombie. He shows Maldonado his phone that reveals the rabbit stamp on the brick.

A somber silence descends. Coated glass crunches beneath Rowan's shoes as she searches for broken-off fingernails, hair, or other elements that could help with identifying a suspect. "What's this?" she asks as she circles back to the body and tugs a card from his shirt pocket.

What happens next seems to happen in slow motion. Kole watches as Rowan unfolds the card. It's a scratch-off ticket, hazmat-yellow, and stamped on top in bright, stinging red are the words KA$H KA-CHING.

His blood runs cold. He knows what the scratched-off numbers will be before he even reads them.

0-5-3-7-3

"Nik?" He feels a hand on his back. Hears a voice. He doesn't know who either belong to, only knows that he's closer to the concrete than he should be. His hands push on his kneecaps. He leans forward and rocks back on his heels as acid surges up his throat. He can't breathe in here. He needs to get out. Get some air.

But the night does nothing to soothe him. Officers are teeming around the scene. He weaves to get around them. His fists are clenched at his sides. He needs to hit something, or yell, or—

"Nik!"

Riley's run out after him. For fuck's sake, can he just have one fucking minute to himself? At his Jeep now, Kole hammers his fists down onto the hood. Forgetting that Hazel is inside. Forgetting everything except those numbers.

Riley catches up to him. She's asking if he's all right when the edges of his vision bleed into vignettes. He should have been more careful earlier when he wished it into existence, because now his whole world is imploding. His awareness is slipping away. Everything is dark and muffled, like he's lying in a casket and someone's dragging the lid over him.

Somehow, it gets even worse.

Vaguely, he hears someone mumbling something about getting back to the lighthouse, hears the driver's side door to his vehicle opening, and Riley's voice begging the million-dollar question: "What the hell is she doing here?"

21
HAZEL

The city zips by in a blur. I ride shotgun while Kole's in the back seat of his own vehicle. Investigator Riley drives. Her nostrils flare. Her eyes are pinned to the road, tearing away only for a split second to glance at Kole in the rearview mirror.

He looks dazed, like someone's just punched his lights out. It isn't like him to be so affected by a crime scene—he's investigated hundreds of homicides at this point—which is how I know there must be more to it. Something personal. At least, that's how it was when he barged into my transcribing office one night, on edge and paranoid upon discovering that his CI had been murdered, stabbed thirteen times and left to bleed out on the floor of her own apartment.

Later, I learned that she was his best friend's daughter.

"You doing all right back there?" Riley asks, her eyes flashing to meet Kole's in the mirror again.

A disembodied growl comes out of the dark. "Fine."

We're outside of the realm of streetlights now. The vacant storefronts. The bums sleeping at bus stops. It's darker out this way and I know that the vast swath of black to the east is Lake Michigan. Even when I lived here, there was rarely any reason for me to venture to this side of the city, toward the yacht club and the lakeside mansions that just reminded me that not everyone was so miserable in Black Harbor. Some people had figured out how to make a living here. Judges. Lawyers. Doctors. Dope dealers.

The lighthouse is a pale beacon in the night. I suck in a breath as Riley turns right and begins a steep descent. It looks like we're about to plummet into the lake, but the road keeps stretching out before us, guiding us to a small parking lot. There are no surrounding buildings, just an endless open space.

Kole is the first one out. He opens his door before the vehicle even rolls to a complete stop. Riley huffs and rips off her seat belt. I follow, caught between wanting to stay close to them and wanting to keep my distance. I shouldn't have strong-armed him into letting me come. Now I'm here, a squeaky fifth wheel to their high-profile investigation, and the discomfort is real. For a second, I consider slinking away. A couple quick steps into the shadows and I could be gone. But I'm afraid I've caused enough trouble for Kole already. He isn't someone I want as an enemy.

I gathered on the way over here that the lighthouse is a clandestine headquarters for their task force. There's the hum of an engine as another car pulls up into the lot and I recognize the two male detectives from Cam's house. Axel is the kinder-looking one, with striking teal eyes and a receding hairline. The other one is Fletcher; bearded, long-haired, and rougher around the edges than any detective I've seen before.

"She shouldn't be here, Nik." Fletcher pushes past me and takes the spiral staircase two steps at a time to catch up to Kole, who turns and grabs a fistful of his shirt.

"She's not a suspect," he seethes. "And last time I checked, I'm in charge. You don't like it, then go home."

I feel myself shrinking, trying to disappear. Riley's behind me, still, while Axel rushes up the stairs to pry them apart. "She's better off with us," he says, appealing to Kole. "Besides, she might know something we don't."

Upon arriving on the third floor, I cast a look around. A cluster of four desks are pushed together in the center of the room. There are four windows, one for each cardinal direction; they might as well be painted matte black for all you can see at this time of night. Taped to a whiteboard on which the whole investigation is laid out, is Tommy's pictures. I startle. Edging closer, I note that there's what appears to be a yellow scratch-off ticket tucked partially behind it.

I frown as my gaze moves across the board. Cam's picture is up there, too. I don't recognize the others; all thugs and snitches, I expect. I let out a breath of relief when I confirm that my own picture is not there.

Kole was telling the truth, then. I'm not a suspect.

Everything is moving so fast. Riley cuts past me and tears the ticket down from the board. "The numbers are the same," she notes.

"The same as what?" I ask, and she explains to me that an identical ticket had just been found in Cam's shirt pocket. My mind immediately starts turning over the puzzle pieces.

Tommy and Cam found drugs floating in the water.

Tommy is dead.

Cam is dead.

Tommy had a scratch-off ticket.

Cam had a scratch-off ticket.

The numbers match.

Which means . . . it must be a message. Or some kind of ritual.

I look up. All eyes are on Kole as he does something that steals all the air from the room. He takes his wallet out of his back pocket and reveals a third identical ticket.

22
KOLE

The ticket he pinches between his fingers is a faded, mealy version of the ones found on Tommy and Cam. Still, it is undeniably the same. Four pairs of eyes pin him in place. He doesn't dare move. The paper is fragile, one chemical element away from dust.

"How long have you had that?" Fletcher asks the question they're all thinking. Next will be *Where did it come from?* Or rather, *Whose body did you take it from?* He's about to answer them all now.

"Nine years." The hush in the lighthouse takes on a haunted quality. He watches their expressions contort from shock to pity, and he hates it. All of them except for Hazel. Her face is frozen in that deer-in-the-headlights look she's worn since they parked outside of Cam's place. She knows as well as the rest of them who the ticket belongs to. She just doesn't know it yet.

Her gaze shifts to his and locks, and this time, he swears he can see her think, the little strobes that flash behind her eyes as her memory rewinds to that cold spring morning when they met at Forge Bridge.

Called there to examine a reported body in the river, he parked in the vacant lot and stifled a yawn as he climbed out of his vehicle, ready to go through the motions of a rote jumper incident. Drag the body onto shore. Check for signs of foul play. Wait for the medical examiner to arrive and bag him or her up. But as he approached the bridge, something in his peripheral vision caught his attention. A flash of red. He homed in on it. Someone was half running, half crawling up the hill, away from the water.

Away from the body.

"Hey!" he shouted, hand moving back to his Glock on his hip. "Police, stop!"

The person kept moving. Kole ran toward her—the banner of dark hair and slim build suggested the runner was a female—and as he started to close in, she chanced a look over her shoulder before vanishing into the thicket.

He chased after her. The trees swallowed what light there was, their branches creating a shelter, a cone of silence. It felt strangely as if he'd fallen into another realm, a peaceful pocket sewn seamlessly into Black Harbor's fabric. Even now, he remembers the sweet, sharp scent of the evergreens, the way his words got swallowed up when he shouted another set of directives. "Police! Stop! I just want to talk—"

His radio crackled, a prelude to the words that dropped him to his knees. "Holy fuck, it's Evan."

The runner got away. For months she haunted him, though. A nameless ghost. But then, one day, as if the universe had finally thrown him a bone, she turned up on his turf as the new police transcriber.

There was no autopsy for his brother. Evan Kole's death was ruled a suicide, as is the case with all jumpers. There was no investigation into foul play. No digging into his personal life or checking his bank statements for financial troubles. No searching his house or his vehicle and so his addiction was kept out of the eyes of the public.

After the funeral, Evan's widow brought him a Ziploc bag full of prescription pills. She found them in a secret cache in their house, behind the milk door that, at one point, had been painted shut.

Sitting in his vehicle, still parked in the cemetery, Kole studied the pill bottles. Most of them weren't even addressed to Evan. Later, he would look up the names and discover one of them to be a cancer patient whose nephew had been stealing her medications and selling them on the black market.

He stayed there for a long time, staring absently at the freshly churned earth of his brother's gravesite. He should have noticed the signs. The mood swings. The way Evan had to chug coffee and energy drinks just to stay awake for a normal shift. The decline in his performance. It all started after the accident, when a vehicle bulldozed into Evan's during a pursuit. He had surgery to mend a disc in his back, and although he complained about pain for a few weeks afterward, things seemed fine.

But they weren't. The thorns of reality were there, rearing their ugly little heads, and yet the truth was that Kole didn't see his brother's addiction because he didn't want to.

Absent-mindedly now, his hand creeps toward his neck, his fingers threading through the black chain he's worn since the morgue sent it home with him among Evan's things: his clothes, phone, wallet, scratch-off ticket. Even through his shirt, he can feel the words carved into the metal.

Vincit omnia veritas. Truth conquers all.

"Nik, what does this mean?" He traces the question back to Riley. They stare at him, waiting with bated breath for him to give the answer. It's an impossible ask, because this is one mystery he has never been able to solve.

For nine years, he has searched for meaning. For nine years, he has failed to find it. The number sequence isn't a combination. Or a date. Not that he's been able to prove, anyway. Finally, he resigned himself to the possibility that Evan simply bought a scratch-off ticket, forgot it in his pocket, and jumped off Forge Bridge.

Except, Kole never found where he bought the damn thing. He went to every convenience store, grocery store, and lottery kiosk within a fifty-mile radius of Black Harbor, and never caught so much as a glimpse of KA$H KA-CHING. Besides, there was the fact that Kole knew in his bones that Evan did not buy that ticket; his brother didn't leave things up to chance. And yet, knowing something and proving it are two different things.

Now, he looks at the scratch-off in his hand, the one he's kept hidden away for the better part of a decade. He's managed not to spare it a thought for quite a while, until Monday morning in the morgue, when he discovered it among Tommy Greenlee's things.

Evan Kole.

Cameron Jeske.

Tommy Greenlee.

Three dead men. Three identical scratch-off tickets.

Two within two days of each other. The other from almost a decade ago.

One body in the river. Another meant for the river, he thinks as he returns to the conversation with Liz, when they talked about the bleach and the garbage bags. *Where does everything get dumped in Black Harbor?*

The river.

Not for the first time, he wonders if his brother's opiate addiction hadn't gone further than hawked prescription pills. He might have gotten himself into trouble, owed a debt he couldn't repay.

They are all quiet. Outside, the lake crashes against the half-sunk piers. Fletcher is first to speak. Cheeky, practically taunting, he addresses the only non-detective in the room. "So what do you make of this?"

Hazel's gaze slides from Fletcher to Kole. Their eyes lock, and the rest of the room falls away. It might as well be just the two of them when she speaks for the first time since coming up here. She's so quiet, he has to read her lips. Still, the message is loud and clear when she says: "The only way out is down."

23
HAZEL

They stare at me as if I've summoned the dead. And I suppose I have, in a way. "The only way out is down" is a phrase that has stayed with me ever since I transcribed my first report of a man who jumped off Forge Bridge. He'd scrawled it on a suicide note that was found with the pullover he'd discarded on the railroad ties.

"He had a ticket, too."

Axel has to pick his jaw up off the floor to ask: "How do you remember that?"

I look at each of them in turn. Their gazes are needle-sharp, sticking me in place. I shrug. "Don't all transcribers remember their first jumper report?"

They exchange glances, and I wonder if they're thinking about their first crime scene, their first dead body, their first overdose. We always remember our firsts and lasts, don't we? It's everything in the middle that ends up in one congealed mess.

Kole's brother, Evan, jumped from Forge Bridge just months before I started at the police department. I didn't see him do it, but I saw his body, floating faceup, empty eyes staring at me from the cruel black water below.

"Do you remember his name?" asks Kole. "The guy who wrote the suicide note?"

I search my memory but come up blank. "No. But he was a white male, ex–Forge Fuels employee. His arms were covered in tattoos."

Riley fires up her computer. Her fingers clack on the keys, perforating the quiet. "You remember the date or thereabouts?" she asks me without looking up.

I give her the year and add: "January 15."

"How?" Axel says again.

So many things about that day are burned into my memory. It was my first jumper report, yes, but hardly an hour after I'd finished typing, my neighbor approached my window and confessed to hiding a body. It was also later that same day, when I clocked in for the night shift, that I heard Nikolai Kole's voice for the first time.

"James Allen Cooper," interjects Riley, eyes glued to her screen. "Forty-six years old. Dead by suicide on January 15."

"He have any next of kin?" asks Kole.

There's a series of mouse clicks as she goes through what I suspect are photos and case files. "Divorced," reports Riley. "There are lots of Coopers. Any one of these could be his family."

"Print that out," says Kole. "That's your roster, assuming the interview with Grayson Jeske is off the table, at least for now. We'll still need to follow up with Aubrey tomorrow. See if she has any information for us . . ." He trails off, thinking out loud. "Regardless, talk to anyone who knew James Allen Cooper. Dude's been dead for eight years and change. If there's any dirt to be found on him, it's high time we dug it up."

Riley tightens her jaw but she doesn't argue. If anything, she looks determined.

He turns to Fletcher next. "Stay on the guns. I want you out at every pawnshop between Milwaukee and Chicago. If we find footage of someone bringing them in to sell, we might have our suspects."

Fletcher nods.

"Axel. Who's that criminal analyst they got up in the bureau now?"

"Gretchen."

"Connect with her tomorrow. I want you two to comb through every DOA—homicides, suicides, natural deaths—from the past ten years, maybe more. If any of those bodies were found with a scratch-off ticket, flag it. After that, you can hop on a canvass. Talk to the neighbors. See if their doorbell cameras caught anything."

"That's going to take forever. There are thousands of DOA reports."

Kole arches a brow. "And you just wasted five seconds complaining about it."

"What about Deschane? I'm working on a warrant—"

"Leave it," orders Kole. "You don't have enough probable cause anyway. As for me, I'm going to head over to SIU, see if they've got a match for that rabbit imprint, and if they've seen hide or hair of Robert Pitts. According to the complainant, he was at the Mineshaft Saturday night with Darren Hogan, who's allegedly split for Chicago, and he's gotten into selling harder drugs lately. He might not be our suspect, but he's worth talking to. I'll call some guys in General Investigations, see if they can give us some support with the tip line."

Silence falls as everyone turns over their respective responsibilities in their minds. These next twenty-four hours are crucial. Not only because hope begins to wane after this window, but come Thursday, the city will literally explode with Fourth of July celebrations.

"What about her?" Fletcher dragging me into the hot seat puts me on edge. I go still, and instantly hate myself for reverting back to my old ways: freeze, faint, fawn, take flight. My gaze wanders to the door, behind which descends the stairwell. He sounds so certain of what he says next, though, that a shiver zips down my spine. "You know she's next."

Slowly, Kole turns. I am paralyzed under his stare, filled with the knowledge that Fletcher is right. Whoever killed Cam killed him because of what Tommy did. Cam was guilty by association. If word gets out that I'm here—Tommy's ex-wife who he'd been communicating with—I'd almost be better off slitting my throat myself.

It would probably be more humane than what they did to Cam. I don't know the details, but I heard some rumors about a blunt-force weapon and a lightbulb.

The way Kole regards me, I feel like a dog left out in the rain. Some pitiful, pathetic creature he now has to take care of. His eyes soften at the edges, sloping like a pair of quotation marks. He doesn't ask what I want to do. Doesn't ask if I need to grab a change of clothes or if there's someone I can call to pick me up.

He knows there is no one.

The pity in his eyes dissolves, then, to be replaced by the same look I saw in Riley. Determination. For what, though? To keep me safe?

I don't want his protection. Or anyone's.

And yet, maybe I need him.

"She stays with me," he says.

It was already after midnight when Kole sent everyone home and told them to start on their marching orders at 8 A.M. At the same time, he made the fact that my options were limited very clear when he unclasped the handcuffs from his back belt loop and showed them to me. "From now until we catch these guys, you and I share the same footprint. Don't make me lock these on us."

Now, the house he's driven me to is the same modest brick Cape Cod that I've been to before. Never inside, though. The one time I came here after shit hit the fan with me and Tommy, his sister-in-law opened the door.

I thought she was his wife. She wasn't, but there was something there.

The memory is a ribbon of smoke that I wave away, along with the notion that even if he didn't have someone then, it doesn't mean he doesn't now. If she's here, I'm about to find out. I take a deep breath as, on my left, a BEWARE OF DOG sign glares from the other side of a window. I feel my eyes bulge out of my head. "Um . . ." I point to it.

Kole waves dismissively. "He's harmless. Eighty percent of the time, the sign alone is enough to discourage a burglary."

I narrow my eyes and hope he's telling the truth, although the statistic sounds spun from thin air. "That's probably what everyone says before their guests are torn limb from limb by a rabid beast."

The metal gate to the backyard groans as Kole swings it toward us. He steps aside to let me through first. The lawn is freshly cut and more verdant than most. As if to assuage my stupefaction, I hear the *chck-chck-chck* of a sprinkler system. The water has an instant calming effect on me. He's got a little oasis back here, complete with an obligatory flower bed, a patio set, a hot tub, and a plastic kiddie pool.

"For the rabid beast," says Kole, when he catches me staring at the pool.

He moves ahead of me, then, to unlock the door. An alarm countdown pulses. He keys in a four-digit code and the white box glows blue. I step in after him and immediately hear the soft thunder of paws on a hardwood floor. The dog slides into me before I see him, sweeping me out at the knees. I crash and take out a shelf of shoes on my way down. My field of vision is entirely obscured by a mane of copper hair and a wet, probing nose.

Finally, Kole manages to wrestle the golden retriever off of me. The dog swivels his head back and forth, tongue lolling, a string of saliva glistening as it reaches toward the floor. "Hazel," Kole says, slightly breathless. "Meet Rocket. Rocket, this is Hazel."

"Nice to meet you," I say through a laugh. I extend my hand as a joke, but to my surprise, Rocket offers his paw. I stare at Kole, incredulous. "He can shake?"

Kole ruffles the fur on Rocket's neck affectionately before standing and helping me up. "You should see him solve a Rubik's Cube."

"Really?"

A blond eyebrow arches. "Are you serious right now, Podunk?"

My breath hitches at the sound of my old nickname. It gives me hope that, although things are different between us, perhaps not *everything* has changed. "What else can he do?" I ask, grateful for the distraction as I take in all that is Nikolai Kole's domain. It's a modern bachelor pad with a seventy-five-inch TV eating up a whole wall in the living room. The others are sparsely decorated with framed sports jerseys, which, upon closer inspection, are autographed. A grey couch with a chaise and matching ottoman take up the entire carpeted floor, along with a blue recliner that looks more worn than any of the other furniture. Rocket's bed and a basket of toys are in the kitchen area. In lieu of a formal dining table, there's a cozy breakfast nook that looks just large enough for two people.

A dark hallway shoots off to the west, leading, I'm guessing, to the bedrooms and bathrooms.

"Roll over, play dead . . ." Kole shrugs. "That would be the extent of his portfolio. Just don't ask him to be civilized during a storm."

"It's okay, Rocket." I crouch to meet him eye to eye. "I don't always like storms, either." Then, to Kole: "I'll bet this week is tough on him, with all the fireworks and all."

"He doesn't seem to mind, actually. Somehow he can't tell the difference between my socks and his toys, but he can discern fireworks from thunder."

"Rocket science," I say, standing back up. I can't help but be pleased with myself for the double entendre.

The dog barks.

"Oh, of course, how could I forget," Kole says to Rocket, then turns back to me. "He's also an excellent swimmer."

"In his kiddie pool?" I tilt my head toward the patio doors.

"We go to the lake. He likes to fetch off the pier."

Rocket stares at me, eyes sparkling, tail slapping against the floor. I reach for him and he comes over to be pet. In my peripheral vision, I catch a glimpse of Kole smiling and a piece of my heart melts. I've dreamed of seeing that smile again.

He snaps back to business mode. "Look, I've got an early start, so I won't keep you up. You can have the bedroom upstairs and I'll take the couch."

"I'm good here," I say.

"Are you sure? I feel like an asshole, taking the bed while putting you out on the sofa."

"You are an asshole. But I'm happy here. Really." I sit down on the ottoman to stake my claim. Rocket lays his head in my lap.

"Okay." Clearly, my host is too tired to argue. "The bathroom's down the hall on the right. I'll bring you a set of clothes to sleep in."

"Thanks."

He's true to his word. When I emerge from the bathroom after washing my face and using my finger as a toothbrush, I discover the couch has been made into a bed with a sheet and a comforter, and a change of clothes is set out. I put on his black BHPD T-shirt and terry-cloth shorts. The shirt is worn gossamer-thin and smells like him. Sandalwood and sage, clean.

I wait for a few minutes to see if he'll come back. But the lights are off and Rocket lopes over to me as if this is his nightly routine. My heart sinks a little as I crawl under the comforter and lay my head down on the pillows. It's much more comfortable than the bed in the apartment. Every ache I didn't even realize I had alleviates. I feel so light I could float. Then Rocket plunks down on the carpet right beneath me and keeps one eye cracked open. The perfect guard dog.

"Good night, Rocket," I yawn. My eyelids feel heavy. I can see my eyelashes closing down like a curtain at a performance. On the ottoman, my phone glows, waking me. I pick it up and read the text message from Kole.

> Goodnight Podunk.

WEDNESDAY, JULY 3

24
KOLE

She was still asleep when he slipped out the door at 6 A.M. He likes to be in the office early, before anyone else gets in. It's stolen time—a window in which his phone generally doesn't ring, and no one's bitching about casework or hounding him about things he needs to do. Of course, the bitching has gotten much better since he founded the VCTF; their cases are all chosen for them. Still, there's something about the morning half-light and the rhythm of the crashing waves that brings him a sense of calm, an opportunity to get his head right before diving back into this mangled mess of an investigation.

Before he left, he paused at the bottom of the stairs when he came down from his bedroom, waiting to see if his footsteps had woken her. But she must have been tired, sleeping off the stress of yesterday, because she remained still as a doll on his couch. Her hair was a dark cloud that cradled her head, her nose but a little scoop before the rest of her sun-freckled face disappeared beneath the blanket.

He resisted the urge to go near her. *Let her sleep,* he told himself. *The less she's awake, the less she'll want to run free.*

If that didn't sound terrible. Like she was a wild animal and he was her captor. It's not like that—this is for her own good—and yet, kidnappers probably have this same monologue with themselves all the time.

He left a note for her on the kitchen counter, then leaned down so he was nose to nose with Rocket. "Keep an eye on her, okay?"

The golden retriever wagged his tail and regarded him with his signature dopey, happy expression. If only people were half as good-natured as dogs, and as easy to please.

Axel isn't thrilled about his assignment, Kole knows, but the fact of the matter is they don't have enough probable cause to write a warrant for Deschane's shop. If the Xombie he and Hazel discovered in the deer head is, in fact, the same stuff Tommy and Cam found in the water a few weeks ago, then that mount left Deschane's possession long before anyone thought of shoving a kilo inside it.

Besides, someone has to look into these DOA reports, and while having blind faith in people would certainly make Kole's life easier, he doesn't 100 percent trust Gretchen not to fuck things up.

The criminal analyst might have some fancy degree, but she doesn't know Black Harbor like the rest of them do. Aside from the fact that she lives thirty miles outside of the city limits, she's never dodged a bullet in its streets, or dove in its dumpsters to dig for a body. She's never dragged anyone off the railroad ties of Forge Bridge, kicking and screaming and biting. She knows Black Harbor as well as someone might think they know jellyfish because they read about them in a textbook.

Now at the VCTF command post, Kole glances at the checklist he's scratched down. They need to get in touch with Aubrey Jeske today. She might be too emotional, but they've got to at least try to have a conversation with her about what she saw and what she hasn't told them about her husband's involvement with the drugs. He was guilty by association, obviously, but could there be more to the story?

Kole crosses the room. It isn't a very large space, or glamorous by any definition, and yet just three years since its inception, his Violent Crime Task Force is responsible for 364 felony arrests, 89 misdemeanor arrests, 11 federal indictments, and 74 seized firearms. The ATF hails it as the best task force in not only Wisconsin, but the greater Chicago area as well, and despite all that, there are days when he wonders if they're not just rearranging the deck chairs on the *Titanic*. While he'd hoped the VCTF's presence and demonstrated ability of not fucking around would put fear in people, encourage them to commit their crimes elsewhere for once, he's afraid that this caliber of criminals enjoys the challenge.

The sun rises across the lake, throwing blades of white across it. Kole's eyes scan the persons-of-interest board where the three scratch-off tickets are tacked up. His gaze skips over them, though, and homes in on the face of Robert Pitts. He's an ugly thing with dark, deep-set eyes and greasy black hair. The complainant from early Sunday morning stated that Pitts had taken her cousin, Darren Hogan, to the Mineshaft Saturday night. If Hogan had truly been Pitts's plus-one, then Pitts was, by default, a member.

As urban legend tells it, there is exactly one way into the club, and one way out: kill or be killed. If Pitts is already a murderer, what would stop him from doing it again?

Unless . . . He studies a grainy photo of Darren Hogan. He's a younger M/B, DOB puts him at twenty-three years old. Could killing Tommy and/or Cam have been Darren Hogan's initiation?

He makes a note of that, and moves on to the next person of interest: Dirty Harriet. Hers is a mug shot from a few years ago, when she got nailed for driving high and possession of drug paraphernalia. She was attempting to sweet-talk her way out of an arrest when the bong she'd been smoking and shoved in her glove compartment transformed her car into a hotbox. In retrospect, it's probably a good thing his detectives weren't able to make contact with her the other day. They don't have a rapport with her.

But he does.

Which is how Kole finds himself on the opposite side of town. He's parked just a block down from where he gets his hair cut, an old Victorian house gutted and renovated into a salon. Lynette's Linzers is on his right. Inside, a handful of patrons enjoy scones and coffee. The building he's interested in, however, isn't as welcoming as either of these establishments. Across the street is a vacant storefront. He can't even tell what it's supposed to be, or what it once was. Maybe a dance studio? A half-naked mannequin leans in the window, strawberry-pink wig askew. Behind her lies a box fan and a broken mirror.

In the story above, a light flicks on.

He takes that as his cue to get out of the car, skirting around a patch of fake hair flattened to the asphalt like roadkill. *Tumbleweave* comes with the territory. It's all fun and games until someone's wig gets yanked off.

The side door to the maybe-dance-studio is locked. The mail slot is one of those old-timey iron ones with the word LETTERS embossed in the plate. Above, in what looks like Wite-Out, someone has painted the word LOVE. He stares at it for a second, the corner of his mouth being tugged into a sad smile, then takes his jackknife out of his back pocket and pops the lock. He's inside in a matter of seconds. A narrow stairwell invites him up, and he does well to avoid the tufts of pink fiberglass bursting out of the drywall in some patches. Just walking past it makes him itch. The rising heat doesn't help. Not that he expected central air, but fuck.

The landing branches into two different halls and what appears to be a shared bathroom. He'd bet his bottom dollar that the units up here are all studio apartments. He knocks on the door to the address Malcolm texted him.

Waiting, he listens to the sounds of communal living muffled by paper-thin walls: slippered feet sloughing on cheap linoleum, snoring, coffeepots gurgling. When the door falls away, Dirty Harriet stands there wearing nothing but a grungy Kermit the Frog T-shirt. Her titian hair is wild, like she just stuck her finger in a light socket, but not as wild as her eyes, which sparkle and swell, as if they are literally drinking him in. She pinches her doughy bicep. "Am I dreaming? Or is this legit? Nikolai Kole, come to my doorstep at the ass crack of dawn."

"Good morning, Harriet." He doesn't bother to mention that 8:15 isn't exactly "the ass crack" of anything.

"Have I been a bad girl?" She slinks against the doorframe, hiking the fringe of her T-shirt up to expose the curve of her butt cheek, confirming his suspicion that she's not wearing anything else. He suppresses a shudder. The truth is, Harriet repulses him. And while he doesn't want to give her false hope, he will never tell her that. She might be a CI, but she has feelings. They're dulled, but . . . they're there.

"I think you know why I'm here."

"Enliven me." She pouts her lips and starts to muss her hair. Not that it needs it.

Assuming she means "enlighten," he presses forward. Lowering his voice, he says: "Malcolm told me Robert Pitts ghosted you after two buys. I just wanna know what you might have seen or heard the last time you saw him. Or what the word on the street is."

Behind him, a door creaks open. Instinctively, Kole's hand goes to his holster. He half turns to see a man with shaggy hair shuffling to the bathroom. "You might want to put some headphones on," he warns, then closes the door.

"Here, come in, won't you?" insists Harriet.

With the symphony of bathroom noises now perforating every regret that has brought him here, Kole reluctantly agrees to enter Dirty Harriet's apartment. "You want coffee?" she asks, pouring herself some.

"No, thanks. What'd you do to your finger?" he asks, noticing a makeshift splint of tape and toilet paper.

"Smashed it in a door." She says it nonchalantly, as if it happens often. The smell of cheap coffee fills the tiny room. Less than six feet away, her mattress is on the floor perpendicular to a TV. A stolen SPEED HUMP road sign is screwed to the wall where the headboard should be. A spider plant hangs in the window. It looks lush and verdant—a stark contrast to everything outside. An ashtray and collection of bongs sit on display in the windowsill, and he thinks about how this little section is a microcosm for the rest of her space, which is essentially Black Harbor's lost and found.

"Did you eat breakfast?" she asks, slapping two pieces of cold pizza on a plate.

"I'm good, Harriet. Thanks."

She smiles, her snaggletooth piercing her bottom lip. "You know, I don't even know why I'm being nice to you. The way you abandoned me and everything."

Kole rolls his eyes. *Here we go.* "I didn't *abandon* you. I got promoted out of the Drug Unit. And Crue wasn't so bad, was he?"

Sulking, she chews her pizza. The cheese is a pale flesh color; a rubbery olive resembles an eyeball, staring at him. He stares back, recalling the time he peeled a dead guy off a radiator in a building similar to this one. His face was melted onto the floor. Who would have thought that, deconstructed, the human face resembles a pizza.

"Milo? He was fine," Harriet admits with a heavy sigh. "And Malcolm's . . ." She shrugs, then waves dismissively as if to say *Let's not talk about them.* "They're not you, Nik. The way you left . . . you didn't even say good-bye."

"I sent you a text."

"Yeah, super lame." She frowns with her mouth full. "I thought we had somethin'."

Kole can't help himself. He laughs. "You were my CI, Harriet. A damn good one, too, if I'm being honest." She perks up at the compliment, but the thing is, Harriet is so good at being a confidential informant, it's disappointing. It's as if she only ever aspired to be a lowlife scoring dime bags and eight balls, and nothing more. Snitching has always been her game, and she plays it well. But now that Pitts has ghosted her, he wonders if she isn't past her prime. That, or something else is going on. And he won't stop digging until he gets to the bottom of it.

"We put a lot of bad guys away, didn't we?" There's a reverence to the way she speaks, a wistfulness for the good ol' days.

"*I* put a lot of bad guys away," he clarifies. "You just bought a lot of dope."

Taking an intermission from her pizza, she sucks on the collar of her T-shirt. He forgot about that habit of hers, but watching her do it, he remembers her sitting in the back seat of his undercover vehicle, chewing on her shirt whenever she was nervous about making a particular controlled purchase. What's got her rattled now, he wonders. The simple fact that he's here or the fact that he's here and she's got something to hide?

"You know I used to get all up in my feelings whenever Sarah told me you were over at her place."

Kole scrunches his eyebrows. "Sarah?"

"Dylan." She supplies the last name and regret slams into him. Sarah Dylan was a CI he never should have flipped. His best friend's daughter, who fell in with a bad crowd after high school. He only took her on because she promised she could get buys on Buddha, the drug dealer Evan had been investigating when he died. He'd been a fucking moron to believe Sarah, to let her play him like she did, because as his informant, she flew under the radar as the Candy Man, selling opiates to kids. How many children died because of his inability to see what was right in front of him?

She's the reason for his cardinal rule: never trust a CI.

"Sarah was paranoid," he explains. "I only went over there for wellness checks, because she was convinced someone was going to kill her."

"Do you blame her now?"

The question is a proverbial frying pan to the face. Sarah Dylan was stabbed to death thirteen times in her apartment.

"Still," says Harriet, deviating from such a tedious topic as murder. "She used to call me just to brag that you'd been there. I always figured the two of you were bangin'. I never said nothin' of course."

"Sarah was a kid." He feels his patience waning. He didn't come here for the third degree.

"So was I when you flipped me."

Another frying pan. *Jesus Christ, it's too early for this shit.* But she isn't lying. Harriet must have been about twenty-one or twenty-two, a little younger than Sarah, even, when he sat down with her on the stoop of a ramshackle house where she'd been caught middling heroin and offered her a deal to work off her charges. He'll never forget the way she looked at him—like he was some sort of savior—and the awful pit he felt in his stomach at knowing he was the opposite. He wasn't offering her a way out; he was offering her a way down, deeper into the underbelly of Black Harbor. And she took it: hook, line, and sinker.

"There was absolutely no romantic relationship between me and Sarah," he states for the record. Truth be told, she'd been like a little sister to him. And he'd let her get murdered. But she'd been playing a dangerous game—selling pills on the side—in a place where the two things people get killed over are drugs and money.

Harriet chews on her collar some more. He doesn't know if she buys his explanation, and he doesn't care. He doesn't owe her anything.

"I know why you're here," she says.

"I told you why I'm here. You were one of the last known people in contact with Robert Pitts, who has become a person of interest in a homicide investigation."

Harriet shakes her head and he'll be damned if a bedbug doesn't fall out of her hair. "No. It's 'cause I've been manifesting you."

When he gives her a blank look, she repeats it, enunciating every syllable. "Man-i-fest-ing." Her shirt's out of her mouth, finally. It's tie-dyed with marinara sauce and God knows what else. "Willing it into existence. Like, if you wish hard enough for something, it'll come true. That's why you're on my vision board."

"Your *what*?"

She grins, giddy like a teenage girl inviting a boy to her bedroom when she grabs his arm and leads him across the room, and he's already imagining scrubbing his skin raw in the shower later. On the wall above the mattress is a heart-shaped monstrosity of magazine cutouts and motivational phrases like BOSS BITCH and YOU GLOW GIRL! There are pictures of palm trees and a Lamborghini that's as bright orange as her hair. A manicured hand with rings sparkling on every finger. A mansion with a swimming pool. Sunrises and sunsets. And him.

Brow furrowed, Kole leans toward it. "How did you get this?" he asks, although he knows. It's clearly a creepshot. He's turned away from the camera, wearing plain clothes. She must have snapped it during one of their buy operations.

"Unimportant." Protectively, she places her hand over it. "The universe is conspiring to make you happy, Nik. But you have to tell it what you want." It's a woo-woo quote she memorized off Instagram or something. She edges closer to him and he knows what's about to happen. He was afraid of this. Call it tenacity or sheer persistence, there's something impressive about how she can always find the courage to bare her soul to him, despite knowing there isn't a chance in hell.

He backs away from the vision board, careful not to trip on the comforter that's spooled onto the floor. "Funny, there aren't any pictures of a legitimate job on that thing. Shouldn't you be manifesting one of those?"

She snorts and goes to twirl one of the tendrils of her spider plant. "Why would I waste my time? The government pays me more to not work. Plus, I got my side hustle with you guys."

"You're not disabled. You shouldn't qualify for a disability check."

"I get headaches."

"You're giving me a headache." He makes a show of checking the time on his phone and starts wandering toward the door.

"I think Malcolm's done with me."

He suppresses a smile. *Finally, here we go.* "Why would you say that?"

"'Cause I can't get no more buys on Robert. That's all he seems to care about, ever since Robert started selling harder stuff."

"What kind of stuff's he been selling?"

"Fetty. Xombie."

He feels the hair on the back of his neck stand up, despite the fact that it's ungodly hot up here. He anticipated this answer. It's just, the confirmation of it is chilling. It makes their dire situation all the more real. "You know who he gets it from?"

She shakes her head. Kole watches for more bedbugs. "When was the last time you saw Robert?" he tries.

"Three weeks ago? Malcolm had me do a controlled purchase."

"What'd you buy? Xombie?"

She nods.

"How'd it go? You think he suspected you of being a snitch or anything?"

That gets her to look at him and stop chewing on her T-shirt again. She's clearly offended. "Please."

"He mention anything to you when you bought off him? About . . . I don't know . . . being under pressure? Maybe having to get rid of someone?"

"You think he murdered that dude at the Mineshaft."

"He was reported as having been there that night with a young guy named Darren Hogan, who, according to his cousin, returned to Chicago. It's just odd that Pitts would disappear for a few weeks, pop up at the scene of a murder, and disappear again. Don't you think?"

Harriet's cheeks redden and her bronze, bloodshot eyes sparkle at being asked a direct question about an ongoing investigation. Suddenly, an ember flickers into existence as she lights the glass bong. She gets comfy on the windowsill, then, and takes a puff. A smoke ring ripples from her dirty little mouth, stretching wider and wider until it dissipates before reaching him. She's peacocking. Which she would only do if she thinks she's got something he wants.

He hopes she does. Taking his phone out again, he scrolls to the kilo of Xombie in his camera roll and shows it to her. "You ever see Robert with something like this?"

She snatches the device with her unoccupied hand, fingers grazing his and lingering. "What's that stamp supposed to be? A rabbit missing a foot?"

"Looks like it."

"That powder's pure as shit, whatever it is. Where'd you find it?"

"Unimportant," he says, mocking her from before.

She smiles with just her top teeth showing and bites down teasingly on the bong. She hands him back his phone and, after another puff, says: "Robert Pitts is dead."

"Why would you say that?"

"What'd you always tell me whenever I got into shit? You play stupid games . . ."

"You win stupid prizes."

She shrugs as if to say *There you go*.

He moves closer to her. He knows he shouldn't. "Why do you think Pitts is dead?"

She doesn't say anything. Instead, she casts her gaze down her arm, out toward the street. The light streaming in through the window makes her hair catch fire. It's moments like this when Kole feels sorry for Harriet. Born to two drug addicts, her entire childhood consisted of getting shuffled from one foster home to another, until she ended up in juvie for stealing from department stores at just fourteen. Hooked on heroin at sixteen and arrested for possession a few years later. Then she met him and he flipped her. She never had a chance.

"Harriet, look at me, please."

Her eyes are wet when she does. Then, her gaze falls just below his waist and he knows it's time to give her what she wants. Taking one more measured step toward her, he reaches into his back pocket, extracts his wallet, and slides out a hundred-dollar bill. He sets it on the windowsill, inches away from her naked knee. She stares down her nose at it, waiting for it to multiply. Cursing silently, he places another hundred on top. The thing with CIs is that, although they can't be trusted, for better and for worse, they're easy to bribe. For a fat stack of cash, they'll sell out their own mother before you even spit out the whole question.

But they'll sell you out, too.

In one fluid movement, Harriet leans slightly forward and slides the money under her pale thigh. Just like that, it's back to being like old times with him paying her for information.

"Why are you telling me that Robert Pitts is dead?" he asks again.

She fingers the bacon-collared neck of her T-shirt, and her makeshift splint comes apart. A streamer of toilet paper unravels, revealing a dark purple bruise on her knuckle, and just before she puts the fabric back into her mouth, she says: "Because Buddha don't play."

25

HAZEL

"Hey, how're ya?" He says it fast, as if it's all one word, then hands me my coffee and a brown paper bag that I assume has my oatmeal and all the mix-ins. I felt awkward—spoiled, even—texting him my Starbucks order, but Kole left specific instructions on the countertop and Axel's phone number. I resisted at first, but then my stomach protested and I remembered it's been more than twelve hours since I put anything in it. And Kole has nothing in his cupboards. I checked. For as nice and homey as the rest of the place is, his pantry looks like that of someone who just moved in.

Axel pauses to take me in, his eyes roaming the black BHPD T-shirt and pajama shorts I put back on after I showered, and I know what he's thinking.

That Kole and I slept together.

It isn't the case, of course. I was out cold, dead to the world until Rocket started licking my face at around 8 A.M. It's the soundest I've slept in weeks, even before coming here, and as I woke, I couldn't help but feel a sense of déjà vu. I know it isn't true; I've never been here before, inside Kole's house, and yet, there's a theory that our memories are stored as holograms, and that a handful of familiar fragments is enough to create a picture. Our imagination just fills in the gaps. It's possible, therefore, that I have encountered a golden retriever like Rocket before, have slept on a couch in a nest of blankets, and experienced these same feelings of confusion whenever I'm with Kole. My mind simply plucked these pieces, put them together, and stitched them into a false memory.

He was gone before I woke up. I never even heard him leave. Just saw the note he left on the kitchen island. *Text Axel what you want from Starbucks, please. Here's his number.*

Normally, I would have slapped on some makeup or at least brushed my hair, but today is not normal circumstances. My things are all a few blocks away, in an apartment that's under secret surveillance. I'll need to return sooner or later, to get clothes, if nothing else, and my laptop. I don't trust Robbie. Everything about him screams *sus*.

"Thank you," I say, and then, because I'm apparently craving human interaction: "How's the DOA assignment going?"

Axel stares at me, deadpan. "It's not even off the ground. I went to talk to Gretchen, the criminal analyst, about it only to find out she's on maternity leave."

I cringe in sympathy. "So now what?"

He shakes his head. "I don't know. It's gonna take me forever and, not to be *that way,* but I think my time is much better spent out here than at a desk, scrolling through decades' worth of dead on arrivals." He rakes a hand through his thinning hair and exhales. "I'm sorry. I shouldn't be venting to you."

"It's okay," I say, perhaps a little too eagerly, and suddenly, I am back to being the old me, the one who so desperately wants to be accepted that she inserts herself into conversations. And investigations. "Is there anything I can do to help?" I ask. "While I'm on house arrest?"

This time, Axel cringes. "Think of it more as witness protection, yeah? I know it's . . . unorthodox. As much as I butt heads with Nik on some things, he's right about you having to stay low. Whoever killed Cam did it because they thought he had intel on Tommy and those drugs. If they find out you're back in town . . ."

"I know." I don't need to hear his conjecture about what they'll do to me. "Maybe I could help with scrolling through decades' worth of dead on arrivals," I offer. "I've got nothing better to do, honestly. And I know the system."

Axel looks as if I've just given him a gift. It's definitely illegal, giving system access to a non–BHPD employee, and yet, his silence tells me he's turning it over in his head. It's been a while since I've logged in to Onyx, but a twenty-minute refresher course on where things are and I'd be off to the races.

"Let me talk to the man in charge," he says.

"Okay," I say pleasantly, and thank him for making the delivery. I meander back toward the air-conditioned house when he stops me.

"Can I ask you something?"

"Of course." *Here it comes,* I think, the beginning of an impromptu interrogation. He's going to demand to know why I'm here, see if he can't draw out on his own what I know about Tommy's death.

"All those animal mounts in the house," he starts. "Did Tommy always have those?"

My body tenses suddenly, slipping into muscle memory as I recall the feeling of being watched by so many glass eyes. Dead creatures that once roamed free, now frozen. Slowly, I nod. My ex-husband was always killing something and nailing it to the wall.

"Did he take them around here to get taxidermied?" asks Axel.

"Some of them."

"Do you remember where?"

"Deschane's," I say as I recall walking into the taxidermy shop on occasion with Tommy whenever he had a new trophy he needed preserved to remind him of his position in the food chain or whatever. "Why?"

Axel pauses and I know he's debating whether or not to tell me, when finally, he says: "You ever get, like, a *feeling* that something is connected and you're not sure how? But you know in your bones that it must be?"

Writing 101. "Yes."

He goes on to tell me, then, about when, not even a year ago, his daughter went missing in the same week two of her classmates were murdered. Dale Deschane, the taxidermist who also worked as an adjunct at the school, rose as a suspect. He admitted to having traps set up all over the city, for taking care of nuisance animals, but that isn't what seems to be troubling Axel. It's the fact that he called the victims bunnies.

"Bunnies?" I repeat.

"Yeah." His voice is thick, and I know it's the trauma that makes it hard to talk. "Because girls are prey." It sounds like a direct quote.

"Damn." I stand six feet away from him, trying to absorb everything he's told me. "The rabbit stamp on the kilo . . . you think there's a correlation?"

"I do. I just . . . don't know how to prove it."

"At the moment," I say, a feeble attempt to give him a shred of hope.

He gives me a fragile smile in return, and tells me to text him if I need anything. Rocket is outside in the backyard, waiting to be let in, his breath fogging the glass of the patio door. I slide it open and he crashes inside. I see, now, why there's no dining room table or chairs. Rocket would take them out several times a day.

I plop down in my nest on the couch with my breakfast and turn on the TV, channel-surfing until I find the local news. Cam's murder is the top story. His picture appears on the screen next to Tommy's—the same one from our wedding with my phantom arm on his shoulder—and it takes everything in me not to look away.

A reporter in a white blouse stands in front of the camera. "The mayor will hold a press conference with the chief of police later this morning, at which time they are expected to share updates on the investigation. In the meantime, the mayor would like to urge people to use extreme caution and remind everyone that possessing fireworks such as firecrackers, Roman candles, bottle rockets, and mortars is illegal . . ."

The footage flashes to a B-roll of past parades and fireworks on the beach. By tomorrow, if not tonight, already, Black Harbor will be a war zone. I snort into my oatmeal. Like that warning will do any good. If anything, it's bound to have the opposite effect. Telling people not to do something only makes them want to do it more.

Like Kole telling me not to leave this house. My toes knead the rug just thinking about it. I need to get out of here, or do something. Watching the news isn't going to get me any closer to figuring out who killed Tommy.

Or Cam.

Or who's probably going to try to kill me, for that matter.

I wander out to the kitchen and set what's left of my breakfast on the island. The stairs to the upper level are a steep ascent, all those steps disappearing into shadow, a euphemism for Kole himself. The embodiment of a mystery, a man who, despite the intense connection we shared years ago, I really don't know that well. This could be my one opportunity.

Before I can talk myself out of it, I'm going up. Kole's an idiot if he thinks he can keep me here all day and I'm not going to explore.

There is no door at the top, just a large open space. The windows are covered with blackout curtains. The walls are painted what appears to be a very dark grey, and the ceiling is stained a cinnamon color that brings out all the knots and striations in the wood. A king-sized bed faces east, its rustic headboard butted up against the sloped wall and flanked by what appear to be decorative streetlamps. A matching TV stand is against the opposite wall, its cubbies holding several different pairs of shoes ranging from sneakers to boots.

The bed isn't made, a detail that surprises me. In all other areas of his life, Kole seems to be a classic neat freak, keeping his house serial-killer clean. It endears me to him, this element of imperfection.

My eyes roam the room for traces of a woman. There are no framed photos, no tubes of lip gloss or pieces of jewelry on any of the surfaces. I wander into the adjoining bathroom where I prepare myself to see an extra toothbrush on the vanity or a skimpy robe hanging on the door. My jaw drops, however, at the sight of the gorgeous shower partition made entirely of glass blocks. They look like ice, sparkling with drops of water from earlier this morning when Kole no doubt showered before work.

Thinking about him naked and wet, I feel a wave of heat flush through my entire body. I press my palms on the marble countertop for something cold and focus on the aesthetics of it—black and smokey grey with veins of gold. It does the trick. My head clears. Reluctantly, I leave the oasis of the bathroom and go to the walk-in closet. My breath hitches in anticipation of what I will find. Dresses? Lingerie? Cute ankle boots? I exhale, however, when it appears to hold only his clothes—hoodies, jeans, T-shirts, and a small selection of button-downs. Exactly one tie hangs on a hook next to his belts.

A men's jewelry case sits on a shelf. I pull it out and observe that there's only a wristwatch inside, and a letter. It's typed, I notice, some of the ink blurred. That odd sensation of familiarity returns, except this time, I know it's more than holograms stitched together in a single mosaic as I read the following text:

I don't know which is more dangerous—him or the bridge. He is at once my salvation and my damnation. At least the bridge offers a way out. Immediate. Dead on impact. With him, the fall would be slow and although sublime, still end in oblivion. I cannot stay here and yet, he makes oblivion look good.

The words are so familiar, I can taste them.

Because I wrote them.

It isn't a letter, but a passage, torn from my old manuscript, the one I'd thrown into the water, a final sacrifice to join the myriad pieces of myself I'd already given to the river.

Final or penultimate?

Would I have jumped, had Kole not intervened? It's a question that rears its ugly head from time to time, ever since he threw me over his shoulder and carried me back to the quiet sanctuary of his car. As much as I would like to say no, I wouldn't have jumped, the truth is that I don't know.

I was a different person then.

Broken, as I've already admitted to myself.

And maybe I still am.

I don't remember writing this passage, but I must have. There are other fragments of the book surrounding it, ones that made it into print about the Candy Man and Forge River—names that have since been changed.

I read the passage again. And again. Tears blur my vision and threaten to spill onto the paper, creating fresh watermarks.

The first sentence cuts into me.

I don't know which is more dangerous—him or the bridge.

It was about Kole, obviously, but why had I written that? Because at one point I had suspected him of having a hand in his CI's death. Even so, on the other side of that coin, I loved him.

Discovering this piece of my own unpublished manuscript feels more intimate than finding a sensual photo. I feel icky, like I'm trespassing in my own memory, and I might just run into Kole there. My heart rate quickens when I consider how he lured me to Beck's last night.

I need you.

Three words that are my kryptonite. Had he not sent them, I might not have met him, and I wouldn't be under his thumb now. He's always been good at getting what he wants—me, in particular. Him keeping this passage all this time is evidence enough that he still wants me. And now he has me.

I stand still, suddenly paranoid that I will turn around to find him watching me, just like I did at the duplex. A dangerous thought screws its way into my psyche. Kole and I have both done untoward things to be together before. Would he kill to bring me back?

26
KOLE

"We haven't had a serial killer before." He traces the statement back to Riley.

"Or we have, and we just didn't realize it," says Axel.

Kole screws up his face as the fan makes a rotation. It peels away before it can wick the sweat from his neck. While the thought of a serial killer is chilling, it does nothing to cool him down. Riley could be onto something. He'd be lying if he said it hadn't crossed his mind between last night and now, when he considered three identical scratch-off tickets that corresponded to three dead bodies. His mouth is dry, his jaw hangs slack when he asks: "Why do you think that?"

"Three's a pattern," she says without hesitation, and he knows she's been mulling this over.

"Is it, though?" challenges Axel.

Riley shoots him a sidelong glance. Kole sees what's going on. Normally, Axel and Riley are in perfect lockstep. Today, however, someone woke up on the argumentative side of the bed. He knows why, of course: the whole DOA assignment.

Riley's eyes are narrowed to paper-thin slits when she says, "Are you gonna just keep questioning shit? Or is there something you'd like to share with the rest of the group?"

Kole snorts. The "group" is the three of them. Fletcher is heavy in the swing of things, knocking on the doors of every pawnshop within a fifty-mile radius. No word yet. But that doesn't mean they're not close. All they need is one of those guns from Tommy's logbook to turn up, and they can start checking receipts, surveillance video, the whole works.

"You make contact with Aubrey Jeske yet?" Kole cuts in, more to get them to stop bickering than anything else.

Riley puts up her hands. "I was checking into James Cooper, like you asked."

"And I was delivering coffee to your girlfriend."

Kole narrows his eyes. Axel is vying for a verbal beating. It just goes to prove his theory that when one force leaves, another will take its place. Fletcher's normally the spiky one. But in his absence, Axel has sprouted thorns.

Riley imitates a cat hissing and sips her iced tea.

"First of all—"

"She's not his girlfriend," supplies Riley.

"And second of all—"

"How long does it take you to drop off coffee?" Riley again.

"Thank you," says Kole. He gestures emptily, giving Axel the floor.

Axel exhales. The simple act of taking a deep breath makes him less rigid. More himself. "Look, I'm not trying to sound like an egomaniac, but—"

"But you're gonna say something egomaniacal—" Riley cuts in.

Kole holds up his hand. "Fight nice, children." Jesus Christ, he feels like a dad driving a minivan with his kids bickering in the back seat. *Don't make me turn this car around . . .*

Axel glares at her, then picks up where he left off. "I think we all know my time is better spent on the street, not at a desk."

Kole sighs, already exasperated. He knows Axel just wants to lurk around Deschane's place, see what kind of probable cause he can scare up to pad his warrant. "So, facilitate with Gretchen . . ."

"She's on maternity leave," says Axel.

"The nerve," jokes Riley.

Kole closes his eyes. Son of a *bitch*. Just what he didn't need. The one time Gretchen could actually prove useful, she's on extended leave.

It doesn't pay to ask when she'll be back; he needs someone now. He starts counting to ten, but only makes it to two when Axel interrupts.

"Hazel offered to sort through them . . ." His voice trails off as Kole fixes him with a look.

"She's not an employee," Riley states matter-of-factly.

"She knows the system. And she knows what to look for."

Kole pinches the bridge of his nose. For the first time today, Axel makes a compelling argument. The countdown is on. They think they're stretched thin now, but tomorrow is the Fourth of July. Most of their patrol resources will be aggregated to work the parade and direct traffic and to tackle the impossible task of keeping people from killing one another.

Someone always dies on the Fourth of July.

It might be Hazel if she doesn't listen to him and stay under the radar. This assignment might just be the perfect job for her.

Axel's arms are crossed over his chest. He leans against his desk. "I'm just saying. Three is hardly a pattern. Especially with, what, nine years between the first ticket, then two within a couple days of each other?"

Kole remains silent. He's got so much chaos going on at the moment—internally and externally—that if Riley wants to fight this battle for him, he'll let her. While three murders might not necessarily be a pattern, it is the minimum number of victims needed to define a serial killer. Said victims will have something in common such as demographic profile, appearance, gender, or race.

Three white males: Evan Kole, Tommy Greenlee, Cameron Jeske. Then there's James Allen Cooper, who, according to Hazel, left a scratch-off in his Forge Fuels pullover when he plunged from the bridge. He was a little older, but still, a white male.

"Four," he corrects, finally. "Cooper makes four."

Riley tosses up her hands as if to say *There you go*. "So far," she adds. "Who knows how many dead bodies were marked with the same ticket, and the BHPD has been glossing over them?"

"What'd you dig up on Cooper?" Kole asks. "Anything?"

Riley shifts and widens her stance. "Parents are both deceased," she confirms. "Divorced. No kids. He's got a sister in Lake Geneva. I spoke to her over the phone this morning. She claims she hadn't spoken to him for years before he died. Same with his ex-wife, who shared, quote: 'Pills and pilsners was all he gave a flying fuck about,' end quote. So that's where we're at."

"Pills and pilsners," Kole mutters under his breath. It sounds like the other dead guys. "She say what kind of pills?" He braces himself for the answer he knows is on the tip of Riley's tongue.

"Opiates: Oxys, Vicodin. That kind of stuff."

Same as his brother. And Xombie, the shit that Tommy and Cam were both killed over, is a mixture of real and synthetic opioids, just ten thousand times worse. The probability that Pitts is dead, too, suddenly feels imminent. Even if he is floating face down in the river or lying in a shallow grave somewhere, it doesn't mean he didn't kill Tommy.

His race in Onyx denotes him as Pacific Islander. If Dirty Harriet is right, and Pitts is dead somewhere with a scratch-off ticket shoved in his mouth or his pocket or an orifice Kole doesn't want to think about, then he's the first one who doesn't fit the bill.

But he was playing stupid games. Maybe that's what all these guys have in common.

"What about Robert Pitts?" says Riley, reading his mind.

Now is as good a time as any to brief them on his conversation with Dirty Harriet. He tells them what she shared with him, starting with her being convinced Pitts is dead, and secondly, confirming the imprint of the rabbit missing its foot is Buddha's signature.

"Buddha?" Axel's eyebrows crawl toward his receding hairline. "That's a name that pops up now and again."

Kole would agree. He's been tracking Buddha off and on for the better part of a decade, keeping tabs on his whereabouts, never able to identify him, which tells him one thing: the guy knows Black Harbor as well as, if not better than, the rest of them.

"Dirty Harriet thinks Buddha killed Pitts?" Riley asks. "I thought they were on the same level."

"Not anymore, apparently." Kole goes to the whiteboard and flips it over. He's had time to think about this, on his way back from Harriet's. On the blank side, he draws what looks like a rough sketch of a family tree. At the top, he writes *Hades*. Then he draws three lines, at the ends of which he writes, respectively: *Buddha, Pitts, Hogan*. He pauses to let them take it in, and when he sees them nodding in his peripheral vision, he crosses out *Hades,* then circles *Buddha* and makes an arrow to the top.

All is quiet in the lighthouse. If Malcolm were here, he would make some shitty comment about how they traded in one bad apple for an even more rotten one. Thankfully he isn't, and it's not as if things were exactly peachy keen while Hades was on the throne. This is Black Harbor. Things only trend one way.

Down.

Unless you're talking about violent crime, then that's definitely up.

"Dirty Harriet mention having any idea where Buddha hides out these days?" asks Riley.

He hears her, but he doesn't respond. His mind has wandered, back to when he stood in the doorway to Harriet's apartment, ready to leave. She sauntered over to him. A thin stream of smoke bled from her lips as she let it out slowly. "I know the only reason you don't want Pitts to be dead is so you can kill him yourself. I would, too, if he killed someone I care about."

He half turned. "Pitts? I don't want to kill him," he lied. "I want to talk to him. Honestly, I could give two flying fucks about Tommy Greenlee, but—"

"Not him. Your brother."

Those two words might as well have been Taser prongs. Kole stopped. His muscles seized. "Evan? What about Evan?"

Harriet took his blank expression as an invitation to move in. He fought not to recoil as he imagined the insects jumping from her body to his. Her lips indulgently grazed his neck when, on a ribbon of smoke, she whispered: "He never jumped off that bridge."

He forgot how to breathe for a few seconds. He just stood there while his soul came unglued from his body and began to float toward the ceiling. Harriet's voice was the only thing that kept him grounded.

She waited a beat, no doubt reveling in being this close to him, in taking more than money from him, and always having something he wanted. "You know, it's kinda sad," she said, tracing a fine line down the center of his chest. "You and your guys, you think you're so much better than everyone. But you're not. You're users, just like the rest of us. You just use people instead of drugs."

Kole bit back a retort. She wasn't wrong. Not entirely. "Harriet, how do you know Robert Pitts killed Evan?"

She smiled, clearly satisfied with her ability to rattle him. "Robert was his CI," she said. "Just like I'll be forever yours."

Hours later, he has not told anyone this new shred of information. After all, a key part of his job is knowing how to play the hand he's dealt, and not showing all his cards at once. But he's going to have to sooner rather than later, because the truth is, he has more than one layer of motivation for finding Pitts and he can't take all this on alone. Not only was Pitts allegedly at the Mineshaft the night Tommy Greenlee was murdered, he was one of the last people to see Evan alive, too.

"Nik." Riley waves a hand in front of his face. "Where'd you go on us?"

He shakes his head. It's all coming back to him. The lighthouse. The whiteboard. The two names, one crossed out and one risen above. Hades and Buddha.

Two parasites who promoted themselves to gods.

He knows, now, that they are not hunting for a serial killer. These crimes, with the matching scratch-off tickets, are more ritualistic in nature. A payment, of sorts, or perhaps a receipt for services rendered.

An offering.

The question is, which false god does their suspect worship?

Find the god, find the killer.

He will reverse engineer this all the way back to Forge Bridge if he has to. But first, he's never been afraid of going right to the source.

27
HAZEL

If all you had to do was one bad thing, and you could leave Black Harbor behind forever, would you do it?

As it did whenever I thought about it, the question sent a shiver down my spine. This time it felt different, though. Whatever substance was in the invisible syringe that cooled my blood was more potent than usual. I felt paralyzed from the neck down, as I sat there on the edge of Kole's unmade bed, ruminating on the words that had unearthed the roots of Black Harbor planted deep in my memory even before I found my old house key, before news of Tommy's murder took over every screen.

I'd assumed it was Tommy who sent the message.

The thought that it might have been someone else had never crossed my mind, until now. But police often use dummy profiles to keep tabs on people of interest. Dope dealers, sex offenders, gangbangers, homicide suspects, and straight-up thugs who do something criminal and boast about it on social media. So, it could have been Kole who sent the message. But why? He doesn't want to leave this place. I learned during my last stint here that his and Black Harbor's atoms are so inextricably entwined, there is no separating them. Like conjoined twins that share a heart, to extricate one would be to destroy both.

Still, could killing Tommy have been the "something bad" he'd been referring to?

I migrated downstairs, recalling the YES I'd sent in response to that cryptic question. Maybe that was all the permission he'd needed to pull the trigger.

A new icy sensation filled my veins as I realized what that meant: We're in this together.

If Kole thought that killing Tommy would lure me back, it worked. I'm here, aren't I? In his house. On his couch. Petting his dog.

"Son of a bitch." The curse was sharp on my lips as I recalled just last night, when I'd spilled my soul to him about the guilt I felt over Tommy's death, that my three little letters of encouragement had been enough to make him take the leap. He'd claimed to know I'd been in contact with Tommy. He'd been so confident, as always, that I hadn't contested him. But now I know he was bluffing, and I fell for it.

He only knew I'd been in contact with Tommy because he'd been pretending to be Tommy, under the guise of a cryptic profile. Cam's was probably a dummy account, too, created just so it could follow @deadmann_walking and further my conjecture that it was Tommy who sent the message.

Rocket's eyebrows rippled as he looked my way. I paced the living room like a prisoner in a cell, or a caged animal, although I suppose they're one and the same. I wished right then that I could unzip myself, leave my flesh and bones behind like a pile of discarded clothes and walk invisible into the scorching daylight.

While I couldn't quite do all of that, I could walk into the scorching daylight. Out of Kole's house. Away from his hold on me.

"Good-bye, Rocket," I whispered apologetically. It wasn't his fault his owner was a psychopath.

The door clicking into the frame sounded like a pair of handcuffs unlocking. My first steps down the sidewalk felt like freedom. Back to the apartment was the obvious place to go. I needed my clothes. My computer. A home base. Robbie was there, but so what? The apartment was safe enough—certainly safer than here—and yet, I felt myself being tugged in the opposite direction, first—one that was away from the lake and farther inward, in the nucleus of the city.

I'm here now. My stomach churns as I complete the descent down

Forge Avenue. A cloud of flies swarms over a diaper that's swollen and fit to burst. I hurry past it, eying it like it's a bomb. A mattress and box spring are discarded at the entrance to the vacant lot. They've clearly been here a while, considering the gaping hole chewed through the center and prairie grass shooting through it.

Everything is still. The air is heavy and electric and so humid that jogging feels more like swimming. I make my way across the cracked asphalt where at the edge lies Forge Bridge, that coal-blackened creature that has claimed countless lives—mine almost among them. It's been biding its time. It grows larger as I approach, filling my frame of vision. I suck in a breath. I have dreamed of this moment, I realize, as I clutch the paper to my chest, my first sacrifice in nearly a decade. There is no way out, no turning back, as I march toward the stretched-wide mouth of Forge Bridge that's been patiently waiting to devour me.

28
KOLE

Involving CIs is at once a dangerous game and a necessary evil. By definition, they're turncoats, which, again by definition, means they can't be trusted. If they'll snitch for the police, for the right price, they'll snitch for anybody. But, if Dirty Harriet is to be believed, Kole's brother was murdered—pushed off the bridge by Buddha or someone in his employ.

Robert Pitts.

Kole turned it over a dozen different ways on his way over here, and the scenario that makes the most sense is that Robert Pitts played a double agent; he acted as an informant for Evan, and then betrayed him. So, if Pitts is still alive, Kole will turn over every crack rock, pipe, and plastic bag in Black Harbor until he finds the rat bastard to wring his neck. Then there's the matter of Tommy's murder. Robert Pitts was at the Mineshaft that night, which means he might be responsible for that one, too.

In the meantime, hopefully Riley and Axel can dredge up some information from Aubrey Jeske. Anything would be helpful at this point. Did she hear a noise the other night when she came home? Was something out of place? Sometimes the smallest detail brings the biggest break in the case.

He parks in the visitor lot. Hazel's bracelet swings softly from the rearview mirror, as it has for years, ever since he pulled it out of the river. Her name is spelled out in beads, prompting him to think of her and wonder what she's up to now. His eyes move to the clock on the dash. It's 11:18. She's probably busy scoping out his place. That's what he'd be doing if he were her. *Curiosity and all that,* he thinks, quoting her from the night before.

For a fleeting second, he considers texting her, and thinks better of it. *Words matter.* She taught him that. And yet, her silence during the past eight years has spoken volumes.

She made it egregiously clear that she isn't here for him. She's here to find out who killed her ex-husband and to collect fodder for her next book. Then she'll leave again and maybe come back in another eight to ten years, when the creative well runs dry again. And he will be here. Still. Always.

The latter seems more plausible with the plan he's about to set into motion. The district attorney wasn't a raving fan when he called her on the way over here to propose his idea, but, like him, she knows how very *between a rock and a hard place* they are.

"The only way this gets worse," he told her, after speaking his piece, "is if we do nothing."

He could hear in her sigh that she knew he was right. All he'd had to do was mention the name Buddha and she was on board. The drug lord who's moved in on Hades's territory has been a topic of various conversations. It's no secret that the only way they stand a chance at saving Black Harbor from sinking any lower is to eradicate him. After a beat of silence, she asked a question that might as well have been a green light: "What happens if this operation goes off the rails?"

"It won't." It sickened him how easily the lie rolled off his tongue. Perhaps it's not so much a lie as it is a formality, a statement of intent made in good, albeit very little faith. They both knew there is only one way this ends—with a body count.

If Hazel isn't one of those bodies, regardless of the outcome of this operation, he will consider it at least a partial success.

"Kill him with fire, Nik." The DA ended the call then.

He sits for a moment in his vehicle, staring at the sprawling concrete facade of Sulfur County Prison, the walls topped with coils of barbed wire, and watching passersby—criminal defense lawyers with their battered briefcases, clerks in pencil skirts chatting with intake officers during a lunch break, a homeless person pushing a grocery cart filled with their belongings—mill about the area. They're at the edge of Black Harbor here, with the city to the east and open fields to the west. What he wouldn't give to move out here, away from the "small city with big city crime" as it's been hailed in the headlines. To have ten acres of his own and to live blissfully unaware of the Armageddon that stalks the horizon.

But he knows what he signed up for, the oath he took twenty-three years ago when the department issued him his badge and gun. His gaze moves to the looming fortress with its towers and teeth, guards with rifles pointed into the yard. If there's a better option than what he's about to do, it has from now until he walks inside to present itself. Otherwise, he has an appointment.

"Well, well, well, look who's still out there, bustin' balls." The man in the grey jumpsuit isn't shackled, per Kole's request. He wants him to associate their meeting today with a taste of freedom, even one as basic as not having to wear chains when alone in a room with somebody. They sit across from each other at a stainless-steel table.

"Hades."

Tobias Shannon stares at him with as much warmth as can be expected from any cold-blooded creature. His tongue flicks between his lips. He's trying to taste fear.

He will return to his cell hungry.

All things considered, however, the disgraced drug lord looks pretty comfortable in prison. He's clearly channeled all of his energy into sculpting his physique. He doesn't have the frame to be a meathead, but he's more sinewy than the last time Kole saw him when he arrested him on drug-trafficking charges. It's been four years.

Seven more to go. But who's counting?

He is, actually. When you come to cut a deal, you have to know your numbers.

The conversation he had with Malcolm on Sunday still chaps his ass. While bagging Hades was a win at the time, in the grander scheme of things, it was bound to have its fallout. He knew it and yet, what was he supposed to do? What message would it have sent if he'd let him go?

For years, Hades was a ghost, as threatening and mercurial as the coal spores in the air. He skated under the radar just enough, getting people dumber and more depraved than him to do his dirty work while he holed up in some obscure hideout, location still unknown. And then four years ago, he wandered out of his den and rolled on his back. When a predator like that is suddenly vulnerable, you're not going to not take your shot.

He knows that Malcolm is right . . . to a degree. Things are worse. Still, he isn't sure Hades's absence is a direct correlation. Who's to say the Xombie doesn't belong to him? Or the scratch-off tickets? People have orchestrated far more elegant crimes from a prison cell.

The rabbit stamp. That's why he's here. If Hades can confirm that the rabbit stamp is Buddha's signature, then Kole will be on his way to solving this investigation. If he's willing to tell who Buddha is and where he hides out, even better.

Either of those things will cost him more than money.

Hades rests his hands on the cold silver surface, long, tattooed fingers intertwined, a businessman waiting to hear a proposal. He didn't rule the underworld for as long as he did by being a total fucking moron; he knows that there's only one reason cops have conversations with criminals. "How's my little brother?"

"He doesn't visit?"

A light dances behind Hades's eyes. "Nah. He puts money on my books every once in a while. Birthdays. Christmas. 'Bout it."

"So, more than you do for him, you're sayin'."

Hades's face splits into a grin. There's just one gold canine now. The grill is gone. He must have pawned it or had the sense to take it out before they locked him up. "He still with that creepy-crawlie, what's-her-name . . ." He snaps his fingers, attempting to conjure it from thin air.

Kole knows who he's talking about, but he won't say her name. As far as he's concerned, she shed her skin and got out of Black Harbor—for good—and while he isn't superstitious, he doesn't want to risk summoning her back here by saying it. It wouldn't be fair to her. "You'll have to give Hudson a call, Hades. Sounds like you two have some catching up to do." But not now, he thinks. Hudson is working the leads desk. Just shy of two hundred tips came in overnight. Most of them are bullshit, but they have to look into every single one, whether it's a local claiming to have seen Tommy Greenlee at the grocery store at 10 A.M. the previous Sunday or a clairvoyant in Arizona claiming to have a vision that sounded ripped from the headlines. Crazies love clogging up the tip lines during high-profile investigations.

"You're a tight-lipped motherfucker, Kole. That's the one thing I like about you."

"You flatter me."

"So, what carrot did you bring to dangle in front of me? An appeal? A credit for time already served?" He pauses and flashes that wicked grin again. "Early release for good behavior?"

Good behavior. That's a knee-slapper. "I don't know if the inmate you beat half to death with a lunch tray would cosign that last one."

Hades has the gall to look taken aback. "We were just kidding around. It was funny. He was in stitches."

"I saw. Sixteen in his bottom lip, another twelve in the roof of his mouth."

Hades shrugs. With that smug look on his face, he might as well be dusting off his shoulders. "I hear it's gotten pretty rough out there." He cuts his chin to the wall to indicate outside. It looks as if it pains him to keep a straight face.

Schadenfreude to the highest degree.

"You'd probably know better than me," says Kole, not taking the bait, because he isn't a total fucking moron, either. He's not going to ask Hades what he heard or who he heard it from. Not until they have a deal.

It doesn't surprise him that Hades knows the state of things. He has access to TV and the internet. He makes the occasional phone call, too. Kole listens to the recordings sometimes while he's driving. He's willing to bet he knows most of Hades's sources, including one named Robbie, who is the reason he knew Hazel was back in town. According to Robbie, she's staying at an apartment building over by the lake. He knows the one.

It was Monday morning when he heard about her arrival. He'd been tracking Hades's phone activity since his conversation with Malcolm, to see if the incarcerated drug lord had anything to say about what went down at the Mineshaft. He remembers the way Robbie described his new temporary resident that not only made his breath hitch, it made him rewind the recording to discern whether or not he heard it right.

Robbie: "Some dime-piece just checked in. Name's Hazel Rydelle."

Hades: "Hmm. Where's she coming in from?"

Robbie: "License states New York. Brooklyn."

Hades: "Any idea why she's here?"

Robbie: "Not yet."

Hades: "Find out. Black Harbor ain't no vacation destination. This bitch is here for business."

Now, Kole's gaze fixes on Hades's throat, on the spot where his heartbeat causes the geometric snowflake tattoo to pulse. Like any reptile in captivity, masking weakness is a survival strategy. Hades's composure, therefore, is a defense mechanism.

Kole tosses a glance over his shoulder at the guard outside the door, nods, and withdraws the kilo he's kept in a paper bag under the table. He sets the white brick between them. Hades stares at it like it's prey.

"So you got a kilo of fentanyl. Who doesn't?"

"Try again."

Hades's eyes squeeze as he regards Kole with suspicion. Then, because he can't help himself, he reaches for the package, studies it corner to corner, then pauses, holding on the rabbit imprint.

Kole sits quietly, watching. He's flipped a lot of people in his day—drug dealers, users, middlers. But Hades isn't a dealer. He's the drug lord of Black Harbor's underworld.

Was.

He's a *has-been*, now.

A new one has risen from the gutter and taken his place.

The name is silent, but he can see it form on Hades's lips. *Buddha.* He spins the brick slowly. "Xombie. One of the main ingredients is carfentanil. Shit's got a half-life of 7.7 hours, almost twice that of Naltrexone," he says, mentioning the opioid antagonist.

"Thanks for the chemistry lesson I didn't ask for."

"What are you asking for?"

"Your help."

Hades scoffs. "No, for real."

Kole clenches his jaw. He folds his hands on the table and leans forward. "At least two men are dead within three days of each other. They found three of these"—he taps the table next to the kilo—"in the water, about half a mile from the shore."

"So where are the other two?" asks Hades.

"That's a good question," admits Kole. "You recognize the stamp?"

Still staring at the brick, Hades says, "I ain't no snitch. Especially not for you."

"There are worse things to be."

"Not in my book."

Kole gets up. He reaches into his wallet for the secret he's kept in his back pocket. He tosses the faded scratch-off ticket on the table.

Hades squints at it, his eyes devouring the red letters at the top: KA$H KA-CHING! "What's that, some kind of calling card?"

"I was hoping you could tell me."

"I don't know nothin' about that, brother."

"You're not my brother."

"Oh right, yours took a spill off the bridge."

Kole lunges, but stops just short of grabbing a fistful of Hades's shirt. The chair clatters to the floor. Behind him, the guard knocks a warning on the door.

Hades's eyes flick from the chair to Kole. "You gonna pick that up?"

No, he isn't. He's done meeting eye-to-eye with this motherfucker. Kole leans forward and plants his hands on the table. "Listen, I'm not gonna feed your ego and tell you that things were better when you were doing your thing in the underworld, but you've got two things going for you. The first of which is that you're a cockroach. As vile as that is, you know your role. And you do it so well."

"Which is what?" asks Hades, unable to resist a compliment.

"You eat shit and you can navigate in dark places." Kole slides the ticket back into his wallet.

"Come on now, you're making me blush."

"I know this kilo belongs to Buddha. I just need you to tell me who the fuck this guy is and where I can find him."

"I think you know where to find him," says Hades. "You just can't get in there. Which is the real reason you're here. Too bad you're a cop. Otherwise, you'd have clearance to become a member. All those dead kids . . . you got more than enough blood on your hands to qualify for a membership. Tell me something. How many lives you think you could have saved had you not been so blind to the fact that your Candy Man was a woman? Does that keep you up at night?"

Kole breathes in through his nose and lets it out slowly. Hades is trying to knock him off his game. He knows that's all it is. Still, he can't help but think of the purple pills that are infiltrating the schools. It's only a matter of time until the death phone rings for a fatal overdose on the playground.

If there are any silver linings to having Hades in power versus Buddha, it's that he never, to Kole's knowledge, sells directly to kids. That isn't to say his drugs haven't occasionally found their way into their hands, but for the most part, the reports of minors overdosing on Schedule II narcotics were less than what they are today. As far as a moral code goes, it's as honorable a one as Kole's been able to find on the streets.

"What you're about to dip your toe in extends far beyond Black Harbor," Hades cautions. "I don't know if you're ready for it."

"Try me," Kole challenges.

Hades leans back. He rolls his neck from shoulder to shoulder, working out the kinks. "Buddha ain't shit, but he's got one thing goin' for him, and that's the fact that he's only got one client."

"How is that an advantage?" asks Kole. "One client hardly seems like enough to keep the lights on."

"It is when that one client is the Mineshaft." Hades pauses for a beat to let that sink in. "To have that contract with the Mineshaft is to hold all of Black Harbor in the palm of your hand. You don't have to peddle your ass all over the city to try and earn your keep. One drop is all it takes. But it comes at a price."

"Give me a number," says Kole.

"A hundred grand a month. That's the cost of doing business. In order to get that contract, Buddha must've had something Big House wanted."

"Xombie." He eyes Hades suspiciously, trying to suss out whether or not he's lying. "And you know about this contract how?"

Hades's eyes smolder. "Because it used to be mine."

Telling him about the contract is a tactic, Kole knows. Hades is giving him a taste of all the information he holds inside, but he won't say another word about it until a deal comes along. Well, here it is. Reaching into his back pocket, he extracts a folded newspaper article that shows a grainy black-and-white photo of the Mineshaft, inside of which is a notecard with a single word written in Kole's handwriting.

This is where people often forget that negotiating is more than being sure-footed on the grounds of an argument. It's being patient, too. Like going to a car dealership, you have to be prepared to walk away. "This offer has a half-life of three hours," Kole informs. He and Hades never take their eyes off each other, not even as Kole backs away and raises his hand to knock—

"Wait."

The word is a pin drop, but loud enough to stop Kole dead in his tracks.

"You said I had two things going for me, but you only named one." A tic pulses faintly beneath the drug dealer's right eye, and Kole knows he'd be hard-pressed to find someone more motivated than Hades to take down Buddha.

Besides himself.

He and Hades are a two-man saw. How fitting that a tool like that is colloquially known as a misery whip. He sighs. He knows better than to trust Hades, and yet, if there's one thing he can trust about him, it's this. "You'll always kill your way to the top," he says, and raps his knuckles against the door to be let out.

Before he can leave Hades to think over his offer, the fallen drug lord says something that makes Kole's internal temperature drop: "Say hi to your girl for me."

29
HAZEL

I'm in the belly of the beast now. The railroad ties are pliant and pockmarked, spongy like a tongue, and covered in light-colored splotches that must be fungus—because this is Black Harbor; not even Forge Bridge is immune to being eaten. The steel beams above form a rib cage. The railing is hot to the touch. I rip my hand away and imagine the rail glowing red as a branding iron.

The air is a warm, weighted blanket. There's no protection from the sun here. It pummels the back of my neck, my nose, the tops of my shoulders. I stand in the middle of the bridge, completely exposed, as I have done countless times before. It feels simultaneously the same and so different. Somehow the bridge seems more perilous than ever. Riddled with rot, the notion of collapsing is now a new and viable threat. The evergreens on the banks are still sharp spires scraping the sky. And like always, I hear the river calling to me, demanding a piece of me.

My gaze drags to the paper that's damp with sweat. I loosen my grip and read the first line again: *I don't know which is more dangerous—him or the bridge.*

I've decoded what it means, now. What I must've been feeling when I wrote it, which is that there are only two forces that can keep a person in a place like this: death and love. Forge Bridge represents death. Not just the death of all who have leapt from its rails, but the death of an economy, the death of a city. It is all that remains of Forge Fuels and soon enough, it will fall into the water like all the jumpers before it. On the other hand, as much as I might have wanted Nikolai Kole to be love, he is death, too. To stay with him would have been to stay in Black Harbor, where I would experience a little death every day until nothing remained. Just like all those sacrifices I gave to the water. Little by little, piece by piece, I began to disappear.

That's why I had to leave.

Except I didn't, did I? Because while physically, I've been elsewhere, contemplating at my writing desk or bopping around bookshops, mentally, I've been here. Tommy was right about one thing. I never left Black Harbor.

I brought it with me.

I think of the key I tossed into the East River. And now the paper in my hand. How will I do it this time? Should I crumple it into a ball and throw it across the water, or let it float languidly like a leaf?

The river is more insistent now. Its myriad voices form a chorus, and although I don't know exactly what they're saying, I know what they want me to do. To join them. Piece by piece. I tear off a corner of the paper and watch it free-fall. Then another, like plucking petals off a daisy.

He killed him.

He killed him not.

He killed him . . .

I lean over the edge and look to see the flecks of white floating on the water, and pause. My hands shake and my breath catches.

The river is bone-dry. What lies beneath the bridge is a hollow valley, a narrow landfill of rusted bicycles and grocery carts. Flattened beer cans almost look like coins at the bottom of a wishing well, mingling with what looks like cobblestones and bleach-white fish skeletons.

My hand creeps to my mouth. I rock back, suddenly charged with the urge to run. What are those voices I hear?

"Hazel!"

Goose bumps erupt on my skin. I turn toward the sound of my name being shouted. Kole stands at the edge of the bridge. His Impala is parked on the scorched grass. I double back, clinging to the unbearably hot railing. My skin sizzles.

"Hazel!" he calls again. "Get off of there!"

Every nerve in my body jolts, urging me to run. I dart a glance to the other bank. It's so far away.

His footsteps are hurried and hollow. The wood creaks.

"Stay away!" I warn. "Please, just leave me alone!" My voice is a shard of glass, tearing at the walls of my parched throat. I'm starting to feel lightheaded. I'm so high up, and it's so ungodly hot out here.

"What is that? In your hand?" Kole asks, ignoring my directives. Funny, he could have me arrested for ignoring his. And yet, my words don't matter. Not to him. Not here.

Déjà vu sets in again. I have been here before. On Forge Bridge. With him. Discarding my words into the cruel, sucking abyss. All these fragments coming together to form a whole, but this time, I won't be thrown over his shoulder and dragged back.

"Deadmann walking," I say, wielding the paper like a shield. "Is that you? Did you kill Tommy and lure me here?"

Despite the urgency in his steps before, Kole stops dead in his tracks. He's so stunned I might as well have hit him with a brick. "Have you lost your mind?"

Immediately, I consider the possibility that I have. That's what this place does to me. What he does to me. They fray my sanity. When I see his eyes soften as he looks upon the shred of paper in my fist, regret instantly sets in. He's so close I can smell the sweat on him, feel the heat radiating off his body, and yet, I can't tell if he's angry or sad when he shakes his head, and that's what scares me the most. That I've hurt him. Spit an accusation at him that can't be taken back. Then, he asks the truest question I've ever had to face: "Why do you always look for the worst in things?"

"I—" I have no recourse. The accusation is a punch to the throat. It's true. Ever since I got here, I have searched for only the shadows that Black Harbor, and all its inhabitants, have to offer. Kole among them. Because if I can convince myself that something or someone isn't for me, it hurts less when it doesn't happen.

"Hazel." He reaches for me.

I yank my hand away.

Kole grabs my arm and shakes. I see red. A shot of aggression spikes my blood. I raise my other hand and I'm not sure if it's to strike him or defend myself when I freeze.

We both hear it—a susurration of voices.

"Nik?" A tremor courses through me, breaking his name into two syllables. I can feel my fingernails gouging into his arm as I hang on to him now. He stands statue-still. A new sheen of sweat beads his lip.

We're not alone.

A tawny hand grapples at the bridge.

"Oh my God," I breathe.

Extending his left arm, Kole guides me behind him. With his right, he reaches into his holster and draws his gun.

Time all but stops.

The hand reaches blindly, fingers stretching, grasping. It looks like something out of a horror movie. The fingernails dig into the grooves of the railroad ties, seeking purchase. My fear is so palpable, it feels as if this hand is needling my skull instead of the bridge.

"Show yourself!" Kole shouts as the rest of the body emerges and I see a head with strings of dark, dirty hair. Half-lidded eyes fix on us, widening upon seeing the barrel of Kole's gun. The man is skeleton-thin, his tanned skin riddled with red craters.

A ruckus breaks out beneath us. Suddenly, like a rodent returning to its hole, the man goes ramrod straight and slides down the hill. Kole tears after him. I stumble forward and fall, catching myself on my hands and knees. My teeth vibrate and I bite down hard on my tongue. Tears blur my vision when I look up just in time to see Kole disappearing into the chaparral. It's just me and the bridge, now, and all the horrors that lie beneath.

30
KOLE

The thicket is a black hole, a tear in Black Harbor's fabric. Its silence is heavy, perforated by an electric buzzing sound. He scans the treetops, fearful that a transformer on a power line could be malfunctioning. All it would take is one spark to raze this whole place to the ground. There's nothing of that nature, though. Robert Pitts is just a few yards ahead of him. Kole recognized him the instant his head popped up over the bridge. Branches rake his face and snag his clothes. This is all too reminiscent of when he chased after Hazel all those years ago, only to be notified that it was his brother's body that had drifted to shore.

Pitts keeps running, legs pumping, and when he reaches the end of the riverbank, he leaps. Kole goes after him, stopping just short of the edge, catching himself on a birch tree. The buzzing is louder here. His eyes stretch wide as he takes in the scene before him.

The river is gone, a scar in its wake. It's screened by a black haze that he immediately recognizes to be flies, the source of the buzzing sound. Beneath the bridge, filthy nylon tents sprout up like an invasive species, and the people lying next to or shuffling between them look as if they've been exhumed from a mass grave.

Kole has eyes on Pitts as he slips inside a blue tent.

He jumps into the basin, kicking up dust. The smell is almost palpable enough to break his fall. It's a thousand times worse than at the Mineshaft. While inside the motorcycle club was the reek of a decomposing body, the dried-up riverbed holds dozens of decomposing bodies. It looks like Chernobyl down here—everyone's skin is pitted and pockmarked. He holds his breath, as if that will be enough to stave off the flesh-eating, mind-rotting disease of addiction. Like all diseases, it doesn't discriminate. Rather, it wends its way through all walks of life. Here is just a concentrated colony of individuals who can't afford to hide it.

They can barely afford to feed it. They trade whatever they have—their souls, their bodies, whatever they can steal—for the purple pills.

He weaves his way toward Pitts's blue tent, watching his step to avoid piles of human waste. Every individual has their own personal cloud of flies, one that hovers over their heads and sucks on their open wounds. Kole takes his phone out of his pocket and starts recording. Although he's wearing street clothes, he looks like the police. Still, no one pays him much mind.

It isn't a crime to be homeless. It isn't even a crime to do drugs. To possess them, yes. To sell them, most definitely. But to inject or ingest them . . . the cops' hands are tied.

He reaches for the zipper of Pitts's tent and reefs it open. Pitts shrieks and scuttles to the back wall. It would be comical if not for the fact that he's a suspect in a murder investigation. Kole pokes his head in, then takes a second to look around as you might when entering someone's home for the first time. "Nice digs you got here. Now get the fuck out."

"You need a warrant!" Pitts kicks the air.

Kole laughs. "It's a tent, dipshit. You gonna tell that to the wind when it blows it over?"

Pitts's eyes skate left, then right. Kole knows that look. He's searching for a weapon. Kole beats him to the punch by bringing his gun into the frame. "Get out of the tent, Robert."

Pitts screws up his face, then spits. It splatters across Kole's cheek, splashing in his eye. Kole grabs him by the scrawny ankle and drags him out onto the clay. Pitts writhes and howls. Kneeling between Pitts's shoulder blades, Kole is intensely aware of the hole someone's been using as an outdoor toilet. He yanks Pitts toward it so his face is inches away from the waste. "It's gonna be hard to talk with your mouth full of shit," says Kole. "And I'm not leaving here until you tell me what the fuck went down at the Mineshaft Saturday night."

"I wasn't there!"

Kole grabs a handful of Pitts's greasy black hair and grinds his face into the dirt. "Wrong answer, try again."

Pitts sputters when Kole pulls his head up again. "You got the wrong guy!"

Kole mashes Pitts's face into the dirt again. "I don't know about you, Robert, but I cleared my schedule. We can do this all day."

"Help!" Pitts cries. "He's gonna kill me! Help!"

No one is coming to intervene, and Kole can't help but wonder how often an altercation like this happens. How many deaths is this little tent town responsible for already?

"I'm not gonna kill you." He has to admit, he doesn't sound convincing. "Just tell me who shot Tommy Greenlee on Saturday night and we can both move on with our lives."

Pitts raises his head enough to spit a gob of blood. "It wasn't me."

"Then who was it?"

"I don't know, man. I left. Must'a been 10 P.M. or so."

"And Tommy Greenlee was there?"

Pitts nods.

"Who was he with?"

"Guy named D."

"D," repeats Kole. "As in Darren Hogan?"

"Hell if I know, sure."

"Describe him."

"Young dude, got one of those flattop haircuts."

Quickly, Kole thinks this through. The physicals are a match for Darren Hogan, who was reported as having gone to the Mineshaft Saturday night with Robert Pitts.

"And you brought Hogan. How do you two know each other?"

"We don't."

Kole's grip tightens. There's a sibilant sound of air through teeth as Pitts winces. "Okay," he admits, "I was his ticket inside that night. That's all. When the boss tells you to do something, you fucking do it."

"The boss?"

Pitts is all but deflated, just a sack of skin and bones. Suddenly, he drinks in a deep breath as if he's been underwater. These mopes can be so melodramatic. Carefully, Kole rolls off him and as Pitts crawls to a sitting position, holds him at gunpoint. "Who's your boss, Robert?"

Pitts casts his eyes down and without looking up, says: "Everyone's got a boss. Even the boss has a boss."

"Who's yours?"

Pitts drags a filthy hand under his nose. There are two silver snakebite piercings that glimmer in his bottom lip. Then, he murmurs two inaudible syllables.

"Come again?" Kole leans forward, the nose of his service pistol plunging toward Pitts.

Pitts's eyes swell, and this time, his voice is loud and clear. "Fuck. You."

Kole lunges. He's stopped midair, though, when a pair of hands grabs his biceps and yanks him backward. Axel breaks his fall, wrapping his legs around him to render him immobile. "He's not worth it," he says.

From the ground, Kole watches Fletcher and Riley move in and detain Pitts. There's a clicking sound as Riley secures a pair of handcuffs.

"How'd you know to come here?" Kole asks, catching his breath.

His detectives all meet his gaze, and then Riley turns toward the bank. Hazel stands at the edge, hair waving in the scant breeze, looking like the maiden on the bow of a ship that's sinking down into the deep, where neither man nor monster dare to go.

"She called us," explains Axel. "But honestly, we were looking for you anyway. Aubrey Jeske's at the police department."

"She wouldn't talk to us within earshot of her family," adds Riley.

Kole works his jaw. He knows what that means: Aubrey Jeske is about to blow the whistle.

31
HAZEL

I ride shotgun in Kole's Impala. The vents blast cool air and lemon scent—a stark contrast from the eye-watering stench below the bridge. My head bobbles with each pothole the tires sink into. A bracelet swings violently from the rearview mirror. I gasp when I recognize my name staring back at me.

It isn't the smell anymore that causes my eyes to tear. A bullet of regret lodges in my stomach. I feel like an asshole. All this time, Kole has kept a piece of me, while I've been building a case against him.

It isn't the first time, either. It was in this same pockmarked parking lot that I accused him of murdering his CI. My heart is still pounding on overdrive, my entire body enveloped in a film of sweat, and I can't discern whether it's from having watched him drag Robert Pitts through the dirt or the realization that I've backed myself into an impossible corner.

"I'm sorry." The words are forced, but sincere.

Kole doesn't spare me a glance. He stares straight ahead as we ascend the hill and turn right onto Fulton Street, where the blue apartments used to be.

I'm afraid he isn't going to speak at all, but as he pulls into the municipal lot, he does something that makes me feel even worse. He loops my bracelet from around the mirror and sets it on my lap. "Here, that's everything I had left of you."

Then, he gets out and slams the door.

I sit, feeling raw from the inside out, as tears stream down my face. Before he disappears via the side entrance, I get out, too, and follow him up the echoing stairwell to the Investigations Bureau where Cameron Jeske's widow is waiting.

The cement-block walls are the same off-white color they were during my transcribing days. It doesn't look as if they've seen a fresh coat of paint since. Hairline fissures make veins throughout. It's so brittle, I bet if you shut a door hard enough, it would shatter.

A metal plate announces GENERAL INVESTIGATIONS UNIT. I follow Kole inside, keeping my head down as I wend my way past desks and filing cabinets. The few detectives in here don't even bother to look my way. They work with headphones on, eyes glued to their computer screens. It all feels so achingly familiar. I've been up here twice before—both times in the dead of night and both times to observe Kole break someone in the interview room.

A few paces ahead of me, he enters an alcove where there are three doors: one for the break room, one for Interview Room 1, and one for the observation room. He opens the third and disappears into what I know is a long, narrow space. My eyes adjust to the dark as I follow him in. From what I can tell, it's just the two of us. Fletcher stayed back at the bridge with Pitts to help patrolmen book him in.

The only light comes from the window that divides the observation room from Interview Room 1. It's a two-way mirror. The aluminum between the glass makes it so we can see them, but they can't see us.

Three people all sit at a stainless-steel table: Axel, Riley, and a woman who I assume to be Aubrey Jeske. Her hair is bright artificial red, grown out at the roots. She looks barely thirty, despite the fact that I know she has a sixteen-year-old son; her cheeks are rosy and round, like she's still got some deposits of baby fat, which will serve her well as she ages. She's wearing a spaghetti-strap tank top and jean shorts. Her leg bounces, her flip-flop making a *thwap, thwap* sound.

"Aubrey, listen. Before we get started, I just want to acknowledge you for coming in to speak with us." Riley's voice is so smooth, she could be a radio DJ like my sister—or a phone sex operator, which, honestly, probably pays more. "Anything you share with us will put us miles ahead of where we were in getting justice for your husband."

Aubrey's gaze lifts to meet Riley's. She gives a solemn nod.

"I'm sorry for your loss," adds Riley. "I'm also sorry for this less-than-inviting space. The soft interview room is under construction."

It's a lie. And a tactic. I've known them to do this before—put someone in here versus the more comfortable, nonthreatening Interview Room 3 where children and victims of domestic abuse are usually spoken to. Interview Room 1 is stark, dread-inducing, and about the size of a shoebox. But it usually does the job. It gets people to talk.

Aubrey takes a deep breath. Her chest is splotchy. "Do I need a lawyer?" she asks.

Beside me, I feel Kole stiffen. If she lawyers up, this interview is over before it even begins.

"Not if you don't want one," says Axel.

She sits silently, chewing the inside of her cheek. Her leg bounces more aggressively.

"How about this," he picks up. "We can just start our conversation, and if at any point you want to stop or you need a break, just let us know, okay?"

Aubrey nods fervently. Everything about her body language says she wants to spill what she knows. But she looks scared. For herself or for someone else?

"You mentioned, when we met you at your parents' house earlier, that you had something you wanted to share with us. Might it have something to do with the night of Tuesday, July 2, when you came home and saw that your husband was . . . ?" Riley tosses her a softball.

Aubrey takes another deep breath. She stares down at her hands, which are folded in her lap. I side-eye Kole, watching him as he watches her. She picks at her cuticles. Then, she nods again, less eagerly this time. When she looks up at the detectives across the table from her, she wears a full-on frown. In the few seconds that transpire, she must give herself a mental pep talk because she shifts in her seat and sits up straighter.

"Cam knew he was going to die," she says. "Whoever killed him . . . he knew they were coming for him. That's why he sent us away. Me and the kids."

Riley and Axel share a look, then Riley leans forward. "How do you know this, Aubrey?"

"Because he was wearing his wedding ring." She loses it. A sob bursts from her mouth and her shoulders shake. Riley reaches across the table and coaxes Aubrey to lay her hand in hers. Axel leaves the room for a minute and they stay like that, Aubrey crying and Riley holding on to her, until Axel returns with a box of tissues. He slides it to Aubrey, who plucks two and immediately dabs at her eyes.

"I take it that was unusual for him," offers Axel. "Wearing his ring."

Aubrey blows her nose. "With his work and all, yeah. He was afraid of catching it in a piece of machinery or something."

"Take us back to that evening," says Riley. "Tuesday, July 2. You'd been at Tommy Greenlee's funeral earlier that day. Now you're home and . . ."

"My mom called. They were having a cookout," says Aubrey. "I figured it'd be good for us to take the kids over there for a while. I wanted Cam to come, too, but he said he wasn't feelin' it. Which . . . I understood. Tommy was his friend and all."

"But not yours?" Riley again.

Aubrey's tongue makes another quick appearance as she wets her lips. "I wasn't . . . unfriendly toward him. It was just, yeah, that whole thing with Grayson and . . . I didn't think he was the best influence on my kids. There's a reason God chooses for some people not to procreate."

The statement rings so true, it causes my bones to vibrate. The decision to have or not have children had been a sticking point in our marriage—Tommy wanted kids while I didn't. He insisted I would change my mind, that I *should* change my mind. That something was inherently *wrong* with me for not wanting to be a mother. Remarkably, suddenly, I feel validated by this woman I've never met.

"Why do you say that?" asks Riley.

Aubrey shrugs. "He just didn't seem to have much regard for anyone's life besides his own."

"Are you talking about the feral kittens incident? The ones he made Grayson . . ."

Aubrey's face contorts. She plants her elbow on the table and sets her forehead into her palm. "He was just a bad person . . ." she mutters. "There was something not right upstairs. And, if you read his ex-wife's book . . . I know it's supposed to be fiction, but, like . . . how much of that shit is true, you know? I bet a lot of it."

Every muscle in my body tenses. I close my eyes, wishing I could disappear. And then, I feel a sensation I wasn't expecting, which is that of human touch when Kole loops his pinkie through mine. Despite the circumstances, I feel slightly euphoric. I fold my other fingers over, protecting and prolonging whatever this moment is.

"Aubrey." It's Axel. "Do you have any reason not to believe your husband's murder could be directly related to Tommy Greenlee's?"

"Oh, I know it is," states Aubrey. This is the most confident she's sounded since she started talking. "Just like I know it's my fault." She breaks down again. Her shoulders shake as she hides her face in her hands.

"Why would you think it's your fault?" asks Riley.

When Aubrey composes herself again, she looks like she's aged ten years. Purplish crescents cup her eyes. Gravity pulls her toward the floor. She looks drained, empty, as all these secrets she's been keeping spill out. "Cam and Tommy found drugs in the water a few weeks ago. Which I know you know about."

Riley and Axel nod in sync.

"Some hardcore shit," acknowledges Riley.

"Hardcore shit," Aubrey cosigns with a sniffle. "Anyway, Cam wanted nothing to do with it. He thought they should turn it in to the police, but Tommy didn't want to. He hated you guys . . . no offense."

Axel shows his palms as if to say *None taken*. "When we spoke with him in your backyard, Cam mentioned to my colleague and me that

Tommy claimed he was going to surrender the drugs at a pharmacy. But he didn't, did he?"

Slowly, Aubrey shakes her head.

"Any idea why not?"

"Because I told him not to."

Everyone's leaning in now. Axel and Riley in the interview room, and Kole and me on the other side of the mirror. Our hands unlink. I dare to look at him. His breath steams the glass as he listens intently to Aubrey Jeske divulging what is hopefully the truth about what happened after Tommy and Cam found three kilos of Xombie floating in Lake Michigan. Once she starts, however, I find myself hoping she's lying. Because what she shares cannot bode well for any of us.

According to Aubrey, Cam had left work a little early that day to pick up one of the kids from school. Upon his arrival home, he told his wife about their discovery, and mentioned that Tommy had volunteered to surrender the drugs at a pharmacy. Aubrey agreed, but the more she thought about it, the more it gnawed at her.

Drugs are big business in Black Harbor. And it sounded like Tommy and Cam had potentially intercepted a drop-off.

"I couldn't sleep," she says. "So, I was up late, just, like, scrolling on my phone. I don't really post on Instagram myself, just watch videos and stuff, but then I saw Hazel's story."

"Hazel," says Axel, eyes widening. "As in . . . ?"

"Tommy's ex. The writer. She had a caption, like, 'ask me anything.' So I did. I was seeking some sort of justification, I guess, for what I was about to ask Tommy to do. From the one person I know who got out of Black Harbor in one piece."

"Aubrey, what did you ask her?" Axel leans even farther forward.

I know what she's going to say before she says it. The handle @deadmann_walking doesn't belong to Tommy. Or Kole.

It's hers.

She looks from Axel to Riley, and says: "If all you had to do was one bad thing, and you could leave Black Harbor behind forever, would you do it?"

"Did she respond?" asks Axel.

Aubrey's gaze drifts to the mirror, and I swear to God she can see me, can see me mouth the one-word confirmation I gave that was apparently everything she needed to move forward with her destructive plan.

Yes.

32
KOLE

Kole pinches the bridge of his nose for the second time today, as Aubrey Jeske furthers his theory that the population of Black Harbor is setting evolution backward.

He fires off a text to Riley and watches as she checks her phone. SHE NEEDS TO LEAVE TOWN. ASAP.

With an inconspicuous glance toward the mirror, Riley nods curtly.

Aubrey wanted a different life for herself and her family—one that didn't have to be here in Black Harbor—and she was willing to play dirty to achieve it. Still, they've got no grounds to arrest her, and considering the fact that her three children are now fatherless, he reasons she's been punished enough. Now she can spend the rest of her life thinking about how, had she not made that phone call, she'd likely be making Fourth of July plans with her husband. Instead, she's planning his funeral.

The wedding ring detail is noteworthy. From a man never wearing it to dying with it on his finger means he knew that whoever killed Tommy was coming for him next. Cam was a martyr. He sent his family away so they would be spared, then he waited for the grim reaper to knock on his door.

"You mentioned you think Cam knew his life was in danger that night," says Riley, reading his mind. "What, besides the fact that he'd been wearing his wedding ring, tipped you off? Did he know your arrangement with Tommy?"

Aubrey shakes her head. She's crying again. "I never told him about it," she admits. "It's possible Tommy did, but . . . I don't think so. When I was at my parents' house that evening, he texted *I love you gummi bear*—his nickname for me—and I texted him back that I loved him, too. That wasn't unusual, we told each other often, spontaneously. And he'd had enough to drink at the funeral. He gets affectionate when he's drunk. *Got,* I mean. And then like a minute later he texted me a random assortment of numbers and stuff. I figured he was drunk or it was a butt dial."

Kole holds his breath, the numbers from the scratch-off ticket shoving their way to the front of his memory. But she says something different. "CD80559."

Axel repeats it and adds: "License plate?"

"I think so?" says Aubrey.

"Illinois," I'm guessing, and Kole agrees. Wisconsin uses the ABC-1234 format, while Illinois and Connecticut default to AB12345. From his phone, he sends an email to the traffic investigations unit, asking them to run the plate. He'd bet his pension it lists to a stolen vehicle.

"Aubrey," says Riley, "we've got a strong reason to believe that yours and your children's lives are in danger. Your parents', too. You need to leave the city. At least until we arrest whoever's behind these murders."

Aubrey looks from Riley to Axel. She's horrified, her eyes as round and bright as headlights, and Kole knows why: it's because right now, the gravity of her actions is being realized. Her face crumples. Her bottom lip trembles. "But . . . what about Cam? I can't leave him—"

"He can stay at the ME's office for the time being," offers Axel. "They'll take proper care of him."

Before they rise to escort her out, Riley has one more question. "Do you have any idea who Tommy was planning on selling the dope to?"

"No." Another sniffle. "But I know he knew people. I didn't like Grayson going over there."

"I don't blame you," Axel sympathizes.

She sits for a minute, numb. Then: "There was a chick around my age, maybe. Harriet? Flaming orange hair. Tommy was sort of seeing her. Cam and I went out with them a couple of times. She was . . . different."

"Different how?" asks Riley.

Aubrey shrugs. "Kinda scuzzy? A far cry from Hazel, if you ask me, but . . . I always thought he outkicked his coverage with her anyway. She was trashy, for sure. Harriet, not Hazel."

Harriet. The name is a brick to the face. Kole thinks back to being at her apartment a few hours ago. She hadn't mentioned that she and Tommy Greenlee were romantically involved. Instead, she'd referred to him as "the dude at the Mineshaft." Apparently, Kole didn't pay her enough to divulge that valuable little detail.

Or there's the simple fact that Dirty Harriet is a dirty liar. After all, she also told him that Robert Pitts was dead. Why tell him that except to deter him from tracking him down?

Because Dirty Harriet and Robert Pitts both had a role in these murders. He's sure of it.

Kole and Riley ask Aubrey a few more questions to wrap up the interview. YOU GOOD? reads the incoming text from Riley.

MAKE SURE SHE GETS OUT OF HERE SAFELY, he replies. Then he turns to look at Hazel. The whites of her eyes are stark, her blue irises as bright as the hottest part of a flame. She's looking at him in that way she was up on the bridge, like she's scared of him. Like she wants to run far, far away from here. From him.

Luckily this time, he knows how to make her stay.

He's going to give her an assignment.

33
HAZEL

We ride in silence. I sneak a glance at Kole, whose jaw is set, his eyes fixed on the scorched landscape beyond the windshield. During the interview with Aubrey Jeske, I'd temporarily forgotten about our dustup until I'd gone to climb into the passenger seat and discovered my bracelet lying there, right where I'd left it. My name, spelled out in white beads, glared at me, calling me out as Kole did up on the bridge.

Why do you always look for the worst in things?

He isn't wrong.

I was, though. I was wrong to wander upstairs and go through his things. I'd been *looking* for something to incriminate him, for a reason to run, and I thought I'd found it. So he kept a piece of my writing. So what? I realize now how impulsive I'd been. I jumped to the conclusion I wanted—one that fit my MO.

By seeing only what I'd wanted to see, I cast him as the villain. Because if he's the bad guy, then I don't have to be.

I swallow. My throat is dry and suddenly I realize it's been hours since I ate or drank anything. A drum beats in my temples. My hand is sweaty from holding the bracelet and deliberating. Just the thought of removing it from Kole's vehicle and taking it with me causes physical pain, a sharp burning sensation, as if someone's driving a corkscrew through the left panel of my chest. It's more his than mine at this point. I only had the thing for a few years—a souvenir from my honeymoon in Jamaica—whereas he has held on to it for the better part of a decade, ever since he fished it out of the river. Finally, even though his body language suggests our quarrel is *to be continued,* I work up the nerve to loop it back over the rearview mirror.

"So, what now?" The question is a dull knife sawing at the tension. "Are you going to interview Robert Pitts?"

He doesn't spare me a glance. I sit, mesmerized by the sharp edges of his profile. The straight slope of his nose, strong chin, square cheekbones. There's a three-day growth of stubble on his jaw, telling how this investigation has so devoured every minute of his life since it started that he hasn't even had time to shave. I don't hate it. I watch his Adam's apple slowly climb up his throat and slide back down. After another beat of silence, he says: "He needs more time," as if Pitts is a child who needs to sit and think about what he's done. But I know what he means. Pitts is an addict. Kole's waiting for him to detox. He's going to lay the hammer down on Pitts when he's in so much agony that he'll do anything to make it stop. Even, perhaps, tell the truth.

"What about Harriet?" I ask.

"What *about* Harriet?"

"Do you think she was the one who stashed the drugs in the deer head?"

Kole opens his mouth to argue, then pauses. I can tell he's thinking out loud when he says: "She middled the deal. Tommy and Cam found three kilos of Xombie in the lake. Whether or not Tommy was actually planning on surrendering it, he didn't, because Aubrey called and proposed they sell the drugs and split the profits."

"Right, to leave Black Harbor behind forever," I say, quoting the message from who I now know to have been Aubrey. A quick search on social media after the interview showed me that *Mann* is her maiden name, thus @deadmann_walking. Clever.

"Did Tommy want to leave?" he asks me as we descend the hill to the lighthouse.

Everyone wants to leave but you, Nik, I want to say, but bite my tongue. "Who doesn't?" I say. People do desperate things to get out of this hellscape—myself included.

Kole's wince is barely perceptible. Still, I take notice.

"You think Harriet set up the deal between Tommy and Pitts?" I ask.

"I guess I'll find out." He sets his jaw again and I know I went too far with that little dig. Our dynamic is thin ice: dangerous, and easy to forget there's no solid ground beneath us. "Does it bother you?" Kole asks as we climb the winding staircase now.

"What?"

"That Tommy was seeing someone else."

The question is unexpected. "No," I say, perhaps a little too fervently. But it's the truth. It makes me feel a little better, actually, knowing that Tommy had moved on after me, that I hadn't traumatized him so completely that he could never have a relationship again. Although, look how well it worked out for him.

The VCTF office is empty save for one lone human, dark-haired and demonstrating hellacious posture as he pores over a spreadsheet on his computer.

"Hazel, this is Investigator Ryan Hudson. He's on loan from White Collar Crimes and he's manning the leads desk for us."

Hudson has a delayed reaction. He makes a few more clicks, hits a few more keys, and slowly swivels around to meet me. I see my reflection in his thick, black-framed glasses. He's attractive in a nerdy Clark Kent kind of way, except ganglier. He offers his hand, which I shake, and he raises his bushy brows at Kole. "*The* Hazel?"

"The one who got away," says Kole, and I'm not sure if he means got away from him or from this city.

"Well, welcome back," says Hudson.

"Thank you?"

"What's the lead situation?" asks Kole, coming around to look at Hudson's computer. "Anything worthwhile?"

"Someone claims to have seen Robert Pitts at a backyard barbecue."

"When?"

"About an hour or two ago."

"Bullshit," says Kole. "I've got him in custody."

"Ohhh-kay," says Hudson, consulting his computer and adding a strike-through line to that entry.

"What else?"

"We've got an ATL on the vehicle you had traffic send over. It's a 2018 Kia Forte. License plate CD80—"

"Yeah."

"Lists to a twenty-three-year-old female. She reported it stolen four days ago. Apparently she came out after work and it was gone. No broken glass, no—"

"There wouldn't be. Those are among the most stealable cars in the world."

"And Hyundais," adds Hudson.

"What time?"

"Between 6:10 and 6:20 P.M."

"Where's work?"

"The hospital. She's a CNA."

"You spoke to her?"

"Yes."

Kole leans over his shoulder and skims the document on his computer. I wander over to the persons-of-interest board, giving them space. My eyes home in on the scratch-off tickets pinned to their respective pictures: Tommy, Cam, Evan Kole, and James Allen Cooper.

Four dead men. Four identical tickets. 0-5-3-7-3. I read the sequence several times. What could it be? A date?

May 3, 1973.

Or maybe a combination?

Or is it some kind of a riddle? Zero of something, five of another, and so on. As I think, my eyes roam the rest of the board, where I see a booking photo of a twenty- or thirty something female. She has wild red hair and salient eyes. She looks happy, as if she's posed for a glamour shot instead of a mugshot. I read the note in Kole's handwriting.

Dirty Harriet. Malcolm's CI. Working Pitts (ghosted).

On the other side of the board, my eyes catch on a booking photo of a bald man. He looks mean, his furrowed brow squeezing his eyes into splinters. Veins make his temples look like a topographic map. "Big House," I whisper. His rap sheet is taped to the board, a portfolio of every crime he's committed since the age of seventeen, boasting everything from arson to attempted homicide. Of course a city like Black Harbor would grant him a business license. According to Kole's notes, he owns the Mineshaft, where Tommy was—

"Hazel." Kole calls for me.

"Yeah?" Trepidation severs the word into two syllables. I'm grateful to walk away from Big House's leering gaze. I start walking back toward them.

"How well do you remember Onyx?"

"Um . . . It's probably like riding a bike, right?" I look to Hudson for moral support, but all he offers is a half smile that morphs into a half frown.

"Here, use my login." Kole pauses and I wonder if it isn't him wondering if he's going to regret these words. *I won't do anything,* I want to tell him, but that makes it seem like I absolutely will. The instructions are fairly simple: "Enter 'DOA' as the investigation type and check every evidence log for mention of a scratch-off ticket. Put an asterisk or something next to any jumper reports."

"Okay." I flex my fingers over the keyboard. It's been too long since they've been useful. They are as anxious to get to work as the rest of me.

Kole regards Hudson, who's now across from me. "You'll help her if she gets stuck?"

From my peripheral vision, I see Hudson nod as I type "DOA" and watch pages upon pages of reports populate. Axel wasn't exaggerating. There are thousands.

"This isn't even all of them," Hudson notes.

"What do you mean?"

"Onyx only goes back as far as the 1990s. For cases that are older than that, the reports are all handwritten and stored in the basement of the PD."

"Dang," I say, my northern Wisconsin accent dragging out the long vowel as I imagine myself standing in what appears to be a library of police reports.

I might be wishfully thinking it, but Kole seems to be holding back a smile. "Let's just hope we don't have to go back that far." He claps Hudson on the shoulder and starts toward me, but stops. Our eyes lock for a second, and just as I feel my lips press together in a soft smile to match his, his phone rings. Kole answers it and a gravelly male voice comes over the speaker. "So, you're who the devil calls when he wants to sell his soul?"

I don't recognize it, but Hudson seems to. His head snaps up. His nostrils flare once, then no more as he holds his breath.

"Hades," says Kole, solving the mystery of the caller. "Think of it as a loan."

"With interest."

"We can talk about that after I bag Buddha."

"All right," Hades says on the other line. "Let's cut a deal."

"I'll send a car for you tomorrow morning. Wear something nice."

When Kole ends the call, Hudson's eyes are on him as if he's just opened the floodgates to Hell.

34
KOLE

He wouldn't say he'd been lying to Hades, or even bluffing, when he slid the offer across the stainless-steel table this morning. More like willing it into existence. *Manifesting*, to take a page out of Dirty Harriet's book.

The DA knows he cut a deal with Hades in exchange for his cooperation. What she doesn't know is that he promised him freedom.

It was a necessary evil. Hades never would have gone for it, otherwise. Had Kole only offered to cleave his remaining sentence in half, it would still be another three and a half years of him trying to survive in prison as a snitch. And snitches get murdered. With a man like Hades, it was all or nothing. The caveat—because all good deals have one—is that Hades's freedom is contingent not only on his cooperation, but on them arresting Buddha. Or, to quote the DA herself: *killing him with fire.*

Kole runs through his mental checklist. Riley and Axel are taking care of Aubrey Jeske and making sure she and her family get out of Black Harbor. Fletcher's chasing Tommy's stolen guns. Hudson's working the leads. And Hazel is combing decades' worth of DOA reports for any mention of scratch-off tickets.

He spared them a glance before leaving the lighthouse, and for the first time since this investigation started, he feels hopeful, cautiously optimistic, almost, that they will find something between the DOA reports and the tip line. Hudson glares at him, but that's all right; it's only because he doesn't understand the full magnitude of just how dire their situation is. Yet. Still, Kole can empathize. Hades is Hudson's brother. They are human examples of oil and water, heads versus tails, for while Hades stuck with the family business of dealing dope and offing mopes, Hudson sought out a more honorable calling with law enforcement. Sometimes, though—and Kole's coached him on this a few times—he's too good for his own good.

As far as character flaws are concerned, however, Hudson's virtuousness that borders on self-righteousness is tolerable. What aren't tolerable are the lies Harriet told him this morning. She's at the top of his shit list for omitting the fact that she'd been involved with Tommy Greenlee. The more he thinks about it, the more he's convinced that Hazel was right about Harriet stashing the kilo inside the deer head.

He parks in front of the bakery, then crosses the street to Harriet's building and knifes his way into the side door. He knows the drill. Lean to the right to avoid the blooms of insulation bursting from the walls. Duck to miss a giant cobweb. Harriet's door is at the top of the landing, on the right. He knocks.

No answer.

Death metal bleeds through the walls of a neighboring unit. He knocks again and presses his ear to the door to better hear. "Harriet," he calls. "Harriet, it's Nik, let me in."

Nothing.

He knocks once more and, after receiving no response, he jimmies the chintzy lock with his knife and lets himself in.

Remnants of a hot-dog lunch grow stale on the table. A fly walks along the crust of what appears to have been a piece of white bread folded in half. A glass bong lies next to it. Kole makes his way through the kitchen, taking in Harriet's menagerie of stolen things—road signs, broken furniture, flowerpots with fissures running through them. He notes how she's mended the latter and painted their scars gold.

None of these are what he's looking for, that being anything that connects her to Tommy Greenlee or the case at hand. *All this junk,* he thinks as he sifts through a pile of old magazines, *you'd think she'd have a scratch-off ticket in here somewhere.* She's made Swiss cheese of the magazines, cutting out pictures of expensive-looking jewelry and cars for her vision board.

Kole turns and looks at the thing. It has a magnetic pull on him, the way he moves slowly but dutifully toward it. The way he flicks through the cutouts. There are layers and layers of them, which he didn't realize earlier. Of course, if Harriet has a scratch-off, why not put it on her vision board so she can manifest herself winning the jackpot? And yet, it doesn't seem to be here. Feeling slightly defeated, Kole takes a step back to better look at the board as a whole.

A blue eye stares at him.

The hair on the back of his neck stands up. It looks as if whoever the eye belongs to is peering at him through a peephole. He unburies it from the surrounding photographs to reveal a portrait of Hazel, the left side torn. Her head is tilted as if she's leaning on something or someone; her makeup is dreamy and dramatic. Her dark hair falls in ringlets, framing her face, and from what he can see of her dress, it's white.

Like a wedding dress.

And there, punched through the center of her forehead, is a bullet hole.

35
HAZEL

After three and a half hours of staring at a screen, scanning rows of complaint numbers and causes of death, my eyeballs have effectively turned to sand.

It isn't for nothing, though. Of the 314 jumper cases I've combed through, four have been found with scratch-off tickets. I made note of their names, corresponding complaint numbers, and dates.

Across from me, a corner of Hudson's mouth picks up in amusement. "Try skimming through bank documents."

"Is that what you do?" I ask. "White-collar crimes?"

"Every day."

After Kole left us alone to our own devices, I had to ask about Hades. "So, your brother. He's bad news, I take it."

"The worst."

"And Nik's getting him out of prison? To help with this investigation?"

He blew out an exasperated breath. "God knows," he said.

"Do you want to talk about it?"

"God, no."

We worked diligently for hours afterward. Now, he's made some headway on the case, at least as far as checking off leads not to follow up on. The phone call I overheard about an old man claiming to have had visions of Tommy's ex-wife resurfacing and killing him was particularly interesting. Now, I shift in my chair, cross one leg over the other. "White-collar crimes, that's corporate stuff, right? Is there that much of it here?"

"Embezzlement, money laundering, bad checks, any type of fraud, really. And yeah, there's enough of it."

"What's the craziest case you've ever worked?"

Hudson frowns in thought. A fog comes over him, then, and he asks: "Have you ever heard of the Reynolds family?"

I shake my head.

On a notecard, he scratches down a complaint number. "Look it up when you've got some time to kill. That one's stranger than fiction. Someone could write a book about it."

Fighting the cringe, I thank him and take the notecard. Cops love to tell writers what they should write about. But this feels a little different. It doesn't come on the tail end of a brag; rather, it feels like a lifeline, something to cling to as I search for what to write next.

I know I have more than one good book in me. I just have to dig deep. And, as much as I'd love to deny it, I also know that if I have to get my hands dirty again, I will.

It worked the first time. While I'd escaped Black Harbor by the skin of my teeth, Aubrey Jeske was apparently so desperate to follow in my footsteps that she was willing to play her part in dropping the atomic bomb of lethal drugs on the city. Kole said just one kilo of Xombie could wipe out fifty million people—more than five times the population of New York.

"Can I ask you something?" says Hudson, and I have to wonder if my thoughts aren't bleeding out of my forehead when he follows up with: "Why are you here?"

It's a fair question, one I've been posing to myself since the second I booked my flight to Wisconsin. Hudson's easy to like. Even though we've just met, I feel, if I asked him the same question, he'd be honest with me. "I need to know how my ex-husband ended up peppered with bullet holes on that bathroom floor."

"Why?"

"Why not?" I counter.

"I think there's more to the story."

"Maybe *you* should tell *me,* then." I lean forward and plant my chin in my palm. "Why am I here, Detective Hudson?"

"For him," he says shortly.

"To see why he was murdered, yes."

"Not him. Nik." When I'm quiet, Hudson leans forward. He has a calming effect, the way he fills my frame of vision. His voice is soft, yet stern, and I get the feeling that this is a tactic he's honed when he really needs people to listen to him. "Look, Hazel, Nikolai Kole loves three things: his dog, Black Harbor, and you."

The statement sends a thrill through my veins. Hudson speaks it as a matter of fact, not accusation or assumption, and I realize how I've missed the two of us being in the same sentence together. "I get the dog," I manage. "But the last two . . ."

Hudson shrugs and relaxes back in his chair. "We don't get to choose who we love. We just do. And if we're lucky enough, they love us back."

The silence that falls is thick and heavy and sucks what little air there is out of the room. I get up and walk to the window, wishing for a breeze and for Hudson not to see the tears that roll down my face.

Sometimes I feel like a heroin addict. If you want to see a portrait of alone, look at them. And yet, the reason they're alone is usually because their addiction has driven everyone else away; they'll rob their own family members blind for a fix. Except I'm not an addict. I'm alone by choice, I remind myself.

Not for the first time, I wonder what's wrong with me. How is it that everyone else can seem to hold on to things when I can't? For as long as I can remember, I have treated everything in my life as temporary. Jobs. Friendships. Relationships. Oftentimes, I suspected that if it wasn't for the participation ribbon get-togethers, I would never have any human contact at all. My world has become quite insular by design, and New York has proven the easiest place in the world to be anonymous.

Everyone is so singularly focused.

Get coffee.

Get to work.

Get home.

It's seamless, like a reel played on a loop, and there's comfort in that. Predictability is an algorithm that doesn't disappoint.

Except when I do a stupid thing like coming back here and planting myself in Nikolai Kole's orbit. I am the wrench in my own plan. Honestly, what did I expect? That he would welcome me with open arms and our sharp edges would wear down as we worked this case together? I shouldn't even be here. I'm a civilian, and I won't, for a second, allow myself to believe that he gave me this assignment for any reason other than to keep me distracted and out of harm's way. With Hudson babysitting me, I am simply one less thing he has to worry about.

Why do you always look for the worst in things?

Because the good things don't last.

I wonder now, though, if that isn't my own fault. If I had allowed myself to believe in the possibility of forever with him, would things have turned out differently? Would I have ever left Black Harbor?

I drink in a deep breath to regain composure. I don't want Hudson to think he made me cry, even if he did. It's not his fault, though. I'm a dam waiting to spill over. Wandering over to the persons-of-interest board, as if this is the sole reason I'd come over here in the first place, my eyes scan the photographs and the notes written next to them. They find Tommy and stay there.

The picture is the same as the one that's been circulating on the news. He's wearing a tux and that *just married* smile. He looks so alive, so happy, so young and carefree. This version of Tommy, the one I fell for, has been gone for a long time.

Our relationship was dead before Kole walked into the picture. Tommy was just too blitzed to notice.

Perhaps the same could be said for the version of me that he'd fallen for, once upon a time. In the years that we moved away to Black Harbor, I'd grown thorny and introspective, wearing my skeleton on the outside like protective armor. So when Nikolai Kole showed me the slightest kindness, made me feel like I was the only thing that mattered if even for a moment, I fell too hard and too fast.

It isn't a justification for cheating on my husband. It's just what happened.

I home in on the scratch-off ticket adhered to the board next to his photo, bright yellow and spattered with blood. My mouth moves soundlessly to map out the numbers, pouting for the zero, teeth lightly sinking into my bottom lip for the five. Where have I seen this sequence before?

As soon as I ask myself the question, I realize where I've seen it before.

It's a date.

Hurrying back to the desk, I scroll through the jumper cases, watching the complaint numbers change as I race toward the bottom. I stop abruptly when I find it.

May 3, 1973.

"Fuck." The syllable is a whisper, almost elegant, as it hangs in the air between us.

Hudson's moved to crouch behind me. "Jumper, dead on arrival," he reads. "Call for service date 05-3-73."

Hand shaking, I click into it and see that he was right about the case files beyond 1990 being empty. I turn to him. The computer screen reflects in his lenses, masking his eyes. "Where did you say the old reports were kept again?"

36
KOLE

The picture he found on Harriet's vision board is the other half of the one that keeps flashing on the news. The edge is torn, as if, in a fit of rage, someone ripped the photograph down the middle.

Harriet, maybe. But he thinks that, more than likely, it was Tommy. Who knows why or when he did it, but at some point, he tore up his and Hazel's wedding photo and used her face as target practice. It's a cold-blooded thing to do, even to a photograph.

He'll address it later. Now, as he has done hundreds of times, Kole wends his way through the desks back to the alcove where Interview Room 1 waits for him. The bureau is empty. There isn't a soul in sight rifling through filing cabinets, tapping on keyboards, or dictating a report for AI software to type. They got rid of the transcribing department last year. Budget cuts.

He texted the photo he found in Harriet's apartment to his detectives, then separately to Hudson with an order:

> Don't let her out of your sight.

Now in the alcove, he cranks the thermostat to the right until it reaches ninety degrees Fahrenheit. If he can't beat the truth out of Pitts, maybe he can sweat it out of him. The manila folder in his left hand feels suddenly heavy. The contents inside will keep dragging him down if he lets them. He has to let go. He has to move forward. The only way to do that is to break the man on the other side of this door.

Robert Pitts cowers beneath the stainless-steel table. His knees are pulled into his chest, his head tucked down in the space between. The backs of his hands are all scratched to hell. He looks like he's having one of the worst days of his life.

Good. Nine years ago, he gave Kole the worst day of his.

The first thing he does upon entering is turn off the camera. Then, he walks over to the table. The chair scrapes across the floor as he pulls it out and sits down. He places the manila envelope on the cold, silver surface and clasps his hands. "Get up," he says.

Beneath him, Pitts doesn't move.

"Get. Up." Kole drives his foot into Pitts's ankle. The mope makes a sound like a feral animal, then slowly crawls out from under the table and climbs into the chair opposite Kole. He looks and smells like absolute shit. His skin is ashen and tinged green. A trail of mucus streams from his nose to his upper lip and glistens in the harsh fluorescent light. There's dried spittle crusted to the corners of his mouth.

"Welcome to the party, Robert."

Pitts doesn't respond. Instead, he looks as if he is going to either projectile vomit or shit his pants. That's if he hasn't already. Kole wrinkles his nose. The stench that clings to Pitts is otherworldly, triggering a memory from earlier today when he mashed Pitts's face into the ground next to a pile of human feces.

He can't say he smells much better. What he wouldn't give to take a shower and rinse the grime of today off his skin. But today isn't over yet.

Pitts sways. His eyelids are heavy, as if they're trying to close to put him out of his misery. To spare him from having to look in the eyes of the man who is going to break him. To give mercy to the merciless.

He's been afforded too much of that already. Mercy. There will be no more, not in this primordial life they've reverted to, where kill or be killed, eat or be eaten, is the only law that reigns supreme.

"You gonna read me my rights?" Pitts mumbles.

"Why? You're not under arrest." This is where most cops fuck up. By reading a suspect their Miranda rights, they doom the interview before it even begins. The key is to give them a sliver of hope, something to grasp on to, a hair-thin promise that if they cooperate, they'll go free. Otherwise, once someone knows they're going to jail, they lose hope. And with no hope, there's no incentive to talk.

It's similar to handling a gun. Don't put your finger on the trigger until you're going to shoot. He will read Robert Pitts his rights only when he's about to slap the handcuffs on him.

Hearing that he isn't under arrest is a shot of elixir for Pitts. He straightens up. "Then why am I here?"

"Because you brought a man named Tommy Greenlee to the Mineshaft Saturday night, where he was shot, wrapped in garbage bags, doused in bleach, and left for me and my boys to clean up."

Pitts shifts uncomfortably. He picks at a scab on his arm.

"My guess is you brought him there knowing exactly what was about to go down. You got a problem with Tommy Greenlee, Robert?" He pauses. "I wouldn't blame you. Because I do. Or did, I guess." When intrigue piques Pitts's brows, he continues, "Guy was a fucking dick."

"What'd he do to you?" asks Pitts.

Kole sets his jaw. For years, he harbored suspicions about Tommy Greenlee. That he was a drunk. A coward. And that he was, at the very least, verbally and emotionally abusive to Hazel; sometimes, it's that specific brand of violence that proves the most fatal—not a single wound, but a thousand slow-turning screws that destroy a person from the inside out. The simple fact that Hazel is back in Black Harbor, after she worked so hard to escape, is proof enough that she's got a screw loose.

While he isn't a therapist or a psychoanalyst, he recognizes behaviors in her that he's witnessed in victims of violent or sexual abuse. Compulsions, like the way she mime-types conversations on her lap or under the table when she thinks no one's watching. Suicidal ideation, because why else would a person continuously visit Forge Bridge? And not to mention her affinity for leaping to irrational conclusions about people who care about her. He didn't want to see them before, but he can't not see them now. Truth be told, the more he learns about Tommy Greenlee, the less he gives a fuck about the fact that he met such an untimely end. What matters to him isn't getting justice for Tommy, but getting to the bottom of who is using Xombie to raze Black Harbor to the ground, one overdose at a time.

"It isn't about what he did to me," Kole clarifies. "But to someone I—" Loved? "—knew. I can only imagine he was as much of a prick to you."

A long, lurid trail of blood trickles from the hole in Pitt's arm where he picked off the scab.

"Why did you bring Greenlee to the Mineshaft, Robert?"

"I didn't."

"Don't fucking lie. There's video footage of you walking in with him." The statement in and of itself is a lie, but Pitts doesn't know that. He makes a futile attempt to wipe the blood off his arm and gets it all over his hands, which he scrapes against the edge of the table.

Kole retrieves something Pitts told him beneath the bridge. "Everyone's got a boss, even the boss, isn't that right? Is Darren Hogan your boss? I know he was there with you."

Pitts snorts, insulted. "No. He ain't my boss."

"Who, then? Or did you act alone? I'm asking because, as I'm sure you're aware, premeditated murder and party-to carry very different charges."

Pitts goes quiet but for his knee bouncing and hitting the leg of the table.

"Look." Kole tries a new tactic. "Unfortunately, you're not unique, Robert. I know—or *knew*, I should say—a lot of guys like you. Guys who fell on hard times. Guys who lost their way and ended up in a place like this." He gestures vaguely to the interview room. "Unfortunately for *me*, we're not so different."

"We're not?" Pitts furrows his brows.

"I'm here in this godforsaken city, aren't I?"

Pitts nods.

"Can I ask you something?"

Pitts drags his gaze to meet Kole's and waits.

"You have family?"

"No."

"Me neither." Kole sighs. "But you must have once, right? So, what was it like for you, when you woke up one day and realized everyone you ever cared about was gone?" When Pitts says nothing, Kole undoes the clasp of the manila envelope and withdraws a single 4x6 photograph that features two young boys—one dark-haired and one blond. They're wearing matching windbreakers with their arms around each other, toothless smiles beaming at the camera.

Kole taps the picture as though pinning the dark-haired child to the table. "Do you recognize him?"

Pitts stares dumbly at it. His mouth hangs slack, a stalactite of drool clinging to his bottom lip. His brows knit as he undoubtedly tries to make sense of how he knows these children. Kole extracts a second photo, this one a professional portrait of a police officer wearing a black dress uniform and an eight-point cap. He slides it across the table toward Pitts, who sucks in his cheeks.

"How about him?"

Pitts is actively avoiding his gaze now, which compels Kole to reach into the envelope for a third photograph. As he does, he can't help feeling like a blackjack dealer, with Pitts being the poor bastard who doesn't know when to quit. The final photo is an 8x10, printed on computer paper. It features the same man who wore the police uniform, who was once the dark-haired boy in the windbreaker, washed up on the riverbank. His skin is pallid, his eyes open and blind, mouth frozen open in a silent plea for mercy he wouldn't receive, the name of his killer trapped on the tip of his tongue. Kole taps the photo, spinning his thumb and forefinger enough so Pitts can see what it is he's using to do the tapping: a purple capsule with CXF monogrammed on the seam.

Carfentanil. Xylazine. Fentanyl.

Better known as Xombie.

Pitts was peddling it until he got hooked on the shit himself. And judging by the state of him, he hasn't had any in—Kole considers the clock—ten to twelve hours. As if the pill has its own gravitational pull, Pitts leans forward.

Kole taps the photo again. "Tell me why we're here, Robert. Who is this?"

Pitts shakes his head, his eyes never leaving the pill. Kole gives him a moment, then he reaches into the envelope for its final content. He places the scratch-off next to the photo of his brother's corpse.

Suddenly, a violent shudder courses through Pitts. Both his knees start jerking as he bounces on the balls of his feet. His skin turns an even sicklier shade of green, and Kole notes how his fingertips dig into the spaces between his ribs. The withdrawal is worsening. In a matter of hours, maybe less, he'll just be a pool of jelly on the floor. Which is fine, but Kole needs him at least minimally cognizant if he's going to get a confession out of him.

Kole leans in, breaking any semblance of personal space. "Why are we here, Robert? Don't make me ask again." He counts silently to ten, then throws an openhanded strike across Pitts's face. Pitts crumples to the floor. He bangs his shin on the way down and lets out a long, pathetic whine.

"Get up," says Kole.

Pitts doesn't move.

Kole grabs the second photo and plants one foot on either side of Pitts. "What's his fucking name?"

Pitts rolls his knees from side to side, his hands cradling his skull, and mutters something unintelligible.

Kole leans down and gets in his face. "What's. His. Na—"

"Evan!" yells Pitts. "Evan Kole!"

Kole steps back and resumes his seat. "Get up or you won't be getting up again." When Pitts doesn't move, however, Kole shouts: "Get the fuck up!"

For once, Pitts does as he's told and crawls back into his chair.

Kole pauses for a beat to compose himself, and then: "Because of you, I know how it feels to be completely alone. To wake up and discover that everyone you ever loved is gone. That they left you. And you know what? That feeling you awoke to becomes what keeps you up at night. It's like . . . living with this black hole inside of you . . . swallowing up every happy thing, every atom of joy." The words catch in his throat. He's never tried explaining it before, and while he'd planned on fake-sympathizing with Pitts, he hadn't planned on sharing his intimate thoughts. "Because of you, Robert, I know what it's like to have nobody. My parents died young. I wasn't close with my aunts or uncles—as if any of them would come within a hundred miles of this place. I mean, look at what it does to people." He gestures openhandedly at Pitts, who flinches, apparently expecting to be hit again. "Evan was all I had. When he jumped off that bridge, I couldn't accept it, I guess, that he was gone. That he had left me here, all alone. I was desperate not to believe it, so for nine fucking years, I searched for a reason, a scrap of evidence that could make a case for his death being anything but suicide. I can count on one hand the number of cases I've failed to solve, and this one takes the cake. Finally, I had to resign myself to the fact that Evan took his own life. That he left me. Until now." He taps the pill against the faded ticket. "Why did you kill my brother, Robert?"

Silence.

"You pushed him off the bridge."

A film of sweat shines on Pitts's forehead. The pulse in his neck races. His tongue looks like a piece of gum that he's about to choke on, when he says: "I didn't."

In a flash, Kole slaps him again. "You were his informant and you fucking betrayed him!"

Pitts is wooden. Then he turns his head to the left and spits a gob of marbled phlegm on the floor. "I did him a fucking favor."

"Fuck you."

A crackling sound comes up out of Pitts's throat as he laughs. "I've been shooting up and popping pills since I was fourteen. You think I don't recognize a user when I see one? He would'a ended up below that bridge one way or another."

The statement is a punch to Kole's stomach. He goes quiet, remembering the Ziploc of prescription pills his sister-in-law brought to him after Evan's funeral, and bites the inside of his cheek until his mouth fills with the taste of blood. He sighs. "Let me make one thing clear to you, shit bird. You're not under arrest for the murder of Tommy Greenlee. Yet. You are, however, under arrest for the murder of Evan Kole. That is, unless you can tell me who put you up to it. Because I have reason to believe that it was the same person who put you up to bringing Greenlee to the Mineshaft Saturday night."

Pitts is contemplative as he picks at more pockmarks on his arms. His breathing becomes more rapid and finally, he says: "It was him or me."

Kole leans back. "You might as well tell me everything. Because right now, I am the only thing keeping you alive. As soon as you walk out there"—he jabs a thumb over his shoulder at the door—"they'll rip you limb from limb. Same as the officers in the jail. You won't last for a second on the streets, either. You're a cop killer and a snitch. So, as fucked up as it is, I'm the best friend you've got."

Pitts turns to look over each shoulder, as though paranoid someone will sneak up on him. He stops then, his gaze fixed on the two-way mirror.

"There's no one back there," assures Kole. "You think I'd slap you around like this if there was?" When Pitts is quiet, Kole taps the Xombie on the table again. "Here's the thing, Robert. I don't think you're an evil person. You remember how I admitted that, unfortunately for both of us, we're not all that different. I think, at the end of the day, we're both just doing our best to survive and sometimes we fuck things up. I've had plenty of fuckups, one of them as recent as this morning when I yanked you out of your tent. I'm sorry for that, by the way." He isn't. "And like I was saying, I think you either got in over your head, or maybe you were just at the wrong place at the wrong time. It happens." He swallows a surge of vomit. Being nice to Pitts is making him physically ill. "Walk me through what went down. Nine years ago, you were Evan's confidential informant, correct?"

Pitts hangs his head. His dark, greasy hair is lank and thin. When he meets Kole's gaze again, his eyes are bleary and bloodshot. "He said it could count as my initiation."

"Who did?"

"Buddha."

The name is a syringe of saline down Kole's spine. Suspecting it is one thing, confirmation is another. He feels hyperfocused as he withdraws into himself, his mind piecing together the clues—the kilos stamped with what Dirty Harriet recognized as Buddha's imprint and the fact that Evan was conducting controlled purchases off of him around the time of his death.

"He found out I was snitchin' on him. So, he ordered me to kill Evan otherwise he'd kill me. It was pretty straightforward. Make it look like a suicide and leave the ticket with him."

"And that was your initiation. For what?"

"The Mineshaft."

Kole's mouth goes dry as he recalls the rumors about there being only one way in and out of the club: kill or be killed. Robert Pitts is a known member of the Mineshaft. And he murdered Evan Kole to get in.

"Which is where you brought Tommy Greenlee," says Kole, stitching it all together.

For the first time, Pitts doesn't argue with him.

"Nine years ago, Buddha told you he was on the come-up and that he'd bring you with him, is that right?"

"He was planning to take down Hades, but you beat him to it."

Kole blows out a breath. This will never not haunt him now. He arrested Hades and things fell to shit. That's typical of Black Harbor. Things have to get worse before they can get . . . worse. Pitts is goading him; he refuses to feed into it.

"Did you know Harriet was a CI?"

Pitts runs his tongue over his discolored teeth. "I figured that out, yeah."

"That why you ghosted her? Lying low 'cause you fucked up with the boss, yeah? But then Harriet called you up and said she had a couple kilos to get rid of. Those were your kilos, weren't they, Robert?" He knows what happened now. It tracks back to one of their earlier theories that Tommy and Cameron intercepted a drop-off. He'd bet any money Pitts was the pickup guy. "How many kilos did she claim to have?"

"Two."

"But you knew you were supposed to pick up three."

A shrug. "That's what she said. Boss said there were three, but I figured two was all they scooped outta the water. I went back and looked myself, to see if one washed up on shore or got stuck in a pier maybe.

Nearly drowned. Fuckin' riptide." He scowls as if the undertow is here in the interview room.

"But you found nothing." Because the third kilo was hidden in a deer head—right where Dirty Harriet had stashed it. "I bet Buddha was pissed, yeah? When you lost his shipment. So you figured bringing him back two kilos was better than nothing. Then what happened?"

"I called up Buddha, told him I had his dope. He said to bring Greenlee to the Mineshaft and we'd make things right."

"And when Greenlee only gave him two kilos?"

"He was mad pissed. Got him good and drunk, followed him to the bathroom then, and popped his dome. Then he turned on me and D, said we better find that third kilo or pay him for it. We searched Greenlee's place to see what we could steal. Harriet said he had a lotta guns. But someone beat us to the punch."

Kole pauses. His whole body seems to glitch for a second as he registers this new information. "You didn't steal Tommy's guns?"

Pitts shakes his head.

"Who else would have taken them?"

"I don't know, man, maybe Harriet? She set this whole thing up."

Jesus Christ. Kole tries to maintain his composure. He can't let Pitts know what a hopeless turn their investigation has taken on the stolen-guns front. Making a mental note to catch up with Fletcher after this, he taps the scratch-off ticket. "What do these numbers mean?"

"I got no idea."

"Bullshit."

"I got no fucking idea!" Pitts screams. Spit flies from his mouth, thankfully not spraying Kole's face this time. His whole body breaks out in tremors. He flings his head back, gritting his teeth so hard they creak as the internal warfare of withdrawal rages.

Kole couldn't care less. Five nights ago, Robert Pitts lured Tommy Greenlee to the slaughter, at a place he only had clearance to enter because nine years ago, he'd murdered his brother.

Evan didn't die by suicide.

Kole always imagined this moment would hit differently. That he would feel some sort of relief when he finally proved what he's been trying to prove for the better part of a decade.

His brother hadn't chosen to leave. He was taken.

And yet, a new weight crushes him. How is it that something as empty as grief can feel so heavy? "Where's Buddha now?" he manages. "Better yet, who is he? You might as well tell me, because I don't believe for a second that you take orders from him and you've never seen his face."

Pitts sucks his cheeks in so hard, he looks like a skeleton. Is he holding his breath, trying to make himself pass out so he'll be spared from answering?

"You're a snitch, Robert," Kole reminds him. "Start snitchin'."

Pitts has pulled his knees into his chest and he rocks back and forth on the chair. "You gotta help me, man. I can't go through this shit. He'll kill me if I tell. He'll kill me!"

"Who's gonna kill you? If you don't tell me, I don't know who to protect you from."

"Please!" shouts Pitts, singularly focused on the purple pill. "Just give me the Xombie! He's gonna kill me!"

Kole erupts. His chair crashes to the floor and he slams his hands on the table. "Who. The fuck. Is Buddha!"

Tears stream down Pitts's face. "I can't tell you, man. I can't. But I'll tell you what. He's dead if he don't find that dope. The cost a living's gotten too high."

"What are you talking about? The cost of living?"

"The cost a living, man. It's too high. We're all too fuckin' broke to stay alive."

Kole's not in the mood for riddles. He'll let Pitts detox and talk to him again later. He slides the first two photos and the scratch-off back into the manila envelope, leaving the third one on the table. He drops the pill inside, too, when Pitts lunges at him, snarling and dragging his jagged nails down Kole's arm. Kole elbows him in the face; pain ignites in his tricep as Pitts's teeth clamp down. Kole pivots and sinks a punch into Pitts's face and drops him. Before Pitts can get up, Kole kneels on his back to immobilize him and begins to lock the handcuffs around his wrists as he states from memory: "Robert Pitts, you are under arrest for the murder of Evan Kole. You have the right to remain silent—"

"Please!" shouts Pitts. "I don't know his real name!"

"Anything you say can and will be used against you in a court of law—"

"Seriously! If I fucking knew I'd tell you! Just give me the Xombie! Give me the Xombie! Give me the—"

"You have the right to an attorney. If you cannot afford an attorney, one will be provided—"

"Buddha don't know about those numbers! He's just following orders!"

"From who?" Kole replays Pitts's statement from earlier in his mind. *Even the boss has a boss*. "Hades?"

Pitts grimaces as Kole gives the cuffs one final click. "Think bigger."

37
HAZEL

I've been to the basement only once before, years ago when my coworker gave me the grand tour of the police department. The evidence room is at the bottom of the stairs, wherein two clerks catalog evidence. The door is shut and there's a handwritten sign taped to it that reads: COME BACK WITH A WARRANT. Past that, there's an old conference room that's fallen into disrepair. The floor is strewn with old wrestling mats and there are folding chairs arranged in a haphazard circle. The SWAT team stages here, Hudson explains, whenever there's a trial going on at the courthouse, or an election, or a press conference, or rumors that someone's going to shoot up a funeral.

We venture farther down another hall. There's a gym on the left with heavy bags on chains screwed into the ceiling. They hang like leaden cocoons, gashes split into the leather, their stitches all ripped and fraying. The rest of the equipment is all primordial and metal, nothing newer than the turn of the century, except, perhaps, for the treadmill.

Finally, we arrive at a door that's unmarked. Hudson inserts a key he snagged from upstairs and we're in. My jaw falls to the floor. Giant shelves loom over us, all stuffed with manila envelopes. In college, I worked part time at the campus library. This room reminds me of the stacks, endless and filled with old, disintegrating books. Except here, there's only one genre: true crime.

"At least it's organized," I say, latching on to the silver lining. Shelf markers denote the years and months.

"This was the default project for off-duty officers for a lot of years."

"To discourage people from getting hurt?"

He shrugs. "I don't know. But I'm glad we're reaping the benefits of their efforts."

"Hopefully." I wince, realizing I sound negative; Kole's critique is still ringing in my ears. But Hudson seems either to not mind or not notice. He's already meandering toward the back of the room, where the older reports have been collecting dust. I follow, stopping in front of 1973-MAY.

"Complaint number?"

I double-check the one saved in my phone and recite it. His long fingers sift through the envelopes, and I can tell he's in his element here. Paperwork. Numbers. He's a few years older than me, but if we'd been in school together, I definitely would have cheated off his math tests.

It's hard to believe he's Hades's brother. But, as he pointed out, with the people we love, we don't choose our family either.

"There!" I say abruptly, causing him to freeze.

He pulls out the corresponding envelope with the complaint number written in marker on the top right-hand corner. Upon opening it, I discover just one single sheet of paper that tells of a detective responding to the scene of a jumper at Forge Bridge on May 3, 1973. Further investigation revealed the decedent had a history of mental illness and the cause was likely suicide. No foul play suspected.

I flip the paper over. It's blank. There's no mention of a scratch-off ticket.

"Absence of evidence isn't evidence of absence," says Hudson, attempting to console me. "Just because there's no mention of a ticket doesn't mean it wasn't there. It could've been in one of her pockets, or—"

"Yeah." I can't help but feel utterly deflated. I was so sure that this was a viable lead. That this was my chance at redemption in Kole's eyes. I acted out of impulse, as I seem to have a nasty habit of doing.

That's how I ended up here. Three days ago I was in Brooklyn, banging my head against my writing desk, going to yoga, and closing down my local café. Now I'm in the basement of the Black Harbor Police Department, playing Nancy Drew and spectacularly bombing at it. I'm no closer to finding out who killed Tommy.

"You ready to get out of here? I can put the key back."

"Can I come with you?" I ask. I'm reluctant to be alone, to let my thoughts gnaw at me.

"Yeah, of course." Hudson's voice is soft, kind as he leads us out of the labyrinth of handwritten reports and back through the basement, up the three flights of stairs to the Detective Bureau.

I remember being up here twice with Kole. Once when I didn't think he knew I was up here, and once when he needed my help to transcribe an interview with a suspect in the Candy Man case. A longing stirs inside me, and I can't discern whether it's a longing for him or a longing for purpose, to be helpful once again.

The sharp slam of a door jars my attention. Next to me, Hudson drops the keys he was returning to the hook. Kole marches in our direction, as angry as I've ever seen him. Then, surprise registers on his face. He stalks toward Hudson and I'm afraid there's going to be a confrontation when he growls: "When they ask, the camera malfunctioned."

"Who's in there? Pitts?"

"Leave him," says Kole. "Patrol's on their way to transport him to the jail."

Next, Kole's gaze moves to me. "You can either stay with him or come with me."

I look apologetically at Hudson, who nods almost imperceptibly. As I open my mouth to voice my decision, I notice a bright red trail snaking down Kole's arm. My breath catches. "Nik, you're bleeding."

38
HAZEL

"Son of a bitch!" Kole clenches his jaw. The muscles in his arm spasm, steeling against the sting of the soap that I worked into a lather before applying it to his wound, a near-perfect dental mold of Robert Pitts's teeth. "What's that laced with? Ghost peppers?"

"Are you sure you don't want to go to the ER?" I ask for the third time.

Sitting on his marble countertop, he leans so far to the left that his forehead is pressed to the mirror. A cloud of fog shrinks and grows with each breath he takes. The black chain necklace hangs to the middle of his chest, the anchor pendant gently tapping against the glass. He side-eyes me, as if I'm the one who got him into this predicament.

I'm not the one who told him to conduct a solo clandestine interview of a detoxing junkie and tease information out of him with a pill. Way to wave a steak in front of a hungry dog and complain when you get bit.

"It's a huge pain in the ass," he says, making his case for why we are upstairs in his master bathroom with the killer glass shower instead of a clinic with medical professionals who didn't have to google *how to treat a human bite at home*. He tried Rowan, but she's at a scene bagging up a body. So here we are.

"Well, if you start foaming at the mouth, I'll level you."

This, at least, draws a faint smile from him. "I'd like to see you try, Podunk."

I melt a little, and a few minutes later, the wound is cleaned and dressed. "I'll send you a bill."

He snorts. "I'll take it off your tab."

"For crashing on your couch?"

"Hey, I offered my bed."

"I'm not gonna take your bed from you. Besides, I have a perfectly decent place to stay."

"Did you forget you're in Black Harbor? 'Perfectly decent' might mean something else somewhere else, but here it just means minimal roaches and maybe you won't catch a stray bullet in your wall."

"Isn't that your department? Violent crime?"

His eyes squeeze into slits, but the amusement simmering behind them tells me he enjoys the banter. "Do you know how many violent crimes happen per year in this city?"

"Enlighten me."

"Last year, there were over four hundred. Do you know how many detectives I have?"

I count, ticking off Riley, Axel, and Fletcher. "Three."

"Three," he repeats. "And I make four. We're outnumbered a hundred to one."

As much of a gut punch as the statement is, I can't help but feel a thrill at the fact that he is sharing a vulnerable moment with me. He used to tell me things. Confidential things. Things he told no one else. "Are you . . . worried?" I ask, treading carefully. The sarcasm has dissipated.

A muscle in his jaw flickers and I can tell he's biting the inside of his cheek. He does that when he's either nervous or about to lie, I've noticed. "I'm tired," he says, his voice gravelly, and I know he isn't talking about being tired at this specific moment, but overall. The years have taken their toll on him. He has less tolerance for bullshit than he used to. And yet, his eyes are the same twilight color they've always been. They search mine with a familiar intensity, for the woman I was before, maybe. The one he knew. The one who left. But he didn't really know her, did he? He knew only the part of her that loved him and the broken part that dropped mementos off the bridge.

The transcriber.

I haven't been her for a long time.

I'm a writer now, a storyteller. My words are my own, not prescribed by someone else who dictates down to the punctuation what must be said. I have sculpted and painted whole worlds with my words, and still, I am here, in this place that refuses to let me go.

Or perhaps, that I refuse to let go of.

"Hazel."

His voice is so quiet it's drowned out by the riptide of blood in my temples, one that carries all the emotions of the past eight years: love, hate, anger, guilt, loneliness, and all the ones that are too obscure to put into words. I've learned that those exist, and I've finally accepted that some feelings are only meant to be felt, not explained.

There is one, though, that clings to me like a shadow, following me no matter where I go. *Monachopsis: the subtle but persistent feeling of being out of place.*

From Black Harbor to Brooklyn and everywhere in between, I don't belong anywhere anymore, and yet, when I'm with him, I don't feel it as much. It's replaced by a different feeling, though, a deep and quiet ache that if there's a word for it, I don't know it, this feeling of missing someone who isn't gone yet.

Kole slides forward so I'm standing between his knees. His left hand comes up and he lightly presses his thumb to my cheek. "You still haven't pierced your ears."

The observation catches me by surprise. I expel a sound that's something between a laugh and a sob. Instinctively, I touch my earlobe to feel the absence of any metal, and as our hands meet again, I recall vividly the night we walked through a creepy apartment, playing Two Truths and a Lie. My lie was that I'd pierced my ears at fourteen.

He lied about being born in Pittsburgh and moving to Black Harbor when he was nine; he's lived here all his life.

"I've gone thirty-four years without," I say. "Can't ruin my record now."

"Fair enough. You know, I used to have an earring. In college." He turns his head slightly to show me where there's a small bump of scar tissue, high up on the cartilage.

"You would," I say, and he laughs.

"One of the douchier things I've done."

"You said it, not me."

"Shut up." He leans forward slightly and I feel myself being pulled into him, as if our chests are each punched through with a cable and it's drawing taut. I can feel the heat emanating from his skin. His heartbeat pulses in his neck and I want so badly to press my lips to it. In a great act of resistance, I lean away and start to pack up the first aid kit.

His left hand comes up and he touches my face again. "Hey. Where did you go?"

"I'm right here."

"No. You were here with me mentally, and then you weren't. It's like you flipped a switch."

I swallow and cast my eyes slowly from left to right, as if searching for a witness to his absurdity. "I'm right here," I say again.

He shakes his head and hops off the countertop. There's a soft screech followed by the spray of water as he turns on the shower. "Get out," he says, and gestures toward the door.

I stare at him in disbelief as he stands there, utterly unreasonable and irresistible in just a pair of dark jeans. A film of sweat makes his skin glisten, highlighting the natural contour of his abs and his collarbones.

Get out. There's nothing I want to do less.

I approach him, then slip past him into the shower, planting myself beneath the stream of hot water.

"Hazel, get out."

"Make me."

He presses his fingertips to his eyelids and massages his face. He rakes a hand through his hair, then leans with his elbow against the glass blocks. He clearly has no idea how hot he is when he's worked up.

"Look." I'm so scared of the words that are about to come out of my mouth, the ones I'll never be able to unsay, that my chest heaves. "I'm so sorry that I left. It wasn't what I wanted. But I—"

He looks up in a *Lord, save me* manner. "That's always the fucking problem, isn't it? You don't know what you want."

"I—" I stop. He's right. I don't know what I want. I thought I did. I thought I wanted to get far away from here, away from him. I thought I wanted to write books and I did. I do. But everything else, it all feels so empty, so devoid of substance without him.

"Why did you come here?" he asks. "And if you try to tell me it's to find out what happened to Tommy, I'll turn this water freezing cold."

I narrow my eyes into slits. "You wouldn't."

He reaches for the knob.

"Wait!" I shout, and immediately cringe at how overdramatic I sound. He's threatening me with a cold shower, not waterboarding.

What do I want?

It's a query I've posed a hundred times since setting foot on Black Harbor's pockmarked and pitted asphalt and now, finally, I know the answer. I want to no longer be haunted by the things I've done. I want to confront what used to scare me. I want not to run, for once in my life. I'm so goddamn tired of running. "I want you to just . . . hear me out. Please, Nik."

"I'm listening."

"I am here to find out who killed Tommy. I need to know, to be able to close that chapter of my life. But I'd be lying if I said it was the only reason I came back."

"To Black Harbor?"

"To you. And I'm sorry about not being honest with you. I was just afraid . . ." I can't finish the thought. My heart hammers in my rib cage as I wait for his response. When he shakes his head, my resolve crumbles. I feel so stupid, standing here soaking wet. This is going to be a legendary walk of shame back to the apartment.

"I don't want you to be sorry," he says after an agonizing pause. "I just want you." If there is one stark difference between us, it's the way he runs toward the unknown and I run away from it. He enters the shower then, and his mouth meets mine at the same time his hand cradles the back of my head. His kiss is deep and life-giving. I breathe him in like I've been drowning. He pushes me up against the glass wall, his body shielding me from the waterfall. I hang tightly to him, my arms encircling his neck. The kiss breaks only so he can plant a trail of them down my neck and collarbones. He peels my shirt up and I help him out. His lips brush the soft swell of my breasts. I slide my hand down, latching on to his soaked jeans, and undo the button.

My shorts are a puddle around my feet. I step out of them and turn around as he grabs my hips with both hands. When I close my eyes and let my head fall back, I feel every inch of him exploring every inch of me and I swear to God I see fireworks.

39
KOLE

Moonlight spills across the blankets. Above, the sky is a quilt of twilight speckled with rare pinpricks of stars. In an hour, maybe less, they will all be lost to the smoke of whatever cheap pyrotechnics people are lighting off at home.

Hazel sleeps soundly, nestled in the crook of his arm, while he lies hopelessly awake. In his head, a tempest of emotions rages. He is at once whole and empty; he is whole at this moment, now that she is with him, but what will happen when she leaves again and he remains alone in this vast bed in a burning city?

For also at this moment, dozens of stolen guns are making their way into the wrong hands. The Xombie addiction is taking the shape of an epidemic. And the identity of the man who's behind it all remains a mystery.

Hazel stirs. Her eyelids flutter softly and when she looks at him, he forgets all the bad bullet points that are running through his mind. Her eyes are pools of hope and peace and calm—although is it the calm that sets in after the storm, or the one that occurs just before everything goes up in flames? As soon as he even thinks the question to himself, he knows the answer.

They haven't seen the storm yet.

They haven't even seen a drop of rain.

"Hey." Her whisper slices clean through his thoughts.

"Hey," he whispers back, then leans in to kiss her, deeply, as if she is the last good thing on this earth. He feels her fingertips in his hair. She pushes against him, rising up until she has one knee pinned on either side of his rib cage. He grabs her hips and she moves freely against him, riding him like a wave and gaining momentum until finally, with a heavy exhale, she collapses into him, biting the side of his neck. It awakens something primal inside him. He tosses her over so she lies on her back, and they make love this time, perhaps for the first time, because how can you know what love is if you've never lost it before?

Afterward, they lie still, listening to the ephemeral quiet. Their limbs are tangled. Bodies spent and sweating. She is a goddess, her hair wavy and cloud-like around her.

"I'm surprised you have one of these," she says.

He rolls onto his back and matches her gaze toward the ceiling. "A skylight?"

"Yeah."

"What, you think someone's gonna break in *Mission: Impossible* style?"

"Maybe."

"Listen." He smooths a piece of hair from her face and tucks it behind her ear. "There are two things you need to know about criminals, the first of which is that most of them are dumb. They're not like the ones in the movies."

"Most," she says.

He side-eyes her. "Trust me, the Black Harbor ones are dumb."

"What's the second thing?" she asks.

"They're narcissists. They gotta put their fingerprint on everything."

"Like the rabbit stamp," she says. "On the kilo."

Yes, on the kilo, he thinks. The one Dirty Harriet apparently stashed. That dirty bitch. And yet, had she not hidden the drugs, Tommy might not have been murdered, which would mean Hazel would probably still be hiding away in Brooklyn.

He knows where she's been. He's always known. Aubrey Jeske isn't the only person on earth who can set up a dummy social media account.

He's never attempted to reach out to her, though; that's where he drew the line. He was avid at first, checking the app every couple hours to see if she posted anything new. But eventually his eagerness to see what she was up to faded, as every smile, every boomerang of clinking glasses, every photo of her dressed to the nines and reigning over New York City from a rooftop felt like a dull knife sawing an even greater distance between them.

But now, a different photo of her troubles him, one with a bullet hole punched through her forehead.

There isn't a doubt in his mind that Harriet swiped the picture from Tommy's residence, which puts her in the vicinity of the stashed drugs and stolen guns, if nothing else. He should show Hazel. She has a right to know. Leaning over the side of the bed, Kole feels blindly for his jeans when he remembers—

"Fuck."

"What?"

Instead of replying, he slides out from under the covers and walks barefoot to the bathroom, where his jeans lie in a damp and crumpled heap in the shower. His stomach flips. He feels suddenly nauseous when he searches the folds, his fingers finally pinching the photograph. It's not all the worse for wear, surprisingly. When he returns to the bed with it, Hazel is sitting up, clutching the sheet to her chest.

"What's wrong?" she asks.

He gives her the photo and watches as her expression changes from one of recognition to confusion to a tinge of fear.

"Where did you get this?" she wonders.

He tells her, then, about how he went looking for Dirty Harriet after Aubrey Jeske had brought her up in the interview. "I was gonna call her out for lying to me," he explains, "for omitting the fact that she was seeing Tommy, that she'd been at the duplex. And I was gonna press her about the kilo, see if I could get a confession out of her that she hid it."

"Did any of that happen?" asks Hazel.

His shoulders sag with disappointment. "No. She wasn't home."

"So you just let yourself in."

"The door was open," he lies.

If she doesn't believe him, she doesn't show it. Instead, she sighs and sets the photo on top of the blankets between them. "Tell me you hate me without telling me you hate me," she says, and he knows she's referring to the bullet hole. "So Harriet wants to off me?"

Kole shrugs. "It was on her vision board, so . . . I'd say that's a pretty strong indicator."

"She can get in line, I guess."

Kole opens his arms. She falls into them and lies with her head against his chest. Holding her, he crisscrosses his arms over her, as if this is enough to keep her safe, and kisses the top of her head. He checks the clock on the nightstand. It's 9:06 P.M. God, it seems so much later than that. In less than twelve hours, he'll meet face-to-face with Hades again.

"That interview with Robert Pitts." Hazel changes the subject. "Did you get anything out of him? Besides a Xombie bite?"

"He killed my brother." Saying it out loud takes something from him. He imagines a jigsaw-shaped hole in his chest. Hazel is silent, waiting, then listening as he tells her everything he learned, starting with the fact that, nine years ago, Robert Pitts was Evan's confidential informant. "It's very easy to get comfortable with your CIs," he admits. "I've ridden around with plenty of them in my day, never really thinking twice about getting stabbed in the back. But Evan was mixed up in some bad shit."

"What do you mean?" Slowly, she untangles herself from his embrace and they lie facing each other again.

He takes a breath, readying himself for something he's never told anyone else. "He was addicted to opiates. Oxys . . . Vicodin, shit like that. He hurt his back once at a SWAT warrant and was never the same afterward. I guess I just didn't know how badly it affected him." A familiar feeling surges through him, uninvited. It's one he's tamped down for years, refusing to acknowledge it when he realized how all it ever did was prohibit him from moving forward with his life. Guilt. Sometimes he swears it weighs heavily enough on him to put him in an early grave.

"It's not your fault, though," she says. "If he hid it from you, how could you have known?"

He stifles a self-deprecating laugh. "I'm a detective. I should have found out on my own."

"So was he. You don't think he knew how to cover it up?"

Kole sighs. The point she's making is one he's argued to himself before. Nonetheless, he should have figured it out.

"So . . ." Hazel continues when he stays silent. "Did Pitts tell you how it went down? Or why?"

"He said it was an initiation," Kole explains, and goes on to share what Pitts told him: that Buddha found out about Pitts being an informant and commanded him to kill Evan. Now a killer, Pitts was in the club.

"The club, as in the Mineshaft?" asks Hazel.

"Correct. Think of it as like a 'gool' where all the bad guys in Black Harbor hang out."

"And you think Tommy was there because he was selling those two kilos of Xombie so he and Aubrey Jeske could split the money?"

"Correct."

"To who? This Buddha guy?"

"You're three for three. I think what he failed to consider was that the drugs belonged to Buddha in the first place."

"And we don't know who Buddha is yet."

"Not yet." He grinds his teeth over that one. While Buddha's identity has been a mystery for years, he's managed to crawl under the radar just enough to evade a targeted investigation. Presumed to be a low-level drug dealer; those guys are a dime a dozen around here. "Anyway, Buddha and Pitts fucked Tommy over big-time. Pitts told Tommy to come to the Mineshaft and bring the drugs there, where they would do the exchange. Tommy did, but he was shorthanded. Whether that missing kilo was the difference between life and death . . . I think they would have killed him anyway."

Hazel's eyes are wet. He slides up toward her and catches a teardrop before it falls. "Hey, I'm sorry, okay? I know this is hard. You loved him, at least at one point in time."

She slumps down into the pillows and turns her body into him so she cries into his shoulder. He holds her as her whole body shakes. "It's not your fault," he whispers into her ear, echoing the sentiment she told him a few minutes ago. "You weren't even here. And you know what?"

he adds when the thought strikes him. "I'm glad you weren't. I'm glad you were elsewhere, living it up and writing and whatever it is you've been doing, because it means you're on this side of things. With me." Suddenly, a grotesque image of her body on the floor instead of Tommy's in that nasty bathroom flashes in his mind, and he holds her tighter. "I'm glad it was him instead of you. I can't fathom—" He can't even bring himself to say it. If it was Hazel lying on that floor, riddled with bullet holes and decomposing . . . he would never forgive himself for letting it happen.

She presses her mouth to his to spare him from having to finish his sentence. He closes his eyes, feeling himself give in again when somewhere in the dark, his phone trills. Kole answers.

"Where's Hazel?" It's Hudson. He sounds on edge.

"She's . . ." Kole locks eyes with her. "With me."

"Okay, good. I'm coming over."

40
HAZEL

Twenty minutes later, I'm on the couch with Rocket's head nestled on my knees when an SUV pulls whisper-quiet into the driveway.

"That's him," says Kole, getting up from his recliner to let Hudson in.

"Hey, Rocket. Hey, Hazel." The nonchalance of Hudson's voice is comforting, as if we've known each other for ages and him traipsing through Kole's living room toting a stack of manila envelopes is a weekly thing. Maybe it is, but I doubt it. Kole seems too private a person to have company over on the regular.

I follow Hudson to the breakfast nook, where he sets down the envelopes. Touching the edge of one, I ask: "Are these—"

"Police reports. Spanning from April 1962 to August 1997. I left out the winter months because, well, I'll explain in a minute."

"Because first you're going to explain what they're doing in my house?" Kole's stare is dead and deadly. He wears the rueful expression of a man who has only recently cracked open the door to his domain, and is now very much regretting all the things that come with that.

Standing proudly next to his leaning pile of paperwork, Hudson looks like a kid presenting a science project. "When you two left, I had an idea. We know, now, that 05373 doesn't seem to be a date. At least, not one on which any criminal incident happened. But what else does it look like?"

Kole exhales. "Ryan, if I knew, you think I'd still be scratching my head over it after nine years?"

"That's your own fault. You could have said something. I would have helped you."

"I know." A look of reverence passes over Kole's face. They've been through some shit together, I can tell.

What do the numbers look like, if not a date? Returning to Hudson's question, my eyes scan the handwritten numbers on the envelopes. The first two digits all denote the corresponding year, i.e., 62, 63, 95, etc., while the last five are all the same: 05373. "A complaint number." I can hear a spark of elation in my own voice as the pieces start falling into place. If the numbers on the scratch-off tickets are derived from a complaint number, then in theory, if we can find the correct report, it should lead us to whoever's behind the murders.

"Right," says Hudson, pointing in my direction.

Kole leans over the table and sifts through the envelopes, homing in on the numbers as I did. After a few seconds, he shakes his head. "These reports are all from before 1998. What makes you so sure that the connection we're looking for happened that long ago?"

"Nothing," says Hudson. He consults his messenger bag and takes out a laptop, which he unfolds and places on the table next to me. "I figured Hazel can start with the ones in Onyx and you and I will go through the handwritten ones. So, start reading."

Kole narrows his eyes, nevertheless sliding onto the bench and grabbing the first envelope from the top of the stack. He looks uncomfortable, as if this is the first time he's taken orders from a subordinate, in his own house, of all places. I slide in next to him and wait for Hudson to log me in to the computer. Onyx is already open. I pull the laptop toward me and type "05373" into the search bar. Within seconds, rows of complaint numbers populate.

24–05373	THEFT
23–05373	ASSAULT
22–05373	FRAUD
21–05373	THEFT
20–05373	HOMICIDE
19–05373	SHOTS FIRED

I click on the bottom-most one and, following Hudson's directives, I start to read. We work diligently for the next hour, during which time, Rocket meanders to his bed, lying next to it instead of on it. From the corner of my eye, I watch Kole skim each report line by line. Across from me, Hudson does the same.

I click in and out of reports. I've got almost thirty complaint numbers to get through, from 1998 to present day. There are most often multiple reports housed under each complaint number, however, not including all the attachments—photographs, evidence logs, and anything police considered noteworthy for the purpose of each individual incident.

Click, skim, close.

Click, skim, close.

It takes me back to my college days, whenever I was cramming for an exam, albeit the subject matter here is far more compelling. But with Onyx open and all the information I could want about Tommy's murder at my fingertips, I start to itch. I turn slightly away from Kole, trying to maintain a cool indifference to the task at hand, and click into the search bar. Reaching into my memory, I open a new tab and type in the complaint number Kole rattled off over the phone, on the way from Cam's house: 24–07185.

There are more than a dozen reports. Scrolling down the list, I can see the evolution of the call-for-service code, from NOISE1 to DOA to HOM.

I know other crime-ridden places exist, but I swear, Black Harbor seems to have an exceptional talent for incidents as benign as a loud noise complaint transmogrifying into a homicide investigation.

The incident report is brief and doesn't delve into much detail. Such is their nature. It's written by a patrolman whose name I don't recognize, and provides a one-page account of officers arriving at the Mineshaft, located at 802 Heeley Avenue, in response to a loud music complaint. The officer ends the report with a remark about the establishment being locked and the need for a supervisor.

Every entry thereafter is a supplemental report. These are where the meat of the investigation lies, the gory details that lay out all the clues for what might've happened. They're written by a mix of patrol officers and detectives who were on-scene. There are names I know: Inv. Riley, Inv. Winthorp, Inv. Fletcher, Sgt. Kole. Lifting my gaze to ensure neither Kole nor Hudson detect my suspicious activity, I open Kole's report.

> *On June 30, I, Sergeant Kole, arrived at The Mineshaft, an "afterset" located at 802 Heeley Avenue, in response to a DOA. Upon my arrival, patrol officers informed me that the body was in the back of the establishment, in the bathroom, and that it was wrapped in black trash bags.*

My stomach tightens. I'd heard about the garbage bags on the news and yet, somehow, reading about this detail in Kole's report makes it feel all the more real. Why shoot someone and wrap the body in garbage bags only to leave it at the scene of the crime?

The answer is as clear to me as if it's flashing on my screen. They got spooked.

I return to the report, reading through Kole's description of the place. He has a way of drawing you in, always selecting just the right details to not only paint the scene, but create an immersive experience: the hundreds of red Solo cups, the sticky floor, the death haze that suffocates and tells the tale of expedited decomposition.

As I read, I imagine my fingers flying across the keyboard as they would have back when I was a transcriber, capturing every word, every letter, every punctuation point. I imagine hearing Kole's voice as he shares this confidential story with me over a headset, all the gnarly details of my ex-husband's murder, and I feel . . .

Nothing.

Not in the sense that I don't care; rather, it's the opposite. Every emotion I've ever felt is colliding, rendering me incapable of sensation. Just . . . numb.

I force myself to keep reading—this narrative that feels as if he wrote it just for me—even as he describes arriving at the back of the establishment, where ME Winthorp has already begun her examination of the scene. When he drags the knife through the plastic to reveal the victim's face, he makes no indication that he recognizes him, instead, stating:

> *The victim, later identified as THOMAS GREENLEE, appears to have sustained five to seven bullet wounds in his upper torso and head area. See photo log for exact locations.*

Scanning through the rest of the report that ends with *Investigation to continue*, I click the little *x* in the right-hand corner and find the photo log.

Do I dare? My breath hitches as the cursor hovers over the first photograph, labeled MINESHAFT-EXT_1. The injuries Kole mentioned are likely in the photos labeled GREENLEE. I feel faint, knowing I'm going to look at every single one of these photos and that whatever I see cannot be unseen.

It might be exactly what I need, though. Photographic evidence of my ex-husband's death could be the missing element to me finally letting go of the fear I've carried with me, the dreaded theory that freedom is only temporary and the certainty that, one day, he will come to drag me back to Black Harbor, just like he did a decade ago when neither of us knew any better.

He succeeded. His death brought me back here one last time, didn't it? I'm here, digging into the why behind his murder, searching for his killer, and wondering, with a shot of anxiety, what will happen when we find him.

Or her.

According to Robert Pitts, it was Buddha who pulled the trigger, Pitts who lured him to the Mineshaft, and Dirty Harriet who set the whole thing in motion. But there was another player—Kole and Hudson seem sure of it.

My fingers work faster than my brain, clicking in and out of attachments. I open the photo log and observe the exterior of the building, with its faded awning and vertical sign that spells out THE MINESHAFT. Ribbons of yellow caution tape warn of the disturbance inside and plastic placards mark possible evidence. There are shoddy pool tables. Dartboards. A cow skull hung crooked on the wall near shelves full of liquor bottles. My heart is a hummingbird as I click click click, suddenly stopping on a photo of a letterboard.

> ## THE MINESHAFT—H0U53 RU43$
> NO
> HANDS ON MY MF DOORS
> FIGHTING IN MY MF HOU$E
> GLASS BOTTLES
> WEAPONS
> PICTURES
> COPS
>
> WHEN THE HOU$E IS TALKING SHUT THE F%CK UP!
> OBEY OR GET YOUR A$$BEAT!

My eyebrows knit as I read the rules over and over. Then, before I can compose myself, I draw in a sharp breath as a revelation strikes me.

Hudson and Kole both snap to attention. Kole frowns when he sees what I've gotten into. "Hazel, don't—"

I zoom in, ignoring him, and with a shaking finger, I point to the top of the board.

H0U53 RU73$

"House rules," I breathe.

"Yeah, we can read," says Kole.

"No." I point at the *O* which is actually a *0*, then the *S* which is a 5. The *E* is a backward *3*, the *L* an upside-down *7*. Another backward *E* rounds it out to reveal our most sought-after clue.

"05373," says Hudson. Only when I look up to find him pinching a single sheet of paper between his fingers do I realize he isn't referring to the letterboard. Under the table, I nudge Kole's foot with mine.

He looks up, knitting his brows in concern. "You got something there, Ryan?"

Hudson doesn't speak. He just passes the paper to Kole. I lean over and start scanning the document.

The case number is 94–05373. A jumper, judging by the DOA code and the address that pertains to Forge Bridge.

The victim is identified as Tobias Shannon.

41

KOLE

When someone jumps off Forge Bridge, they become one of two types of bodies: floaters or drifters. Floaters stay stranded in the middle of the river, usually because they're caught by a current or because their clothing snags on something that's been discarded; that's how police found all those stolen bikes last spring. Drifters wash up on the banks.

Tobias Shannon was a drifter.

This report is from thirty years ago, which means that the thirty-seven-year-old jumper must have been Hudson's and Hades's father.

Years ago, when Hudson first applied at the BHPD, it was Kole who conducted his background investigation. Later, Kole would supervise him in the bureau, and while working a cold case together, the fact that Ryan Hudson is the full-blood brother of Tobias Shannon, aka Hades, would come to light. He adopted his mother's maiden name. Kole doesn't fault him for it. He might have done the same if he had a family like that—a brother who tried to drown him and a deadbeat drug-dealer dad who took the coward's way out of this world.

Unless he didn't.

Kole searches the narrative for any mention of a scratch-off ticket. When he doesn't find one, he lays the paper down in the middle of the table. "I'm sorry, Ryan."

Hudson exhales and Kole watches the silver glimmer of hope in his eyes, faint as it was, dim. "Don't be," he says.

His disappointment is two-fold, Kole knows. Not only would a scratch-off ticket have been another lead—perhaps a starting point, even—the fact that his father didn't have one means he more than likely died by his own volition. Kole's gaze drifts to the report again, where the words NO SIGNS OF FOUL PLAY stare back at him, and he cannot help but compare their situations. Here they both sit, each of them invisibly tethered to a jumper. Except, Evan didn't jump by choice. Tobias Shannon did. He doesn't have to imagine what it feels like to sit with that knowledge. He spent years accepting the fact that Evan willingly left this world, and while he presumes Hudson has done the same—for even longer, as he would have been ten years old when his dad jumped off the bridge—he also knows that, until you're presented with indisputable evidence, there's always a *what if* gnawing at your brain stem.

What if it was an accident?

What if he changed his mind and it was too late?

What if . . . what if . . . what if . . .

"What did you tell me about criminals earlier?" Hazel's voice pulls him out of the dark confines of his own head.

"They're dumb."

"Not that. The other thing."

"They're narcissists."

She points to the image of the letterboard still on the computer screen. "They've always gotta put their fingerprint on everything."

He sees where she's going with this, and while he loves a connection as much as the next person, this is typical Hazel; if given the chance, she would find a way to connect everything in this room. She proved that earlier today when she accused him of killing Tommy to lure her back here, simply on the basis that he'd kept a shred of her manuscript. All he'd wanted was a memento that served as a glimpse into that beautiful, tenebrous mind, evidence that the two of them had existed together, if only for a short time. And she wanted to crucify him for it.

"Let's not get ahead of ourselves," he cautions. "I know you're seeing that the complaint number of Hades and Hudson's dad jumping from Forge Bridge matches the numbers on the scratch-off tickets, but it doesn't necessarily mean something. That jumper report you guys dug up from May 3, 1973, had fuck all to do with any of this." As soon as he plays his voice back to himself, he instantly feels bad for the tone he's taken with her, as if she's one of his detectives. She hasn't built up a callus for being under this kind of pressure. Still, she is harder than she used to be, more guarded. She cuts her chin and sits stiffly. Her eyes find refuge in Hudson across the table.

"It's not nothing, though," says Hudson. "Shannon not having a scratch-off ticket doesn't necessarily rule him out as being the . . . inspiration . . . behind what's going on here."

Kole does the math as he thinks back on what Robert Pitts said about Buddha ordering him to kill Evan for initiation into the Mineshaft. It doesn't add up. If the scratch-off tickets are connected to both Hadeses—he considers the DOA report—and Big House—he considers the H0U53 RU£3$ sign—then why would Buddha have given the order for Pitts to kill Evan?

The answer drops into his head as whole as an egg.

Buddha didn't give the order. Hades did.

Hades was top dog before Buddha. Mainly because he held the exclusive contract with Big House and the Mineshaft. He steals a glance at Hazel, as he realizes why she brought up the whole fingerprint thing: if Hades and Big House were business partners, more or less—one managing the drug trade and the other harboring a den of Black Harbor's most violent criminals—it stands to reason that Hades hid his numbers in that sign.

Because he's a narcissist.

And to show that even Big House's turf was part of Hades's playing field.

Kole's investigative mind goes to work, piecing together everything he remembers of his brother's final days, weeks, months, and it all seems to point to the fact that Evan hadn't just been looking into Buddha; he must have been looking into Hades, too. While he might have started out digging into Buddha for selling dope, his investigation would have inevitably led him to uncovering Hades and his partnership with Big House.

He wonders if Evan ever figured out Buddha's identity. What secrets did he take to his watery grave?

"Buddha's got the Xombie hookup," he says. The more he plays the statement back to himself, the more sure of it he becomes. "That's the only reason he's alive and why he's been able to rise to a position of power." He grabs the salt-and-pepper shakers and sets them on top of their paperwork. "Buddha." He taps the salt. "And Big House." He taps the pepper. He sets them about six inches apart. "Ten years or so ago, these guys were on a level playing field. Big House owns the Mineshaft, where all the Black Harbor baddies have started hanging out. Buddha's among them, but he's just a dealer."

"Neither of them is in power at this point?" offers Hudson, following along.

"Correct," confirms Kole, "because they both work under the umbrella of"—he sets his phone on the table, forming a triangle—"Hades."

Hudson's gaze is fixed on the pieces, as if he's locked in an intense game of chess.

"Hades is . . . the lord of the underworld, if you will," narrates Kole. "He's calling all the shots. Until four years ago, when I locked his ass up. But before that, while Hades was in power, Evan must have gotten a wild hare or maybe was tipped off by a CI to start looking into Buddha for selling dope. He employs Robert Pitts as his CI, who gets caught while conducting a controlled purchase. Hades catches wind of all this, and he's pissed, because if Buddha goes down, Hades does, too, which means he'd lose his contract with the Mineshaft, and therefore, his position of power. He gives Buddha a scratch-off ticket, which is clearly some sort of ritual or ceremonious thing, and orders him to get rid of Evan. But Buddha's a little smarter than the average mope. He finds Pitts and decides to make him loyal. He passes the scratch-off on to him along with the order to kill Evan, which he does. Fast-forward a few years, Hades gets arrested . . . by yours truly." He drags his phone away. "Now Buddha's got the contract and it's him and Big House running the show."

"An equal partnership," offers Hudson.

But Kole shakes his head. "No. Because while Buddha might control the drugs"—he slides the pepper shaker above the salt shaker—"Big House controls all the crime. He's the shot caller now. And the Mineshaft is a mecca of malintent."

"And the scratch-off tickets?" Hudson asks. "There's no way Hades could have left them with Tommy and Cam. He was locked up, as you said."

"I have two thoughts on that," prefaces Kole. "Hades has loyal followers. He could have orchestrated those murders from inside. Or . . . old habits die hard. I'd say these scratch-offs are vestiges of a tradition long upheld, one of the longest-running, best-kept secrets of Black Harbor. Why do away with it?"

All falls quiet. Even Rocket seems to give this moment its deserved silence as the vile contents of Black Harbor are spilled out onto the kitchen table.

Kole glances at Hudson, who seems far away, and he knows that as different as they both are, they will forever be bonded by the fact that they each have a brother who Black Harbor turned for the worse. Except Hudson's is still alive.

Only because his brother gave the order to kill Kole's.

Hades might as well have pushed Evan off the bridge himself.

It will be a miracle if Kole doesn't wring his neck tomorrow morning.

THURSDAY, JULY 4

42
HAZEL

"The truth conquers all and yet . . . everybody lies."

Hudson went home about an hour ago. Now Kole and I are upstairs in his bed, our faces inches apart. Moonlight knifes through a gap in the curtains. I lift the black chain that loops around Kole's neck and disappears into the dark, liminal space that exists between his body and the mattress. Holding the anchor-shaped lavaliere, my thumb traces the engraved words: VINCIT OMNIA VERITAS.

I've never seen him not wear it.

"You learned Latin?"

I feel my mouth curve. "I looked it up." The truth is, this anchor and this phrase have been burned into my memory since the first time we lay like this, in a sketchy hotel, listening to the shushing of traffic on the interstate. Finally, I'd solved the mystery of what hung from that black chain. Since then, I have displaced my disappointment on this pendant, blaming it for the reason he stays in a city that's capsizing. But, as much as anchors are symbols of stability, they also go where you go.

He doesn't leave because he doesn't want to.

And I can't stay. At least, that's what I spent years convincing myself, and when all was said and done, it turned out that I can't stay away.

"What does it mean, though?" I ask.

He peeks at me from beneath one eyelid. "It means the truth isn't always what you want it to be. It just is what it is. Either you bend to its power, or you break."

"But it will also set you free," I say.

He doesn't say anything back. I swallow the spiky bramble of dread that's crawled halfway up my throat. "Tell me something confidential."

A lifetime has passed since we last played this game. It's a trust fall, really—sharing secrets and having faith that the other person will keep them safe. Collateral, too, because when you know someone's deepest, darkest secrets, they're less apt to fuck you over. There's only one rule: no matter what, you have to tell the truth.

"Do you want me to stay?" I ask.

His eyes are fully closed now. I think he might be asleep when he says: "I want you to stay alive."

With daylight comes a heat so blistering, you'd swear the earth split open, the fires of Hell rising through the fissures. The AC blasts full force on the drive from Kole's house to my rented apartment. Axel's behind the wheel. He coasts to a stop along the curb, and my eyes automatically lift to the second-story window that was mine for a fleeting minute.

Kole's side of the bed was empty when I awoke. There was no note, not even a text waiting on my phone. Downstairs, the vestiges of our investigation were still scattered on the surface of the breakfast nook—stray papers, mug shots, notecards.

Rocket was nowhere to be found, and that's when I knew something was awry—before I looked out the picture window, squinting into the already harsh sun, and observed an SUV parked in the driveway. From behind the windshield, Axel gave a half wave.

He walks beside me now, escorting me to the entrance of the apartment building. "I only have two bags," I tell him. "You don't have to—"

"Trust me, I do," he says. "Nik will have my head if something happens to you."

It isn't much cooler in the lobby. The air is still, fetid. There's a smell of old carpet baking in the sun.

"After you." Without pausing to look around or get his bearings, Axel gestures to the caged elevator. The door rattles closed.

"You seem to know your way around," I comment.

He shrugs. "We've done, like, a million search warrants here."

"Really?"

"Well . . ." He closes his eyes, as if counting. "Probably not a million. But a lot."

"For what?" I ask, grateful for the conversation as we ascend. The ancient elevator groans as it climbs up the cable.

"Oh, I don't know if we have time to cover all that. Domestic abuse. Guy took a hostage here, once. Mostly, it's drugs, though."

"Xombie?"

He shakes his head. "I'm sure it's here, but we haven't had probable cause for a warrant yet."

"Probable cause" reminds me of his investigation into the taxidermist. "Were you able to scare up enough PC to search Deschane's?" I ask.

"I'm working on it," he replies as the elevator jars to a stop and the cage opens to spit us out on the second floor. As I've gotten used to doing, I hold the key between my knuckles as I make my way down the hall. The hair on the back of my neck rises, despite how hot and airless it is in the building. I walk straight, my muscles clenched, as if I'm bracing for a knife in the back. I know Axel's right behind me, but still. The sense of unease I felt around Robbie remains.

The walk to the door seems never-ending. When I finally arrive at it, I stand on tiptoes and sweep my fingertips across the ledge.

"What's wrong?" Axel asks.

"Nothing," I say a little too quickly. My eyes flit, searching for any place a tiny camera could be stuck. I don't see anything, though. Holding my breath, I listen. There's no feedback coming from the other side of the door. All I hear are the sounds of whatever's going on outside—grills sizzling, beer cans cracking open. It isn't even 9 A.M., but around here, people seize any excuse to drink beer for breakfast. Birds sing. The waves of Lake Michigan lap against the pier, daring some naïve out-of-towner to jump in.

I insert the key and turn the knob. The door swings inward, inviting us in. Cautiously, I cross the threshold, finding reassurance in the sounds of Axel's subsequent footsteps. "Not bad," he muses. "Got a nice view of the lake."

I smile to agree with him, but I'm on edge. And so is he. I can tell by the way he works his jaw, the way he traipses around woodenly. His ears are red, too. Maybe it's the heat, or maybe they're sunburned. Or maybe he's nervous about the fact that he knows something I don't.

The place appears as I left it. My laptop is on the bed, tucked behind the pillows. Articles of clothing are either in my duffel bag or discarded on the floor or hanging on the back of the bathroom door. I pick them up and swipe up any toiletries in the shower or crowded on the sink. As I'm wrapping up the cord to my straightener, the sound of footsteps snags my attention.

The gait is different than Axel's.

"Hello? Oh, shit. You're that cop."

It's Robbie, I can tell by his voice, and he's just discovered I'm not alone.

I step out of the bathroom, gripping my flatiron tightly, in case I need to use it as a weapon. "You two know each other?" I point the straightener at each of them in turn.

"You were at Tommy Greenlee's funeral," Axel says to Robbie rather than to me.

"The fact that you're still alive tells me you didn't try to take Big House down for the murder," says Robbie. "He's got guys out here who have killed for much less than that. Same as Hades." Then, turning to me, he says: "I know who you are."

Stunned, I open my mouth to speak, but no sound comes out.

"You're Greenlee's ex-wife. The one who wrote her way out of here." Slowly, he advances toward me, this shiny thing he wants to touch.

Axel holds his arm out ramrod straight. His palm presses up against Robbie's chest, preventing him from getting any closer. My eyes automatically scan him for any bulges or sharp edges, anything that might be a concealed gun. Dread is a jagged thing I force myself to swallow. I've feared this day would come, when someone who recognized Black Harbor in the book comes after me for painting such a grim picture of their hometown. It's not like I deterred people from coming here. Black Harbor does that all on its own.

"He's been watching me," I tell Axel. "He fitted a camera in the doorknob." *And God knows where else.*

"You failed to mention that when we talked at the funeral," Axel says to Robbie.

"I keep an eye on the place," Robbie replies. By "place," I get the hint he's referring to more than the apartment building. His gaze swivels back to me then. "Most of the time, when people leave Black Harbor, they don't come back. There's only one reason you'd be here now. You know something about why your old man got capped and who pulled the trigger."

"I really don't—" I start.

"It's an ongoing investigation," Axel cuts in. "We can't share any information."

"Then I guess I can't, either," says Robbie.

They argue, and I feel my consciousness lift from my body. The details of the room fall away as I float, untethered, grasping at bits and pieces of what all has transpired over the past few days, along with my unanswered questions.

Robbie fits like a key turning into a lock.

"You work for Hades," I say, grounding myself in certainty. "What are you, like, a messenger?"

"More like a conduit. I keep him connected to the goings-on."

"Don't kid yourself," warns Axel. "You're probably one of a dozen."

Robbie ignores Axel's bark. "Let me ask you something, Hazel. If all you had to do was one bad thing, and you could leave Black Harbor behind forever, would you do it?" His lips stretch as he grins. He's enjoying every second of my discomfort.

I think back to the one time I repeated those words out loud. My stomach drops. "You followed me to Beck's the other night," I say.

Robbie doesn't even try to mask his smugness. "You should be more careful. You never know who might be eavesdropping."

In my mind, I conjure the setup of Beck's, with the partition that partially walls off the area of the arcade games. On the side with the Pac-Man machine is a worn leather couch where Kole and I sat and I spilled about what brought me to Black Harbor. On the other side is a table where Robbie must have sat, listening to every word. Then the call about Cam came in and we didn't even spare a glance over our shoulders.

I take a deep breath to calm my heartbeat. Even if Robbie overheard that conversation, all it did was make him a valuable asset to Hades. Unless . . . "Are you a double agent?" I ask.

Robbie has the gall to look offended, then he rolls up his sleeve to flash an old tattoo. I squint at it. The blurry image resembles a three-pronged crown. "I used to be one of the Nightmare Kings. I aged out of the gang, got my shit somewhat together, but I only have allegiance to one lord in this city, and that's Hades. Imagine his intrigue when I told him the ex-wife of Buddha's latest kill has come to town. And she's staying right in his building."

"This place . . ." I spin slowly . . . "belongs to Hades?"

"Probably one of a dozen." Robbie cuts a sharp look at Axel. I meet Axel's gaze, too, and while he looks fairly nonplussed, something ominous brews behind his eyes. His expression is that of someone intensely aware of the ground steadily concaving beneath him.

"So, what?" I turn back to Robbie. "You've been . . . following me, going to Tommy's funeral . . . to feed information to Hades? But he's in prison."

"Not forever. When he gets out, there'll be a turf war. And I'm not gonna be caught on the wrong side."

"There already is," notes Axel. "Your alma mater, the Nightmare Kings, and the East Side Anarchists have been terrorizing the streets all summer."

Robbie looks amused. "We ain't seen nothin' yet. Especially now that the Kings have all that firepower."

Axel knits his brows. "What are you talking about?"

"Kid named Grayson, one whose dad got capped the other night. He's one of them."

Axel stands frozen, but his eyes flicker back and forth, processing this information. "Grayson Jeske raided Tommy Greenlee's place?"

Robbie nods. "Poor bastard must've trusted him enough to give him the keys to the castle."

The world stops. I've retreated so far inside myself that the sounds of the lake and the sizzling of the grills have all gone silent. Of course. Grayson had keys to Tommy's house. And probably the combinations to the safes. Considering what Aubrey Jeske shared about how close Tommy had been with her son, if he would have trusted anyone, it would have been him.

And Grayson robbed him blind the second he had the chance. I wonder if he knew about his mom and Tommy's plan to sell off the Xombie. If he did, I'd bet it was because Tommy had been stupid enough to confide in him.

Guilt is an ice chip melting in the pit of my stomach. Not stupid. Trusting. We should be able to trust people we care about. But sometimes *what should be* and *what is* are worlds apart.

As with Grayson, Tommy should have been able to trust me, his wife, not to betray him. And yet, I'd trusted him, too, so much so that I followed him to a place as dismal and dangerous as Black Harbor, where he became someone I no longer recognized. Or even liked. He hurt me in ways I cannot even begin to explain, and I hurt him back.

Now he's dead, forever remaining in the place he warned I'd never leave.

Maybe I won't this time.

"I'll be watching," Robbie promises. "I can't wait to see how this ends." He dismisses himself with a sneer and I wait to leave until I no longer hear his footsteps. Outside, there's a black car parked behind Axel's SUV, a rideshare sign in the window. The driver steps out, as though to help us with our bags.

"Oh," I say, waving him away. "We're this one." I tip my chin toward Axel's vehicle.

The driver says my name, and the sudden realization that I'm not going to the VCTF office to be reunited with Kole is a sucker punch to the stomach. I've been played. I turn and glare at Axel.

"Please don't be mad," he says, handing my bag to the driver. "Nik asked me to do it."

"He asked you to get rid of me."

"He just wants you to be safe, Hazel. We all do." When the driver attempts to take my bag from me, I wrest away from him. I could stand here forever, anger and betrayal turning my bones to lead.

Axel nods at the driver, a gesture that tells him to give us a minute. "Look, I'm sorry. I really am."

I shake my head. My throat is so dry and tight, I couldn't speak if I wanted to.

"I think it's a good idea. If this plan goes to hell . . ." He stops like he doesn't want to finish that train of thought. "These are dangerous guys, Hazel. As long as you're in Black Harbor, you're nothing more than a moving target to them. They will catch you. And they will kill you . . . slowly. You've been incredibly helpful, but now, it's time to go." He opens the back door of the black car. "Your sister's expecting you."

43
KOLE

> You lied to me.

Kole's phone lights up with what he's sure will be a saga of inflammatory text messages from Hazel. He leans forward and plants his head in his hands. Outside, firecrackers are already popping off. It will be a miracle if the city doesn't burn to the ground before noon, which also makes today ideal for a very not ideal operation.

Breaking Hades out of jail is the epitome of playing a stupid game. But it's the only way they can get into the Mineshaft. If there's any chance of stopping the flood of Xombie and putting a cap on all the violent crime, he needs to know who Buddha is so he can take him out, once and for all.

Better the devil he knows.

Even if it means partnering with the asshole who killed his brother. Whether by his own hand or indirectly, Hades is responsible for Evan's death. As much as it pains him to do so, he has to zip up that anger and stow it away on a high shelf where he can't readily access it. Anger will get him nowhere right now.

His phone vibrates again.

> You used me.

He sighs. The fact that Hazel's angry means Axel followed orders, at least.

He called her sister, Elle, this morning on his way to drop Rocket off at daycare. He didn't dive into details; Elle's a smart person and she's been keeping up with whatever parts of the investigation are on the news. She didn't seem terribly surprised when he told her Hazel was in town, either. "Just . . . don't let her out of your sight, yeah?"

"No tall task," Elle snorted, and he was glad for the levity it brought to the conversation. It also made him realize the sheer impossibility of his request. He might as well have asked her to find an honest lawyer.

Still, he felt better after the phone call. Having assurance that Hazel is out of harm's way will free him up to be singularly focused on the shit show that's about to unfold. He's playing with fire today, perhaps more than he can handle, and he doesn't want Hazel anywhere near him when this all goes to hell.

Because it will. It has to.

Unlocking his phone, he taps an apology:

> Hazel, I'm sorry. But it's for your own good. Please.

Her response is immediate:

> Liar.

He tosses his phone and it smacks hard against the surface of his desk. Then he stands and walks over to the persons-of-interest board, where he tacks up a new photo—a mug shot of Joseph Orien, aka Big House, as Riley emerges from the stairwell. "Hey, boss. Word on the street is you taste like chicken."

"Who does?" Fletcher arrives next, Axel right behind him.

"Nik." She cuts her chin toward Kole.

The wound in his arm pulses as if in response. He changed the dressing this morning. The skin around the puncture marks was red and bruised. If it's thinking about becoming infected, it'll have to wait.

"Who bit you?" Axel wants to know.

"Robert Pitts." Just saying the guy's name sets his blood to a boil. "Yesterday, after I interviewed him."

"We'd all better watch our backs," says Fletcher. "Now that mopes have got a taste for human flesh."

Right now, Pitts will be curled into a fetal position in his jail cell, cursing the world and him, most likely. That's one of the fundamental problems with guys like Pitts. Nothing is ever their own fault.

"Where's the footage from the interview? I wanna see this shit go down." Riley again.

"The camera malfunctioned," offers Hudson, who enters the command room.

Riley rolls her eyes. "Sure it did."

"How'd it go?" Kole addresses Axel, who shrugs.

"She wasn't happy."

"No, I'm getting that." He nods toward his phone, which flashes with what he assumes is another cutting string of words from Hazel.

"But I came across some new information."

"Oh?" Kole listens, then, as Axel fills them all in on his and Hazel's encounter with a guy named Robbie, one of Hades's lookouts.

"According to him, Hades owns the apartment building where Hazel was staying," he adds for Riley's and Fletcher's benefit.

"I know," says Kole. "It's how he washes his money." He looked into the place after tracing several of Hades's jail phone calls to a Robbie Berhardt. "What else did this guy have to say?"

"Aside from the fact that he's been keeping tabs on Hazel to see what intel she might lead him to, and that Grayson Jeske is the one who stole Tommy's guns, not a whole lot."

"Wait, how does he know that?" Fletcher steps forward, and Kole is just as eager for Axel to explain. "He belongs to the Nightmare Kings. They're basically Hades's street team . . ."

As Axel talks, Kole's mind works on overdrive, fitting all the pieces of the investigation into their proper places. Tommy and Cam intercepted a drop-off, for which Pitts was the pickup guy. He was meant to bring the three kilos of Xombie back to Buddha. Aubrey found out about the drugs, knew the value, and convinced Tommy to hold on to them for resale. Tommy then confided in Harriet, who offered to broker the deal, meaning she'd take a percentage of the profits for connecting Tommy with Pitts. By the time Harriet hid one of the kilos in the deer head so she could later sell it on her own and come out ahead, it was too late; the deal was already in motion. Tommy went to the Mineshaft to do the exchange one kilo shy. He must have shared with Grayson what he was about to do, and Grayson gathered up his gang to strike.

At the mention of Hades, Hudson takes the floor. It seems he made more out of a sleepless night than Kole did when he fires up a presentation. The first slide is a photo of a scratch-off ticket and a case report side by side. Digital red lines encircle the numbers on each: 05373.

"We can't choose our family," he prefaces. "As you all know, Tobias Shannon, better known as Hades, is my brother. In 1994, our father, Tobias Shannon, Sr., jumped off Forge Bridge."

In his peripheral vision, Kole watches as Riley's hand slowly covers her mouth.

"We believe it was this incident," Hudson continues, "that sparked the inspiration behind these scratch-off tickets. Our running hypothesis is that Hades created these tickets, and the ritual of leaving them with murder victims, as a way to pay tribute to our father's memory."

Slowly, Kole feels everyone's gaze fall to him. Finally, Riley speaks. "Does that mean he killed Evan?"

"Robert Pitts killed him," clarifies Kole. "But Hades ultimately gave the order."

"To Buddha," Hudson explains. "Who then turned and handed the deed off to Pitts when he caught him in the act of conducting a controlled purchase on him."

"What about Tommy Greenlee? And Cameron Jeske?" Riley asks.

"Buddha," Hudson and Kole say in unison. The next slide is a visualization of the power shift that's occurred in Black Harbor since Hades has been locked up. Kole and his detectives watch as the slide containing Hades's photo fades to black and is replaced with the names of two new thugs: Buddha and Big House. He subsequently offers a thorough explanation of each one, identifying Buddha as being responsible for the bulk, if not all, of the Xombie being distributed in Black Harbor.

"Well, fuck me sideways." All heads turn to Riley, who makes a face. "Relax, boys, it's an expression. I don't really want any of you to . . . You know what, never mind." She takes a step back, as if dissecting a figure of speech for them is below her pay grade, which it is.

Axel is the only one willing to ask the question they all must be wondering: "So, how do we stop them?"

Fletcher, who's clearly been strategizing during Hudson's presentation, adds: "We can't just take out Buddha. We tried that with Hades and we all know how well that worked out. No offense." He darts a look at Kole.

What cut him deeply the other day is now but a glancing blow. Although Kole will never agree that he shouldn't have put Hades away for selling narcotics and operating a drug house, he can admit that Black Harbor is worse off without him than it is with him. At least if Hades is running the underworld, a more sinister party can't come in and take over.

Besides, his arrest only came on the heels of Kole and Hudson getting him acquitted of murder. So with that logic, the bastard owes them.

"As soon as we arrest one"—Axel points dually at Big House and Buddha's photos—"the other's as good as gone. We need to make contact with both of them at the same time."

"The Mineshaft . . ." Riley's voice trails.

"It's members only," Fletcher reminds them all. "We'll be killed."

"What about Pitts?" says Axel. "He's a member. He could get us in?"

Kole shakes his head. "Even if Pitts could function like a normal human being for an hour or so, the whole world knows he's a snitch. They wouldn't let him come within a hundred feet of the building before blowing his head off."

The room falls silent again. Kole leans against his desk and exchanges a look with Hudson, watching as his task force deconstructs the case, working toward the same conclusion they arrived at last night, which is the same conclusion that drove Kole to Sulfur County Prison Wednesday morning: there is only one person who can get into the Mineshaft and gather intel, and he happens to be Black Harbor's most dangerous criminal.

Suddenly, their ears perk to the sound of tires crunching on gravel, then the slamming of two car doors.

"Are we expecting visitors?" Riley asks.

No one answers. They wait, listening, everyone tense. Kole feels his heart beat to the cadence of footsteps taking the stairs. He tastes the saltiness of his own sweat as it beads on his upper lip and trickles into the crevice of his mouth. Waves crawl onto the shore outside, whispering *So it begins* as Hades, exiled lord of the underworld, materializes on the landing. He's a silhouette at first, hardly more than a curl of smoke distorted in front of the windows. Then, the tendril cracks a smile and as he begins to close the distance between them, Kole can see that he's replaced his gold grill when he says cheerily: "Honeys, I'm home."

44
HAZEL

A few years ago, I ran my first marathon. It was November. It was raining. And for half of the race, you had to run into a wind that gusted at sixteen miles per hour. About three or four miles in, I realized I had a shadow. A little shorter than me, she stuck to me like a tattoo. She trailed me so consistently that I sometimes forgot she was there, and then with two miles until the end, she veered out from behind me and shifted into high gear to finish eleven places ahead of me.

She'd used me to block the wind. I was a bit salty about it afterward, but all she'd done was employ a tried-and-true strategy. Robbie had done the same thing, trying to get me to do the brunt of the work so he could report his findings to Hades.

His findings.

I think back to my conversation with Kole at Beck's. Depending on how much Robbie overheard, he would have gleaned that I'd gone into Tommy's residence in search of a gun, and that Tommy and a coworker had discovered drugs in the water, all of which he would have relayed to Hades.

This whole situation makes me sick, or maybe it's just the skunky smell of weed that's woven into the fabric of the back seat. My head swims in an herbaceous fog.

I glance at my phone.

Kole's stopped responding.

I know that sending a storm of inflammatory text messages is toxic, but it feels good, like peeling off a scab. It takes me back to the months when we first met, two strangers thrust into each other's orbit, our relationship new and tumultuous and fragile. Each of us was always just one wrong word from the other person walking away. And yet, as if connected by an invisible cable, we inevitably found our way back to each other.

It's almost romantic, when you think about it that way. But ours isn't a love story. It's a story about addiction, one so palpable you could taste it.

I send him another scathing text, justifying to myself that I have every right to be angry. He betrayed me, the one person in this godforsaken place I dared to trust. But I knew better. Which is why I should have predicted he would pull a stunt like this, colluding with Elle to yank me out of Black Harbor when I'm *this* close to getting to the bottom of Tommy's murder.

It was Aubrey Jeske who coerced Tommy into selling the Xombie instead of surrendering it, and it was Tommy's girlfriend and Kole's former CI, Harriet, who brought Robert Pitts into the mix. After hiding a brick for herself, she sent Tommy off with Pitts to sell the two that he had.

I pause.

What if that's where we're wrong? It isn't completely outside the realm of possibility that Tommy agreed to hold one brick back for himself and Harriet. Who knows what kinds of visions of grandeur she fed him. It raises another, more dissonant question: Were things so awful that Tommy was willing to go on a suicide mission? He should have known there was a 90 percent chance they'd kill him for coming up a brick short. And yet, maybe the reward was worth the risk.

I stare at my phone again, willing it to light up with a new message from Kole. I should tell him what Robbie said about Grayson Jeske and his gang being the ones to steal Tommy's firearms. But Axel is on his way to tell him all that, if he hasn't already.

Axel. There's only one explanation for him knowing to bring me to the apartment building, and that's from Kole, who, I now have no doubt, learned it from Robbie, who's been in contact with Hades. Kole's been a silent third party, listening in on all of Hades's phone calls for God knows how long. Robbie must have told Hades I was in town. The instant it pops into mind, it makes sense.

You think I don't have eyes everywhere? Kole said to me once. Ears too, apparently.

He has a maddening way of making me feel stupid. And yet, I am the one who discovered the numbers of the scratch-off tickets hidden in the sign at the Mineshaft. If it wasn't for me, he and Hudson would still be spinning their wheels, trying to figure out how Hades connects to Tommy's murder.

It's because Hades has the exclusive contract as the wholesaler for the Mineshaft. Or *had,* until Kole arrested him four years ago and Buddha took over, proving his worth by bringing something even better to the table—Xombie.

Tears sting my eyes and I don't know if it's from smoke or frustration. I open the window to get some air flowing and lean my head out when I see her.

Dirty Harriet.

I recognize her from the persons-of-interest board in the VCTF office. She's the same orange-haired woman I saw outside the duplex the other day.

"Wait, can you pull over?" I ask the driver.

He flicks a bored, dazed glance at me in the rearview mirror and keeps driving.

"Pull over," I tell him. "Please. I need to talk to that woman."

His small eyes remain focused on the road now.

"Pull over!" I shout, smacking the door with the heel of my hand.

Instead of finding a curb to park alongside, he turns the knob on the radio, drowning my request. My blood starts to boil. I peer past him, through the windshield, and notice a traffic light. It's yellow. There are two vehicles in the lane in front of us, another to our right. The vehicle rolls to a stop when the light deepens to red. I unlock the door, and, grabbing my two bags, I make a break for it. The driver barks after me but I can hardly hear him with all the blood rushing between my ears.

Running feels like wading through quicksand. I make my way toward

Dirty Harriet, who is two and a half blocks away. She's picking through junk that's been set out on the curb. Her arm is half-buried in soiled couch cushions when I approach her. She reels it back in and scrutinizes her findings: a stale Cheeto and a dime. She pockets the dime, pops the Cheeto in her mouth before making a face and immediately spitting it out.

"Excuse me," I say, fighting to catch my breath. "Are you . . . Harriet?"

Slowly, she rises to her full height, which isn't very tall, and wipes orange dust on her bare thigh. She's dressed scantily in an off-white camisole and shorts that look as though she outgrew them in middle school. On her right hand she wears a checkered oven mitt. She keeps the arm tucked close against her body, as if minding an injury.

"Listen, I'm sorry to bother you," I start. I unshoulder my bags and let them sink to the sidewalk. "But I'm—"

"I know who you are."

Jesus, she sounds like Robbie. "You do?"

"You're Tommy's old lady."

I blanch as if I've been slapped upside the head. "I heard you might've been seeing him . . ." I start.

Harriet pouts her lips. "Yeah, we hooked up a few times. Nothin' too serious." She smiles, then, and her snaggletooth pokes out. "Ooh, don't tell me you came back here to get into a catfight with me. I've always wanted to be in a love triangle." She looks genuinely happy, as if she's truly living out some sort of fantasy.

"No," I say. "Just . . ." The gravity of my mistake sets in. I should be halfway to Elle's by now, not . . . Where am I, exactly? I turn around. The buildings look familiar in the sense that all of Black Harbor looks familiar, with everything leaning a little to the left and in desperate need of a new coat of paint—or a demolition. "I just have some questions," I recover.

Harriet holds out her hand. I stare at it, then up at her. "You got cash? I don't light up for free, doll."

Feeling like I'm in a foreign country where cash is still king, I dig into my pockets and am relieved to pull out a crumpled twenty-dollar bill.

She shoves it down in her cleavage, where it vanishes like a magic trick.

Not putting it past her to charge me by the minute, I cut to the chase. "Who killed Tommy?"

A laugh bursts from her mouth. "Well, that's the million-dollar question, ain't it?"

"Harriet, please. I saw you at Tommy's house two days ago. What were you doing over there? You weren't looking for something of yours, were you?" As soon as I say it out loud, I'm more confident than ever that she's the person I saw ambling down the sidewalk. She'd been making a beeline for the duplex, but stopped dead in her tracks when she saw Kole and me in the entryway, and pretended to peruse a discarded couch.

Her eyes squeeze into slits. "Looking for something like what?"

"I don't know," I say, feigning nonchalance. "A kilo of Xombie."

"Bitch, I don't know jack shit about no kilos. I think the real question is what were *you* doing at Tommy's house with Nik?"

There's so much to unpack in that rebuttal. I stutter as she throws the question back in my face, and spit out the only thing I'm able to say: "How do you know Nik?"

Her smile is feline and feral. "We're lovers." She runs her tongue over her teeth and shrugs as if it's *no big deal*.

It's a lie. Kole wouldn't fall for someone this low caliber. She's clearly on something and she doesn't look—or smell—like she's showered yet this month. Still, my cheeks burn as if it were true. "I thought you were with Tommy."

"Who are you, the monogamy police? Shit. If I'd'a known I was gonna get the third degree out here, I never would'a left my luxury condo." When I don't say anything, she starts to move away. "Look, sweetie, I'm a very busy woman. So if you don't mind, good riddance to you and I'd appreciate it if you kept your dick beaters off my man—"

"His blood is on your hands," I say, anger making my voice jagged. "You connected Tommy with Robert Pitts, who brought him to the

Mineshaft, where he was murdered over the kilo you stashed in the deer head."

She's so stunned, I might as well have stuck her with a Taser, and I know I'm right. I saw how her green eyes glowed just now at the mention of the hidden kilo. "You know, it's only a matter of time until Buddha links it back to you. If he hasn't already. Do you have any idea what happened to the last guy he interrogated?" Dipping into writer mode, I unnerve her with every gritty, gruesome detail about what happened to Cam.

Harriet gulps. She looks like a goldfish gasping for oxygen. Finally, she checks slyly over one shoulder then the other. It seems one of the details I've given her has tipped her off. "A blunt-force weapon," she repeats. "Like a mallet?"

"Maybe."

Harriet goes still. All but her right hand, which starts to shake.

I dare to take a step closer. "Harriet, do you know who killed Cameron Jeske? Was it the same person who killed Tommy? The same person who hurt you?" I ask, glancing at the checkered oven mitt.

She's shaking her head, but it looks like more of a glitch than her telling me no. If she demands another twenty, I don't have it. But I didn't jump out of a rolling vehicle not to find out the truth. Then, to my horror, Harriet grasps my hand. "I can't tell you. Not here. There's eyes on every corner. But I can show you."

45
KOLE

"Oh, hell no," says Riley, indignant.

"Normally the trash gets taken out, not brought in," says Fletcher.

Hades's smile stretches. He presses his hands together in mock gratitude. "Thanks for the warm welcome."

Hudson is notably quiet. He stands rigid, remaining in front of his presentation of Black Harbor's baddies, which includes Hades's mug shot. Hades here in the flesh gives the illusion that the presentation has come to life.

"Nik." It's Axel. "Care to tell us what the fuck is going on?"

Kole plants himself between Hades and his task force. He knew they'd demand answers; he'd be disappointed in them if they didn't. Still, as much as he values his detectives, there's a reason he's in charge and they're not. It's because, even in a shitstorm where visibility is limited, he can see the bigger picture, the leverage that a cockroach like Hades affords them, because the fact of the matter is that cockroaches eat shit for breakfast.

"Listen." Kole takes a steadying breath. "We cut a deal. Sometimes things have to get worse before they can get . . . worse." He makes eye contact with each of them, commanding the room. "This isn't ideal, but we're long past anything being ideal. I know he's a nasty—"

"—spineless," supplies Riley.

"—snake," adds Hudson.

"I'm right here," says Hades.

Kole ignores him. "But he still has loyal followers. While they might be bending the knee to Buddha at the moment, Hades is and will always be the drug lord of Black Harbor's underworld. If you haven't noticed, our city is on the brink of destruction. We've been minding our manners for too long."

"What are you proposing?" Riley widens her stance, crosses her arms over her chest.

"We need intel," Kole states plainly. "Which means we need someone who can get inside. We already know what Buddha wants—"

"His missing kilo," offers Axel.

"But why?" says Kole, stabbing the air. "Of course, he's a drug lord, he wants his drugs. I get that. But why is he so goddamn desperate?"

"It's 'cause he's got debt," says Hades. All heads turn, and Hades explains: "When you live among spineless"—he flicks a glance at Riley—"snakes"—another at Hudson—"debt is the only thing that keeps you alive."

Kole nods, listening, as puzzle pieces of the last couple of days start fitting together. Pitts was ranting about the cost of living when he locked him in handcuffs. What he'd written off as nonsense in his fury then, now makes perfect sense. Since Pitts failed in delivering the Xombie to Buddha, he owed him a debt. Buddha, in turn, owes a debt to Big House, his boss. *Think bigger.*

"So who does Big House owe, then?" says Kole, thinking out loud.

Hades closes his eyes and Kole can only guess that he's debating whether or not it's too late to pull the plug on this whole deal. But the deal is clear—information in exchange for freedom. If he reneges now, Hades will return to his cell branded as a snitch. Former drug lord or not, snitches have the shortest life expectancy of any creature in Black Harbor. Finally having made up his mind, he says: "You people have all been living under a goddamn rock if you don't know it's the cartel that's running the show. They've got hubs in all port cities, including Chicago, thanks to that little waterway," he adds, his gaze flicking to the lake. His eyes are pitch dark, his pupils dilated to eclipse the surrounding iris.

"The coasties mentioned this," says Riley, "about how the Great

Lakes enable drug traffickers to move inland. So, you're saying that the cartel has a remote location set up in Chicago, and they got mopes transporting drugs across Lake Michigan to Black Harbor?"

"She's pretty *and* smart," Hades says to anyone but Riley.

Rolling her eyes, she rebuttals: "I've got a mean roundhouse kick, too, dickhead. Don't make me prove it."

Hades grins but it doesn't last. "This whole drug business is a franchise, with the cartel at the top"—he raises both arms, illustrating an umbrella—"with remote sellers like Buddha reporting to top-tier bosses. Buddha gets the drugs for one price, pays to have them delivered to him, and he upcharges when he sells to the guys at the Mineshaft, so he can make enough to cover the cost of doing business, i.e., the contract, and keep some profit for himself. Can't imagine taxidermy pays too well these days."

Taxidermy. The word knifes down Kole's spine.

Axel steps forward, closing the distance between himself and Hades. "Dale Deschane, the taxidermist, is Buddha?"

Hades points a finger pistol at Axel, and says two syllables that make Kole see red: "Ka-ching!"

46
HAZEL

I called Elle and told her I would be late. My friend wants me to swing by her place in Milwaukee, I explained, and while my sister huffed about it, she didn't have a solid leg to stand on. After all, she'd gone behind my back and orchestrated Operation Get Rid of Hazel with Kole, who's made it abysmally clear he neither needs nor wants my help. *Let him bark up the wrong tree,* I think as I step over a spent firecracker, my thoughts soured by vengeance. My stomach churns, though, upon realizing this could be his fatal mistake. From where we left off last night, I would assume he's going to the Mineshaft, where both Big House and Buddha will be, and where Hades, as a known murderer among men, has access, otherwise, why else cut a deal with him?

I should warn him, but first, I need to be sure. My toxic trait of jumping to conclusions hasn't benefited anyone thus far and, even if Harriet is right about there being a third player in all of this, Buddha and Big House need to be taken down anyway.

So, in this regard, maybe I can help. Kole can't be in two places at once, but I can be his boots on the ground on this path of the investigation. "Are we almost there?" I feel like a child in the back seat of a vehicle. I check my phone. Nothing from Kole, just a text from Elle reminding me that dinner's at 7 P.M. I reply with a thumbs-up.

We've been walking for almost an hour, throughout which time,

Harriet has made no gesture to carry one of my bags for me. Not that she has to, but if the tables were turned, I would offer. I keep two steps behind her and let her lead. She seems to be driven by some internal GPS, taking us through alleys and across parking lots of buildings with all their windows either boarded up or busted out. Gang signs graffiti every brick in certain pockets of town. I stare at them as if they're lenticular artwork, the kind in which all it takes is a different angle to reveal something meaningful.

"Almost," she assures me, marching forward, and I never thought of how subjective a word that is until now. "Almost" as in a couple more blocks or "almost" considering how far we've already come?

The Fourth of July parade is over; evidence that it happened lies in the form of candy wrappers shoved against the curb, cigarette butts stomped to smithereens, and the occasional broken lawn chair that will remain until trash pickup next week. Or until someone like Harriet comes along and pillages it.

We're near the lake again, and I see I've essentially made a giant loop. The apartment building is just a few blocks south.

"Here we are," Harriet announces finally. I pause to take in the place where she's brought us. My duffel bag slips from my shoulder and plunks to the asphalt parking lot. The exterior of the building is wrapped in cedar-shake siding, the kind that looks like the roofer got carried away and nailed shingles all the way down. They're faded, all the color beat out of them by the sun. Above the entrance is a yellowed sign that reads, in red letters: DESCHANE'S TAXIDERMY.

"It's closed," I note, and point at the CLOSED sign in the window. The observation is a tactic to buy myself a second to think. I've been here before, years and years ago, and yet, none of those memories are what's setting off the current alarm ringing between my ears.

Harriet waves dismissively. "Closed to randos," she says, walking toward it with all the confidence of someone about to be admitted into an exclusive nightclub. "Which we're not."

"We're not?" I ask.

She throws me a look that says I know nothing, and raps her filthy knuckles against the glass. I stand a good six feet behind her, my hands loosely wrapped around the straps of my bags that might as well be stapled to my palms and filled with sand.

It's just stuff, though. I can replace it.

My face feels hot and it isn't just from the sun. My internal temperature has skyrocketed as my most primal instinct to run engulfs me. But I'm not that person anymore. I came here to stand my ground, to face my fears.

A man materializes on the other side of the door. He's wearing a red flannel, despite the heat, with the sleeves pushed up to his elbows. A soul patch sprouts from his bottom lip. He looks irritated, but when Harriet jerks a thumb over her shoulder at me, his eyes brighten, like a hunter who's just noticed a doe walking into his sights.

He flips the lock and pushes the door open.

"Come on," Harriet coaxes.

The man in the red flannel smiles. "Well, well, well, Mrs. Greenlee. Have I got a bone to pick with you."

47

KOLE

"We fucking had him!" Axel smashes his fists onto his desk. His frustration is palpable. His vindication, too. He paces like a fighter in a ring.

Kole can only imagine how he's never going to live this one down. It isn't just that Axel was onto Dale Deschane this time around; he was onto him ten months ago, too, back when those girls were getting murdered.

Or rather, *bunnies,* as Deschane called them.

"So much for there being no loyalty among thieves," Fletcher directs at Hades. "You knew Buddha's identity and you kept quiet this whole time."

"You know, I normally get water and a bag of chips when I'm being interrogated."

Riley frisbees a rice cake at his head. It glances his temple and breaks on the floor. Kole shoots her a dirty *You're cleaning that up* look.

Hades flashes her a grin, then replies: "And give up my get-out-of-jail-free card? Keeping that little secret to myself is what got me out. Isn't it, Detective?"

Kole feels Hades's gaze needling him. It's a petty, albeit effective tactic—antagonizing a law enforcement officer by addressing them as a lower rank. Journalists do it all the time.

Looking pointedly at Axel, he says: "Draft a warrant for Deschane's. Let SIU know we're gonna need as many guys as they can give us." The simple mention of SIU sparks a realization that he can't believe he didn't see until now. The night Tommy was murdered, there had been a shootout on Geneva Street between the Eastside Anarchists and the Nightmare Kings—the latter of which is Grayson Jeske's gang.

Perhaps "Uncle Tommy" wasn't as much a threat to Grayson as Grayson was a threat to him. If Grayson was the one who stole the guns from Tommy's residence, it explains why the place was unlocked and the safes were opened instead of smashed or stolen altogether.

"Fletcher, have you memorized Tommy's logbook yet?"

Fletcher nods.

"Tommy had some obscure calibers in there. Name a few."

"Let's see, there's a .450 Nitro Express, .250 Savage . . . he had a .338 Spectre . . ."

Kole had been right to go to SIU and inquire about the casings they collected off the street. However, instead of trying to match them to the ones he fished out of the toilet at the Mineshaft, he should have sought to match them to the guns in Tommy's logbook.

"A couple of the Nightmare Kings hang out at 211 Roulette Court. See if you can't get one of them to squeal about the guns. Remember," he adds as Fletcher already bolts toward the door, "they won't talk in front of one another, so get one alone. Chase him. Just make it look legit. Scare him."

"Don't threaten me with a good time," says Fletcher, and he's already got one foot out the door when Riley snatches her keys. "I'm going with him," she says.

Now there are three. With the rest of his task force off on their respective missions, Kole looks from Hudson to Hades—one brother on the right side of the law, the other living far, far below it.

"Are you ready to make a deal with Big House that he can't refuse?"

Neither of them answer. They're both smart enough to know they don't have a choice.

48
HAZEL

A bone to pick . . . My lips move soundlessly. I have no idea who this caveman is, let alone what problem exists between us. But, he called me Mrs. Greenlee.

So this is about Tommy.

That bastard. Even after death, my ex-husband will find ways to fuck me over.

Before I know it, Harriet is behind me, shoving her shoulder into the small of my back so I practically fall into Deschane's arms. I recognize him now from when I'd tag along with Tommy to bring in his latest kill.

"Your husband owes me fifty thousand dollars."

I can practically hear my eyeballs bulge out of their sockets. My heart crawls into my throat. I try to swallow it back down. My cells vibrate with the urge to run, but where? If there's another way out, I can't see it. As far as the door I came in, all Deschane has to take is one giant step and he'll beat me to it.

Just more than an arm's length away, Harriet looks smug, like she's waiting for Deschane to give her a pat on the back. I wish I had something to skewer her with. My eyes pinball around, seeking purchase with a pair of antlers or a needle-nosed fish. Then I hear a sound that makes the hair on the back of my neck stand on end.

The click of the lock.

Harriet's hand hovers by the door. Her face is all teeth as she stares at me, excited to see me ripped apart.

"I d-don't have fifty thousand dollars," I stammer. "But . . . I can get your kilo. I know where it is."

"Let me guess," says Deschane, "you found it shoved inside a deer mount."

My mouth falls open. The word is silent. *Yes.*

Deschane looks at Harriet. "I had a hunch as soon as those cops came by and started asking questions. There's only one person who would have thought to hide drugs in a place like that."

Harriet's smile shrinks. I watch how Deschane holds her with a reassuring gaze, like he's praising her instead of preying on her, the way a hunter might coax a fox out of its hole so he can kill it for its pelt.

"See, Harriet, here, is a greedy little pig," Deschane explains to me. "She gets herself tangled up with Tommy Greenlee, and as luck would have it, he and his buddy scoop three kilos of Xombie outta the water. *My* kilos." He thumps his fist against his own chest. "Tommy gets the bright idea that he should sell 'em. So, Harriet calls up a pissant named Robert Pitts and sets up a deal for two of the three kilos, all the while intending to keep one for herself. Ain't that right, Harriet?"

Harriet's face is beet red. Staring down at the floor and digging the toe of her shoe into the thin carpet, she nods and looks very much like a child being scolded. She shifts, and I catch a glimpse of the oven mitt she hides behind her back, as if she's protecting it.

"What she failed to consider," Deschane goes on, slowly starting to circle Harriet, "is that Pitts was the designated pickup guy. He'd been searching for the kilos because I'd already threatened to skin him alive if he didn't find them. I hear he's in custody now, so I missed my chance."

Deschane threatened Pitts. Which is why Pitts was hiding out under the bridge—he was hiding from Deschane. This revelation sparks another. "You're Buddha," I say.

Deschane grins and I swear I can see tobacco grime dripping from his teeth. When he moves, I catch a glimpse of the handgun holstered at his side. It's a six-shooter with a blued steel cylinder and classic wood grip. Suddenly, I remember years ago, watching over Tommy's shoulder as he marveled at this practically antique handgun that could shoot the same bullets as the revolver he bought me—.38 Special.

"You know, I remember when you used to come in here with your husband. You were this meek, mild-tempered little thing. Always reminded me of a bird with clipped wings, the way you followed him around . . ." Deschane is still circling. He's talking to me, but his eyes are trained on Harriet. His hand morphs into a claw, then, and he brings it down over her head as if she's some cheap toy in a crane game. Her eyes swell with fear.

"Pitts told me what Harriet was up to. So I paid her a visit. I'll admit, I didn't believe her when she told me that Tommy's wife was back in town and that you must have taken the kilo. But, here you are. Sorry about that. I'll sew 'em back on for you if you want." He stares down his nose at the oven mitt on Harriet's right hand.

"You cut off her fingers?" A sour taste surges up the back of my throat.

"Smashed 'em with a rawhide mallet. One for each day the kilo remained missing. I was gonna find her again today but this is even better."

He yanks, pulling Harriet to the floor and twisting her hair around his fist. She yelps and kicks, but he's too strong. He drags her toward the back of the shop the way I've seen Tommy drag a deer carcass through the woods.

"Let her go!" I drill a punch into his back but his mass absorbs it. He turns and smacks me with the back of his hand. I spin to the floor. The world teeter-totters and when my vision steadies, I look up to see a pair of double doors, above which is a metal sign that reads NO TRESPASSING—I'M TIRED OF HIDING THE BODIES.

The doors swing gently. In the space between, I can just make out the figures of Harriet and Deschane. He hauls her past long wooden tables with reloading presses clamped to their edges. Then he lifts her so her head is on what appears to be a literal chopping block.

I can't look.

It's quiet for a blessed second, and then I hear a feral scream and the crack of mallet against bone.

I clamber to my hands and knees. Still dazed and dizzy with fear, I stagger to my feet, but Deschane is faster than he looks. He crashes through the double doors to wrap an impossibly large hand around my ankle and pulls. I smack the floor. I feel the blade before I see it, the cold kiss of the metal against my shin. When I look down, I observe that the edge has teeth for sawing through tendons and bone.

"Shh . . ." he whispers. "You know what I've always found to be so . . . ironic?" A low rumble comes from deep down. His breath is rancid and thick. "Lucky rabbits' feet come from unlucky rabbits." I can hear the morbid amusement in his voice, and yet what unnerves me most is the scent he gives off. It's a musk, like I imagine predators emit when they're about to go in for the kill. "So what do you say? Are you gonna be an unlucky bunny today?"

49
KOLE

You have debt, you stay alive.

That is the unspoken code of the kingpin. Major drug dealers are millions and millions of dollars in debt at all times, otherwise, they get killed. If you take their life, you take their debt, too.

Debt is one thing that Buddha has going for him. The problem, however, is that by losing those kilos, he's proven he's the last thing a guy like Big House wants to do business with: a liability.

Thus is the basis for Hades's proposition to Big House. He will offer to take on Buddha's debt in exchange for the contract. It will be in Buddha's best interest, then, to vanish, reinstating Hades as top dog of Black Harbor's underworld.

They're parked in the lot by Forge Bridge. There's a trail in the woods that will spit Hades out two blocks from the Mineshaft. Kole takes a deep breath. This is just like a controlled purchase, he reminds himself. He's done hundreds of these. The only difference is today they're working with varsity criminals versus low-level dealers, and Hades won't be fitted with a camera, which means they will have to trust his word.

Their plan sounds ludicrous as he plays it back to himself, but Hades is the only person who can get inside the Mineshaft, and they'll frisk him the first chance they get—if they don't blow his head off first.

"You know, we might be sending him in there to get killed," says Hudson, echoing Kole's inner monologue.

"It's a win-win." Kole shrugs. "Either he goes in there and gets information, or they kill him and now we've got a reason to arrest them. No offense," he adds, meeting Hades's gaze again. He hasn't forgotten who ordered his brother's death.

Hades makes eye contact with him for a fleeting second, then resumes flicking a Bic lighter. He strokes the flame like it's a cat's tail. "Let freedom ring, boys."

"Where did you get that?" wonders Hudson. He's half-turned around in the passenger seat.

"Who are you, the police? Don't worry about it."

"You got the kilo?" Kole asks.

Hades makes a show of patting his pockets. "Phone, wallet, kilo." He lifts up his shirt to reveal the last item, the white brick that's tucked into his waistband.

"So when they ask, how'd you get out of prison early?"

"I've forsaken my evil ways and I'm working with the cops to fight the war on drugs."

Kole nods his approval. In a place where everybody lies, what better cover story is there than the truth? Big House will never buy it. All they need is for him to be intrigued enough by Hades's offer to let him inside, where Hades will turn over the kilo in exchange for the contract. If all goes according to plan, Kole can write up a SWAT warrant to be served as soon as the fireworks show is over.

"All right, get out," says Kole.

Hades steps out onto the asphalt, but before he slams the door, he leans into the opening. "Hey, Ryan."

Hudson's jaw is set, like he's waiting for a slap to the cheek.

"You deserve better than me, you know. I'm sorry I'm not one of the good guys."

Hudson folds his lips in. He looks like he might say something when Hades closes the door and heads into the thicket. The silence is loud as they watch him disappear.

Kole bites the inside of his cheek until the taste of blood fills his mouth. Three minutes stretches for an eternity when Malcolm finally radios in. Kole recruited him to assist with surveillance. "We've got eyes on Hades. He's just turning on Heeley Avenue."

"Copy." Moving the shifter into drive, Kole presses the gas pedal. Forge Bridge shrinks in the rearview mirror as they ascend the hill. Hazel's bracelet swings back and forth, like a wagging finger, scolding him for what he did. He lied to her. But it was the only way he could get her to leave. She will either forgive him or she won't. And if she doesn't, he's still glad he shipped her off; there's no way she'd make it out alive now. A capsule of dread seeps into his bloodstream as he remembers the photo he found in Harriet's apartment, the bullet hole through Hazel's forehead.

Someone wants her dead. And once it's discovered she doesn't have the missing kilo, there's no reason for her to stay alive.

"You think he means it?" Kole asks as he pulls into the gravel lot of an auto repair business. He parks between a black sedan and a red pickup truck with a shattered windshield. The mirror on the door closest to him is held on by duct tape and a prayer.

"Means what?" says Hudson.

"That he's sorry."

Hudson laughs humorlessly. "If he was sorry, then he would do something about it."

"Maybe this is him doing something about it."

Hudson says nothing. His eyes are glued to the middle distance, where the Mineshaft cuts more of an imposing figure than it should. A faded brick exterior that stands only one story tall, it isn't the least bit intimidating at first glance. It's only because they know what evil lurks inside that it raises their hackles.

The binoculars are in the center console. Kole picks them up and peers through them, finding purchase on Hades's white T-shirt. He follows him as he approaches a man wearing all black, a cigarette clamped between his lips. With grey shoulder-length hair, a long nose, and deep-set eyes, he isn't a match for Big House. He must be the doorman. A silver wallet chain glints in the sun, blinding as the man moves to regard Hades, no doubt surprised that he's out of prison.

Kole passes the binoculars to Hudson, who leans forward, practically stamping the windshield with them. "God, I wish he was wearing a wire," says Hudson.

"Me, too. But you know they'll frisk him."

Proving Kole's point, the man pats down Hades's shirt. He pauses, though, when he discovers the brick. The two men level their faces with each other. Hades's lips move. The other man's eyebrows knit. He looks down at the brick again, and up at Hades's face, and Kole knows that Hades is in. Tipping his head toward the entrance, the man peels away, Hades following two steps behind.

"He's inside," Kole communicates over the radio, then to Hudson: "Now, we wait." He just settles in when a truck pulls up to the curb. Hudson frowns.

Kole snatches the binoculars back from him and watches as a man in a red flannel gets out of the driver's side. He recognizes him immediately.

Deschane.

The taxidermist moves to the other side of the truck and opens the passenger door. A shrill scream pierces the air as a woman is dragged from her seat, kicking and flailing like a fish out of water. She's wearing an oversized black BHPD T-shirt, the one he let Hazel keep this morning when he—

Fuck.

The epiphany hits him with the force of a bullet. Kole erupts from his vehicle and careens into the street. Hudson bolts after him but Kole's too fast. Thirty feet away . . . now twenty . . . Deschane drags Hazel into the Mineshaft. He pumps his arms. His hands are blades slicing through the viscous air.

"Nik!" Hudson shouts.

But they are already a world apart. He chases after Hazel as he did the first moment she appeared in his life, when she dodged him in the copse on the cold, grey morning his brother's body washed up on the riverbank. Now it's broad daylight and he might as well be running into the fires of Hell because he cannot let her go down like this—not after all the nights he prayed for her return.

The door is closing.

Kole's lungs burn as, with a final burst of adrenaline, he propels himself forward, barreling into the Mineshaft just before the door closes.

Darkness.

Fireworks explode in his vision. Before his eyes can adjust, he reaches for Hazel and yanks her away from Deschane. Her nails rake across his neck as he pushes her backward, out the door. She tumbles into Hudson. The last thing Kole sees are their faces, eyes like orbs, mouths frozen in terror as the door closes between them, locking him in with Black Harbor's most heinous criminals.

His own heartbeat is deafening.

Slowly, he turns to check out his company, his hand reaching for his holster.

Big House is a planet of a man. His mug shot doesn't do him justice. Bald with bulging biceps, he has the kind of presence that fills an entire room and a shifty gaze that penetrates every corner. He stares into Kole, nostrils flaring, a bull about to charge.

"Motherfucker, you brought the cops!" the doorman shouts to Deschane.

What happens next happens all at once.

The doorman's gun is the first to go off, followed by a series of muzzle flashes. A rocket of pain takes Kole out at the knees. He drops and his whole skeleton vibrates as he smacks the floor. He is all instincts now, rolling onto his elbows and crawling behind the bar where the doorman is bleeding out, a pool of crimson spreading across his chest. Using the bar for cover, Kole leans out and fires three rounds into Deschane.

The big man dances. A revolver flies out of his hand and topples end over end on the floor where it lies like a lead weight. He notes the wood-grain handle, the antique look of it as shadowy tendrils creep into his vision and he realizes with a shot of sadness that this is it. The job has finally come to collect.

His head is both heavy and weightless. He's floating, leaving this hell behind now that he has finally made good on the deal he cut with Black Harbor twenty-three years ago—his life in exchange for the keys to the city.

But it isn't done with him yet.

"So what do you think of the place, Detective?" Big House's bodiless voice booms. It fills every inch of space in the clubhouse, screws itself into the fresh wounds in Kole's leg. "I know you and your boys have been wanting to get inside for years. You violated my House Rules, though, so unfortunately, I'm going to have to kill you. No cops," he adds.

No glass bottles, either, Kole thinks, and yet shards of glass stick into his palms as he tries to keep himself from falling face first onto the floor. Where is Hades? His gaze leapfrogs from one body to the next—first the doorman, then Deschane—but Hades is nowhere to be seen.

He hears him, though, when Big House grabs the drug lord by the throat and pins him against the wall. Kole peeks around the bar to see that Hades is suspended, his feet inches off the floor, face fire-poker red.

"Get out here!" Big House throws his voice over his massive shoulder. "I want to see this great Detective Kole, the one whose Violent Crime Task Force is locking up all my customers. You're the wrench in my business model, you know that?"

With his left hand crushing Hades's windpipe, Big House raises his right hand and fires a round into the bar. Wood splinters in all directions. Kole shields his face with his forearm and hunkers down as a shock wave pulses throughout the place. The ringing threatens to split Kole's skull down the center.

"I've been at this a long time." Big House's baritone commands the room when the ringing finally dissipates. "Spent a good chunk of my adult life in and out of prison—for stupid shit, mostly. Opportunistic, like stealing cars and beating the piss outta someone 'cause he looked at me cross-eyed. Finally, I got tired of living in a tiny cell and eating cardboard food, so I created this place, a clubhouse where people like me feel . . . welcome. Wanted, even. Safe. A place where the cops got no reason to come sniffing around. A lot of seedy characters have been through these doors. Present company not excluded. This guy"—he points the barrel of his gun at Hades as if about to tell a joke—"comes to me one day with a proposal. How'd you put it?" He shakes Hades, whose eyes are rolled so far back that just the whites are exposed. "A hundred grand a month in exchange for exclusive rights to sell to my club members.

Well, I think you initially said fifty, we landed on a hundred. Anyway!" he shouts, getting himself back on track after that little tangent. "That worked out well, 'til he got his ass thrown in the slammer. Thanks to you, I understand. No Hades, no contract. No contract, no money. And I got my own debts to pay. People think the cost of living is high, I guarantee the cost of operating a place like this is ten times higher. I was worried I'd have to shut it down, but then along comes Buddha with the hookup for a new drug that's sweeping underworlds across the nation. Xombie." He pauses as if reminiscing about all the money that arrangement has brought in. "That was all fine and dandy, too, until a shipment goes missing and some bastard ends up dead in my bathroom. That's the problem with criminals: we just can't play nice."

Without warning, he fires another round in Kole's direction. The bullet punches the wall behind him. He rolls away, accidentally taking out a stool.

Shit.

He's given up his position.

Big House guffaws and fires another three rounds.

A bottle of vodka slides into him. Miraculously, it's still in one piece. Still full.

If it weren't for his ears ringing, he knows he'd probably hear a death rattle from Hades, unless the drug lord is already unconscious. Kole grabs the closest thing to him—a broken chair leg—and whips it across the room. Big House pivots and shoots. It's the split-second diversion Kole needs to drag himself to his feet, raise the vodka bottle like a sledgehammer, and smash it over Big House's head. Glass rains everywhere. Stunned, Big House drops Hades, who crumples to the floor. Big House barks out a laugh. "Criminals don't play nice, but you know what I learned about you good guys?" His mouth stretches into a jack-o'-lantern grin. "You don't always win."

He squares up and extends his arm, pistol pointed at Hades's chest. It happens faster than the muzzle flash. First instinct, now pure rage, Kole rushes Big House, forcing him up against the wall. The bullet ricochets into the dark. Liquor bottles crash and shatter. Wood splinters. Everything goes pitch-black as Kole takes a fist to the face, a knee to the ribs, and suddenly . . . it all stops. A squelching sound makes him crack an eye open to discover that Big House is pinned to the wall, the hook that once held the cow skull impaling his chest.

He doesn't see that Hades has risen to stand next to him until the drug lord strikes the cheap lighter and tosses it. Soaked in liquor, Big House catches fire.

"Come on!" Hades shouts as smoke thickens the air. He fits his shoulder under Kole's armpit and, careful not to trip over the bodies of either Deschane or the doorman, they fall out of the Mineshaft rather than walk out.

The outside world is impossibly bright. Kole inhales, each breath a thousand pins stabbing his lungs. He slips off of Hades and falls to the ground. Shapes move toward him but he can't make out who or what they are.

Two words ring in his ears. "Officer down!"

Someone is shouting them over and over, as if it's an incantation that can bring him back to life. A grimace snags his mouth as the abysmal truth of Black Harbor rings true. *The only way out is down.*

"Officer down! Officer down!"

The shouts fade, growing distant—or perhaps he's the one growing distant, drifting toward some unknown shore—only to be severed by the song of sirens as the taste of blood fills his mouth. Darkness devours his vision like a flame eating the pages of a book, and he is blind to everything except for a pair of startling blue eyes.

No one named Hazel has a right to have eyes this blue.

EPILOGUE
HAZEL

"If I don't make it out alive, it's all yours, Grayson."

So begins the video that police discovered in Grayson Jeske's email when executing a search of his things. In it, Tommy speaks to the camera—his phone propped up on the mantel in his living room—and fills in the gaps surrounding his death.

He has a cabin in the Missouri Ozarks, bought and paid for. It's outfitted with a security system and stocked with nonperishables. "Everything a person would need to survive indefinitely off the grid," Tommy explains. He stifles a derisive laugh, then stares hard at the phone, as if he's really making eye contact, less a recording and more a real-time conversation. He looks around, the whites of his eyes glowing as he tilts his head back to take in his surroundings. "That's one hard truth about this place. Most of us don't make it out of here alive. But you will. Now, listen carefully, because I'm about to tell you the combinations to every safe . . ."

I only watched the video once. It was so filled with dramatic irony, watching Tommy confide every secret to a boy who would ultimately betray him. The guilt that weighed on my shoulders was enough to sink me into the ground, especially when I observed that it was shot the same day Tommy was. He's wearing his Alpha T-shirt, the one that hours later would be riddled with bullet holes and stained with his blood. But as

Kole reminded me on numerous occasions: *You play stupid games, you win stupid prizes.*

The video ends on a blurry frame of the deer mount, the one I blasted with my .38 Special revolver. It's obvious, now, how Dirty Harriet came to the idea of hiding the kilo inside. She was aware of the operation Deschane was running, with the dead animals in his taxidermy shop made into morbid piñatas, their hollow insides stuffed with Xombie all packaged into little baggies and ready for resale. They were collected as evidence when police arrived to examine the body of a "30-yo F/W," later identified as Harriet Marie Wright.

It isn't all of the Xombie, not by a long shot. But, it's a start to eradicating this disease that has taken the lives and livelihoods of too many. The bodies under the bridge are starting to wake up, seeking refuge in shelters and mobile health centers. The mayor has finally been persuaded to invest in sustainable resources. There are plans to erect a rehab facility on the charred patch of earth where the Mineshaft once stood.

The rain came this morning, just before the memorial. The denizens of Black Harbor filed solemnly into the chapel, bowing our heads as the chief of police stood at the lectern and read Matthew 5:9: *Blessed are the peacemakers, for they shall be called the children of God.*

Beside me, Kole was a stoic shadow. He wore all black and linked his pinkie finger with mine as we endured the ceremony for his brother. The world knows, now, that Evan Kole's death was not a suicide. The day after everything went down at the Mineshaft, Robert Pitts, sober enough to be remorseful, confessed to murder. After getting the order from Buddha to get the cops off his back, he'd gone to the bridge and feigned distress. He called Evan, who came to his aid, and when they were both in the middle of Forge Bridge, Pitts pushed him, not before shoving a scratch-off ticket in his back pocket.

We watched the video of the confession from Kole's hospital room. As ragged as he was, twelve hours out of surgery and being monitored for smoke inhalation, the change in him was immediate, as if someone flipped a switch. The darkness behind his eyes dissolved, as the truth behind his brother's death was finally brought to light.

Buddha, or Dale Deschane, was identified as the sole shooter in

Tommy's murder. The gun recovered at the Mineshaft was a Smith & Wesson Model 10 revolver. It was a match for the bullets that Kole fished out of the toilet Sunday morning—a Smith & Wesson .38 Special. Hades had the sense to retrieve it and dump it on the ground before vanishing into the cracks for good.

Well, not for good.

He slithered away before the fire department arrived to douse the flames, but he will surface eventually. Even the most veteran cockroach can't play dead forever. At which time, I presume Kole will pick up the hunt. Hades might have helped dismantle the Xombie operation, but he ordered Evan's murder. They're not even—not even close. As morbid as it is, there's something comforting about their dynamic. Hades will continue to wreak havoc, and Kole will continue to keep him in check. The friction between them is what keeps Black Harbor in precarious balance.

The truths about both Tommy's and Cam's murders continued to unravel as Darren Hogan was caught and questioned after wrapping the stolen vehicle around a light pole. Once he was cuffed and placed in the hot seat, it was easy to see why he'd disappeared as quickly as he had; he couldn't keep a lid on it to save his life. Hogan spewed information like a shaken can of soda, spilling everything about how he'd been the one to drop the Xombie in the water for Pitts to pick up, only to learn it had been intercepted when Buddha ordered him to return to Black Harbor to make things right. He and Pitts had gone to raid Tommy's place after Buddha shot him, searching for anything they could sell to recoup the loss of the missing drugs, only to discover that the Nightmare Kings had beaten them to it. Some of the stolen firearms have since been recovered but the rest are on the streets, their serial numbers scratched into oblivion.

So it goes, the nature of Black Harbor.

The nature of you.

Thunder rolls. We sit in the liminal space between two storms, parked in the vacant lot of Forge Bridge, its iron, coal-blackened rungs rimmed in silver whenever lightning skips across the sky. I watch as a black plastic bag tumbles over the asphalt, diaphanous and pitching with a subtle blow of the wind.

"You know what's funny about all this," Kole says, still dressed in his funeral blacks. "I don't even drink and I still ended up in a bar fight."

"*Afterset*," I correct.

He smiles. It's the first real one I've seen since everything went up in flames. Then he says something that surprises me. "Tell me something confidential."

I take a deep breath. "What do you want to know?"

"What's that in the back seat? That Hudson gave you."

My gaze moves to the rearview mirror, on which my beaded bracelet hangs. "The Reynolds case," I say, alluding to the cardboard box that Hudson gave me one evening after we had dinner at his place.

"You going to write a book about it?"

"Maybe," I admit, although the truth is, I've already started, because while Kole's been busy wrapping up this investigation, I've ventured to the crumbling shore to observe the Reynolds mansion, a sea glass–colored masterpiece split by a fracture right down the center as the east-facing wing slips off the edge. It's abandoned now, vacant as a haunted house. My fingers twitch, already mime-typing the story that's waiting to be exhumed.

I feel my teeth sink into my bottom lip. There's something I've been dying to ask him, but I haven't had the courage to, until now. The ground feels more solid beneath us. "You're never going to leave Black Harbor, are you?"

He's quiet for so long as he stares into the middle distance that I wonder if he's staring at the ghost of his younger self from the morning his brother's body washed up on the riverbank. I match his gaze out the windshield, trying to see what he sees. Finally, he says, "I know that everything I've done doesn't really matter. Not in the grand scheme of things."

"How can you say that?" I ask.

He turns to look at me and I feel our irises lock into place, like a combination. "Because for every action, there is an equal and opposite reaction. So, we cut the Xombie operation off at the head. It's still here, and when people get bored with it, a new, more dangerous drug will come along. There will always be guys like Buddha and Big House and

Hades, thinking they can make the city their own personal hellscape. But there are good people here, too. People who are trying to make the most of their one and only life that happens to be in Black Harbor. And that's why I've got to be here, too. I'm not built for anywhere else, Hazel."

My vision blurs as I hold back tears. I knew the answer. I just needed to hear him say it. He knows where I'm headed first thing in the morning—up north to see my family. My life in Brooklyn is on pause. I'm subletting my apartment for the rest of the summer. Which means I have another month to drift, to float like a dandelion seed and see where I land.

"I'm not asking you to leave," I preface. "But maybe you could come north with me? Just for a few days."

When he looks at me, there is something different shining in his eyes. Something warm, like sunlight melting frost. "Okay," he says softly. Then, gently tugging my bracelet from the mirror, he loops it on my wrist as he asks a single question: "When we come back, will you stay with me then? Here in Black Harbor?"

I stare at the bracelet. The white beads are stark against my skin, the letters of my name carved into the plastic of this memento I once discarded. It found its way back to me, as things that are meant for us have a habit of doing. His question echoes in the silence while he waits for my answer, a single three-letter response.

"Yes."

He cups my chin and kisses me hard, with the same vigor as if I will be ripped away from him any second. But I'm not going anywhere. Not this time. Because even though I can't pinpoint when it happened, my bones have shifted as I have been remade for Black Harbor. I lay my head on Kole's shoulder, breathing in his cologne of sandalwood and sage. My fingers find the anchor pendant beneath his shirt.

"We should get home," he says when raindrops start to tap-dance on the windshield. "Rocket."

Lightning illuminates the world again as if to punctuate his point. It draws my eyes to Forge Bridge and perhaps for the first time, I see it for all that it is: a skeleton of wood and iron that stretches from one riverbank to the other. And perhaps also, for the first time, I see you for what you are not.

You are not the villain in this story.

You never were.

You are as grim and unrelenting as the truth, blunt and bulletproof. Yes, you swallow some people whole, but for those of us who survive, you strip us down to our very essence, forcing us to see all the frightening, remarkable things we are made of. We either bend to your power or we break.

And if we're lucky, we are set free.

Years ago, I thought you were the beginning and the end of everything. But now, as Forge Bridge shrinks in the rearview mirror, I am dangerously aware of the fact that I know just one thing for certain: we are far from the end.

ACKNOWLEDGMENTS

I always suspected Hazel might return to Black Harbor. Whether or not she would stay this time remained a mystery until the very end. That's one of my favorite things about writing—unraveling the mysteries of each character.

I'm so grateful to the whole team at Minotaur, most notably Kelley Ragland and my editor, Leslie Gelbman, for urging me to write a proper, potential send-off for this series that has changed my life in the best ways. To Kayla Janas and Stephen Erickson: you are weapons and you make this whole marketing thing even more fun than it has a right to be. Thanks also to Grace Gay, for keeping things on track and running smoothly.

The team at LGR Literary, especially my superstar agent, Stephanie Kip Rostan, are everything I could have hoped for and more. Thanks for always being down to throw ideas at the murder board with me. Of course, we might never have connected if not for Leslie and the inimitable Elle Cosimano (who's every bit as kind as she is hilarious). Elle, you've become a mentor to me in more ways than you probably realize. "Thank you" isn't enough, but it's a start.

Audiobooks have made novels more accessible and immersive than ever before, and I'm so fortunate to have such a fantastic team with Macmillan Audio. Shout-out and major thank-you to Angela Dawe, for reprising the role of Hazel, and Robb Moreira, for giving a voice to Nikolai Kole.

ACKNOWLEDGMENTS

I want to acknowledge a few people who are all too willing to help pull me out of a plot hole, including my friends and early readers, Nicole Sharon Schultz, Alissa Stormont, and Elenna Garrett. More early readers include authors Mary Kubica, Kimberly Belle, David Ellis, Kimi Cunningham Grant, and Charlie Donlea, who so generously shared blurbs for this book. I'm such a fan of all of your work and I hope you know I'm always happy to return the favor. And to my friends Tessa Wegert and Danielle Girard—I'd plot murders with you any day.

I love interviewing people who've got their boots on the ground in the landscape I'm writing about. On that front, I want to thank Special Agent Jim Krueger, from the Wisconsin Department of Justice, who shared his extensive knowledge with me about drugs, cartels, and the chilling notion that if you have debt, you stay alive. Thanks also to my phone-a-friends, former medical examiner Becky Porcaro and dispatcher Jody Howell, for weighing in on the gory details.

I'd like to give a special shout-out to my sister, Miranda @novel_vfx, who makes the most killer book trailers. She is also the designer behind the Midwestern Noir merch on my website, so if you want to lurk (or lounge) around in Black Harbor's finest apparel, you know what to do. On that note, I just want to acknowledge my whole family for being amazingly supportive and for never telling me to go out and get a real job.

The absolute best way to support an author is by reading and recommending her books. I'm so grateful to all of the Black Harbor diehards—the Bookstagrammers, reviewers, libraries, bookstores, and anyone who has read and recommended my books. Thank you for following me into Black Harbor.

Speaking of bookstores, I've got to shine a spotlight on my go-to indie, Blue House Books, in Kenosha, Wisconsin. If you haven't been, add this one to your bookstore bucket list. They pull out all the stops for author events, and the whole team is just awesome. Say hi to owner Sam Jacquest for me—she's the one with the bangs and the main character energy.

Finally, to my husband, Hanns. We both know that Nikolai Kole wouldn't exist without you. For four books now, you've graciously let me steal the words right out of your mouth and give them to this character who, in myriad ways, you brought to life. On top of that, you're always there to help me untangle the mess I've made of my own investigations, like when I bring the murder board to the kitchen table. I love you, I love our life, and I love our boys. Griswold, Muffins, and Kevin: you keep me honest with the 5 A.M. wake-up calls and make sure I never write alone. I'm so lucky to have you all in my corner.

ABOUT THE AUTHOR

HANNAH MORRISSEY studied English and Creative Writing at the University of Wisconsin–Madison. Her first novel, *Hello, Transcriber,* was inspired by her experience as a police transcriber. She lives in Wisconsin with her husband and pugs.